JACOB DADDY

—— a novel by ——

Barbara Randall

Published by

Culturatti Ink, *a social entrepreneurship of Culturatti Kids.*

www.CulturattiInk.com

www.CulturattiKids.net

Inquiries should be emailed to: Orders@CulturattiInk.com

ISBN: 0-9712383-3-2
LCCN:2006920004

First Printing 2010
Second Printing 2012

Printed in the United States of America

Cover design by Ryan Alvis.

To the children

Jacob Daddy

The basement was musty and dark, but Ada wasn't afraid. She had gone to the basement with Jacob, and she wasn't afraid of Jacob. She was not yet acquainted with fear, the awful irrational thoughts that would cause someone to dread the dark…to be unnerved by loud voices…to feel anxious in cramped places…or to be crippled by ordinary smells. She hadn't yet learned to value distrust, or the merit of suspicion. Her innocence was unbroken; she had never been betrayed.

Jacob bounded the basement steps with Ada pressed against his chest, her stubby legs wrapped tight around his middle. At the bottom of the stairs, Jacob lifted Ada into the air high above his head and held her there a few moments. Excitement caused her feet to kick, and she giggled in disbelief when Jacob threatened to 'drop her on her head.' This was a game they'd played before. Jacob was being silly and Ada wasn't afraid.

Ada sighed her disappointment when the game ended, and Jacob planted her on the surface of a makeshift table in the corner of the dimly lit room at the back of the basement where the furnace was housed. Jacob told her, "Be careful—sit still so you don't fall off." Ada leaned back on the dusty table, supported by her sturdy little arms, while her legs dangled over the edge. It was a long way down to the floor, but Ada was a big girl, and she knew how to sit still. And though the table wobbled a bit on its tall, rickety legs, she wasn't afraid. Absently, Ada watched Jacob's back as he strode away from her and toward the archaic coal furnace. Almost every day when he got off work, Jacob came to their place to stoke the beast.

He was a big man, tall—with wide shoulders, hard muscles in his arms, and huge, strong hands. He would kiss their mother, and he greeted Ada and her two brothers and her sister by swinging them from his big arms and tossing them into the air.They would all jump on his back, wrestling him until their mother made them stop. Ada thought she was his favorite. She coveted his attention and she competed shamelessly for it. But Jacob never seemed tired or cross, so she attacked him every chance she got.

Jacob had a look, revealing Indian or maybe Chicano blood in him. His eyes were gray and somnolent, like everything else about him. The movement of his eyes was slow. And yet for all their lack of fervor, they were omniscient, as if he could see you whether he looked at you or not.

His teeth were more brown than white, stained from the Copenhagen he chewed, and from the fat cigars he always smoked. He would spit the thick black liquid from the chew into their yard, or into a tin cup their mother provided.

Ada had never seen anyone chew tobacco before. She thought it was curious and a wee bit alarming. And the spitting grossed her out, but still she thought he was a handsome man.

And it never bothered Ada that Jacob's fingernails were rimmed with black. She mentioned to her mother once, just in passing, that Jacob's hands were dirty. "Jacob's hands aren't dirty," her mom explained. "He's a very clean man. The stains on his nails are from his job at the factory. They're permanent. He could scrub them from now 'until kingdom come' and they'd never look any cleaner. But they are clean," she said. "He has a good-paying job, but he works very hard with his hands."

That answer satisfied her. Ella did start to buy Lava soap for Jacob to wash with. The commercials said that Lava was made from pumice, which came from volcanoes. It promised to remove the stains from the hardest-working man's hands, leaving them spotless and clean. It didn't clean Jacob Wright's hands. But Ella was always neat and clean. She didn't mind the stains on Jacob's nails so Ada tried to ignore them, too.

There was always beer on Jacob's breath, but that didn't bother her, either. Her mother would sometimes offer Jacob a beer, or sometimes he would send Ada to get him one from the icebox. And she felt proud when she delivered it to him. He would call her his big girl, and reward her with a small peck on the cheek.

Now she watched him as his long legs covered the distance to the furnace in a few short steps. When he crouched low to the ground beside it, and began tinkering with it, Ada lost interest and allowed her eyes to explore the unfamiliar surroundings. She had only been to the basement a few times before, and she'd never seen it as a potential playground. Now as she surveyed it, assessing its many nooks and crannies, she perceived the possibilities. "This'd be a good place to play hide and seek." Ada spoke out loud, but more to herself than to Jacob.

A sudden whooshing sound caused Jacob to stand up. He turned toward her, wiping the soot from his hands on his dark blue work pants. "Heat!" he said, with eyes that managed to twinkle.

All at once, Ada smelled the heat and the warmth of it caused her to return his smile. He was pleased that she was pleased with him. "Well," he said, "I couldn't let my little girlfriend freeze."

Jacob came back to her side. He scooped her up from the table and with one quick motion he swung her in the air. Ada giggled. She was kicking her feet again, this time in mock anger; striking him with her hard little shoes. Jacob lowered her until they were face to face. Touching her nose with the tip of his nose, he gave Ada a counterfeit scowl, and then brought her back close to him, back flush with his body.

Ada figured they were through playing for now, so assuming her usual position she threw her small self against him, and prepared for the ride back up stairs. Instead, Jacob hugged her too tight for a moment, and then returned her to the surface of the crude, old tabletop. He stood her there on her feet. This time, his grasp was rough. And when he pulled her against him, Ada wanted to say he was hurting her. One big hand seized the back of her head, pressing her face forward against him. She couldn't speak. With her nose buried in his shirt, she struggled even to breathe. Her heart was pumping so violently she could hear it. With his free hand Jacob started to tug at the elastic waistband of her little wool skirt. The garment slid down her legs, to rest on the tops of her shiny black shoes. Ada was confused. And then she began to feel something else, something unknown.

A moment later, when a splinter from the wood snagged her plump thigh, Ada realized that Jacob plopped her on her bottom again. Then maneuvering her legs, he opened them. He was squeezing the tops of her uncovered thighs…he was pinching her flesh with his tobacco-stained hands. And then he was touching her there….

Her mind was a jumble of thoughts, but none of them made any sense. What was he trying to do to her? He leaned close to her ear, and he told her, "You're my big little girl."

The words ran around in her brain, but she didn't know what to do with them; she didn't know how to answer. His mouth was too close to her neck, and his damp breath tickled her ear. She ducked her head, trying to get herself free, in response to it. Ada realized once more that she couldn't breathe. Jacob pulled her forward again into his massive chest. She wondered if he knew he was killing her. She fought once more to turn her head; she opened her mouth wide against his shirt, trying to catch a breath. Jacob's grip was too firm. She was pinned against him, searching for hard-to-find pockets of air. She shuddered because of the potent emotions that assailed her brain. Great pangs of panic washed over her in erratic waves. Ada felt as though a heavy weight had been placed against her chest. Then she realized that Jacob had thrown her on her back, and his was the weight that crushed her. He was hurting her. His hands groped beneath her, and he squeezed her hard on her bare bottom. Then his hands somehow slid lower, and he prodded her hard with his long fingers. He was poking her where she went pee, and his dirty fingernails scratched the soft flesh hidden there. She tensed as searing pain tore through her. Ada was now crying hard, trying to tell him to stop, to let her go. But she wasn't sure words emerged from her mouth. She couldn't be sure of her voice. She couldn't be sure of anything. She felt imprisoned, glued to the stiff fabric of Jacob's work shirt. And then, abruptly, he released her.

Ada found her breath—and Jacob's breath, suddenly rancid, was all around her. It permeated the room, and she gagged on it. And now his shirt stank like tobacco and sweat and stale beer. And it was wet. Ada had dampened it with her tears, and with slobber and with snot.

Jacob's hands were gentle once more when he pulled her back to her feet. With soft words, he consoled the little girl while he tugged her cotton panties and her thick tights back up her thighs. As he smoothed her clothing, Ada realized she was wet. She had peed on herself.

Jacob wiped her face with a dingy cloth he pulled from his pocket. He wiped her tears and dried her runny nose, but she still felt grimy and unclean. As he straightened her clothes, he instructed her in a too-soft tone, "Don't cry, Ada. We'll get you into some dry clothes, and mommy won't know. You won't get into trouble."

Ada knew she would be in trouble. But Jacob repeated, "If we don't tell mommy you won't get into trouble."

Ada sniffed, but when she still didn't answer, Jacob lifted her head. He removed the saccharine from his voice. "If you tell your mommy about the basement, you'll get into trouble. The basement is our secret." Jacob's features had always been cheerful, but now they were severe. And he was piercing her with his darkened eyes. He repeated, "You can never tell mommy, Ada!" This was a voice she had not heard before. His words were firm, precise.

He captured her jaw with one big hand. The pressure did not cause pain, but the words were cloaked in an ominous tone. They mirrored the message that sprang from his eyes. The feeble up-and-down motion of her head told him she understood. She understood, but she couldn't speak. Jacob was satisfied, and he loosened his grip.

Ada merely sensed that Jacob was speaking again. She sensed the familiar tone she knew. But his voice had grown vague, distant; and she couldn't hear him. When he reached for her this time, Ada flinched. But Jacob just tossed her into the air, like he'd done a thousand times before. When he lowered her to his middle, Ada drew in a shuddering breath. Still, she straddled his waist like she always did. She coiled her arms around his neck as he carried her up the steps. She was holding on tight so she wouldn't fall. At the top of the stairs, just before he threw open the basement door Jacob paused. He tilted his head back and studied Ada's face, to see what was written there. He found her expression was veiled. That pleased him.

From over his shoulder, Ada caught sight of her mom. The light from the kitchen bathed the top of the basement stairs. Her mother was near the stove wearing a bright apron that said it was mealtime. Despite the enticing aromas being cajoled from the stove, a strange knot grew in the pit of her stomach, and tightness in her chest made Ada think she didn't want to eat.

The house felt warm. It made Ada remember the furnace and drew her back into the basement. She hated the smelly old basement. She would not go there again. Her mom crossed the room to peck Jacob's cheek.

Ada watched as her mother returned to the stove. She noticed the warmth in her eyes…then her mind drifted away.

As she grabbed a firm hold on nothingness and her vision started to dim…a strange new emotion was born—one she couldn't then name.

In time, though, she would know in intimate detail this strangeness that helped to make her separate and distinct.

And this emotion born in the basement that day that she would know for the rest of her life…was fear.

Enigma

Ada was born Adalia Annabelle Reynolds. She hated her name. She saw it as strange, old-fashioned—a stain she was given at birth. "Nothing good can come of a child named Adalia Annabelle," she used to protest whenever she begged her mother to change her name, which in her early years, was often. She was named *before* she was born by her grandmother's aunt, Great-aunt Augustine, who would knowingly pat Ella's belly and declare, "This one will be a special child."

Augustine died before Ada was born, a fact that Ada deemed peculiar. Nobody knew how the old woman developed her opinions but Augustine was 97 years old when she foretold the unborn baby's future. She was as sharp as a whip, so her prognostications were never challenged.

She was full of proclamations, both bad and good. She had been born, Ada's grandmother explained, with a veil over her face, so she could see 'haints' and she *knew* things. Still, Ada entered the world in the usual way, and nothing extraordinary attended her birth to signify whether her life would be exceptional or otherwise.

She was a pretty little girl and like the previous Reynolds babies, she was quick. But when she stood on her little feet and walked at eight months, eyebrows were raised. And when she started saying the cleverest things as soon as she could form sentences and displayed an astuteness that defied her years, her family regarded her with questioning interest, and began to wonder if perhaps old Augustine's predictions might just come true.

Ada was born into a large and boisterous northern black family whose roots still connected them to the rich values and traditions of the South. Her mother's mother, Big Mama, would often announce, "She's been here before." All the aunts would at least agree that she was older than her years, and precocious. Big Mama said when Ada was born she'd been touched by God, or at any rate, it seemed she had found Him by the time she was three years old. Proof, for Big Mama, came in the form of a car accident that occurred when Ada was not quite four.

The Reynolds were traveling a deserted country road, heading home from a trip down south, when Ada's dad lost control of their old car. They skidded over an icy embankment and rolled top over bottom, landing wrong side up in a desolate, snow-covered field. Amazingly, no one was hurt, but they found themselves trapped in their mangled car for hours, and obscured from the view of travelers on the distant icy roadway.

There was frozen, snow-covered land beneath them and biting mid-winter winds howling around them, and they all were certain they'd freeze to death before they could be found.

The entire family was in that car, the mom and dad and all four of the young kids. While their desperate screams pierced the frigid night air, Ada, in a calm voice demanded, "Everybody, let's just pray. We just need to pray." Of course, they were discovered in time and the only real casualty that night was her daddy's car. Still, the story is told. Ada's mother said it proved two things: that both religion and an inexplicable strangeness were programmed into Ada's life.

Ada's earliest memories were fragmented and incomplete, a mystery, like a puzzle with missing pieces. Much of her life, with days, months, and even years misplaced, rushed by her in a blur. She was forgetful. She wouldn't remember people she had met, or visiting places she had been. To save face, and to hide her embarrassment, Ada learned to joke at her own expense.

Ada was an enigma, even to herself. Great lapses of memory caused her to be that way. She could exude ego and ooze self-control, or be too sensitive and unsure of herself. She laughed too easily and cried too easily. She could be profound and cerebral, intrigued by thoughts and ideas. And yet with her next breath, she was shallow and lost in triviality. If she had been asked to describe herself, it would have been a daunting task. But here's what she might have said: think of the silliest, the most serious, nicest, vilest, truest, phoniest, bravest, most fearful, pettiest, vainest, most modest person you've met. Ada was easy to read and impossible to know. And those who thought they knew her well, did not.

The Early Days

Ada's mother and father were Ella and Thomas. In primary images, Ada saw them all in the big, old house they rented on East 42ⁿᵈ Street. When she thought of that house, it brought back the happy, contented times she'd known there. She thought of the early days with her mom and dad and her older sister, Angela, and her two brothers, August and Anthony. If she could have suspended time and preserved those days, life for all of them would have been different.

With all of her senses, Ada remembered her father. She could see him clearly, hear his rich voice, and his scent was still sweet in a spicy way as it drifted back to her. She remembered the feel of his calloused hands, which were gentle when he touched her. She thought he was positively jolly. He was never in a bad mood, and she knew that he loved them. She could still see his face. He would always be young and strong to her. His complexion was fair, and his jet-black hair was bone straight except where it formed soft curls at the nape of his neck. He was so handsome that he commanded attention by just walking into a room. Ada loved looking at him.

He always had a joke to tell and he never got tired of their nagging requests for bedtime stories. When his children talked, Thomas listened to them with a smile in his eyes and he sang to them with his beautiful baritone voice, especially at bedtime, when they'd fall asleep sprawled across his lap or nestled in his arms. Thomas and his twin sister, his only sibling, surprised their parents late in life. His sister died in infancy, and Thoma was raised alone, and lonely. He was proud of the good-looking brood of children he produced with his pretty, young wife. Ada adored this wonderful man who was perfect to her in every way.

To Ada, Ella was near perfect, too. She was much younger than her husband but Ada thought they looked great together. Ella was more than pretty. Her chocolate-colored skin was flawless, and her soft hair fell in waves to the middle of her back. She never needed to press it. Ada and her sister loved to sit behind their mother on the big, old mahogany bed that often accommodated the entire crew, and they would chatter childishly as they combed the soft tangles from Ella's hair.

Their mother did not quite have their dad's easy sense of humor, but she *could* be provoked to smile, and she had a steady, rock-like quality that made them feel safe and protected. Ella was young, but she was capable. She provided old-fashioned, home-cooked meals. No one could out-cook their mother. They were neat and well dressed, and their house was always clean. Ada and her sister Angela inherited their mother's long thick hair, which Ella divided into smooth braids that ran over their shoulders and down their backs.

Every few days, Ella took their braids down and scratched and massaged their heads so gently that they had to fight not to fall asleep before she could finish re-braiding their hair. Ella could be very stern, but her children never questioned that she loved them as much as their dad did.

Red Clay Dirt

Ella Josephine Douglas was born in rural Arkansas, in the late 1920s. She grew up in the proud, sturdy little house her father built from the tall trees that covered his land. The lofty oaks and the pine trees shedding their cones, and the vast fields of cotton, and crops of tall golden corn and beans, and the red clay dirt that dusted everyone's feet; this was the scenery that landscaped Ella's youth.

It was a time when families were close and strong. Work was purposeful, and life was both hard and good. Ella's father, Luther, was a farmer from his heart. His father had been one, too, and his father before him. He had owned that proud land long before his birth, an inheritance, and a legacy from a guilt-ridden white great-grandfather who could never have claimed him in life.

Luther worked the land with his pretty young wife, Mattie, and together they produced the crops that sustained them. And year after year they brought forth an even more precious yield—sturdy little boys and girls, a total of sixteen of them, who would become aunts and uncles to Ada, and one of them, born second to the baby, would become Ada's mother.

On Luther's farm, life was typical. The long days began when the rooster crowed, and ceased only when the moon declared that the day had seen its end. Luther and Mattie rose with the sun or before it, to begin the hard tasks before them. And their children, once they were big enough (and they were almost immediately big enough) were also given appropriate daily chores.

Work was plentiful and no one was idle. There were hogs to slop and fussy hens to be fed and cows to be milked. The little ones made a game of feeding the chicks while beans were snapped or corn was shucked, and clothes were scrubbed by hand with the harsh lye soap that Mattie made. There were meals to plan and foods to can and wood to chop and fields to plow, and most hated of all, there were long hours spent under the mean midday sun, in those dreadful white fields of cotton that were so crucial to the economy of the Douglas household.

The chores varied from season to season, but they never ended. Bad times hounded the good ones, and the living went on. Ada's ancestors were toughened by the unforeseen occurrences that peppered their world. Like their neighbors and friends, they developed a stoicism that was spawned by the racial and economic injustices of the times. They faced the losses of children who were never allowed to taste life and of those who tasted it too briefly. They suffered the painful loss of their oldest daughter, Helen, who died unexpectedly just before her 19th birthday. There was something about Helen's solemn photograph, the only relic belonging to her that survived, which always haunted and fascinated Ada, and would set her mind racing to games of 'what if.' She stared at the faded picture of the somber young woman in the old-timey dress, and wondered what kind of life Helen would have lived; if she had lived.

Throughout the hard times, the Douglases were bolstered by their faith in the Bible and in God. Their coping skills were extraordinary. The strong sense of family, so scarce today, was a dominant force in their lives, and so there was constant support from close and distant relatives who would rally in times of trouble. And except for the compulsory adherence to the Baptist faith, the Douglases were convinced that secular education was the greatest gift any parent could bestow upon a child, so they worked hard and planned diligently to provide their children with the promising futures that they themselves had been denied.

Tragedy

Ella was six months old when tragedy struck. It was a day like any other when Mattie took the large bundle of just-washed clothes out of the kettle she used to boil them in. She boiled them to get them white. The big iron pot always sat in the back yard, just a few feet from the porch. She then hung the laundry in the sun to dry. It was a terrifying sound, the scream that snatched Mattie from her monotony, a scream unlike any she'd ever heard before. She raced into the house and found Ella where she left her, on the floor in front of the fireplace, but she was horrified to see that the smaller caldron of scalding water that been sitting on the burning logs in the fireplace had tipped over. All of its boiling contents had spilled onto the floor where Ella was sitting.

Luther was in the field working when he received the message from his daughter, Ethel, that baby Ella had been severely burned. Luther rushed from the fields to find his household in a panic. Nearby neighbors were summoned, and arrangements were made to get the baby to town, to the nearest available doctor, but only after one of the neighbors, in an effort to survey the extent of the burns, removed the cotton stockings that Ella had been wearing. When the leggings were removed, and the cooked flesh of Ella's legs was exposed, the critical nature of the situation became more obvious.

For the Douglas family, from that day on, life would not be the same. Neither financially nor emotionally would they ever recover from that devastation.

In time the wounds healed, but Ella's legs were left twisted and disfigured. The scars on her body were easy to see, but even deeper and more damaging were the scars that weren't visible to the eye. These scars, more than the physical ones, would mar her personality and cloud her judgment, and when she had children, *they* would be hurt by a tragedy that had damaged their mother when she was a child.

Daddy Leaves Home

Thomas and Ella had four kids, two girls and two boys. They were stair-steps. August was born first, a namesake of Great-aunt Augustine, and then Angela. Ada was their third child and when Ada was two years old, Anthony was born, and he was *her baby*. Now her family was ideal, perfect and complete. But those were the very early years.

Ada was four years old when her father left home and her world changed. He left with a bang, showing a side of himself that none of the children had seen before, and their existence was altered, with a jarring act of violence that embedded itself with permanence in Ada's brain.

Ada remembered that night. Supper had been eaten, the dishes were done, the children were upstairs, ready for bed, and still Thomas hadn't come home. She recalled the sudden pounding on the door; it came out of the blue, and took them all by surprise. She remembered being glad to hear her father's voice, and yet confused that it sounded so angry and loud. She remembered her father demanding that her mother open the door and let him in. She remembered him calling to her, August, and Angela to let him in, and her mother was warning them not to. She recalled how anxious she was when she heard her father calling her name, and she remembered her feet finally flying to the door and flinging it open. She remembered her surprise when he brushed past her, almost knocking her over, ignoring her up-stretched arms, and Anthony was in the playpen on the living room floor, crying, but Thomas rushed past him too, and the house erupted into chaos and the kids were screaming and Ada's mother was screaming and then she was running with all the limited speed that her crippled limbs would afford her, and her husband was hot on her heels, with the kids stampeding behind them.

And Ada vaguely recalled that there was a shadow, a tall dark silhouette of a man on the wall near the living room door. This man played no part in the unfolding drama. He was not part of their family, and Ada didn't know why he was there. This unnamed figure stepped aside when her father rushed in and chased their mother through the house and out into the alley behind the house and then choked her until her body appeared crumpled and lifeless.

And when Thomas carried Ella's still form back into the house and laid her motionless body on the weathered couch and then calmly walked out into the tranquil night, leaving the chaos behind, Ada recalled that this strange man, who had first appeared to her as a shadow on the wall, and who would soon become her father—was gone.

Jacob Daddy

None of them ever spoke of the incident that had almost ended their mother's life. Like unwanted trash, this unpleasant occurrence was discarded. Later that year Ada learned her mother had a boyfriend. Their father was gone and a new one had taken his place. And although trauma must have followed those events, Ada so cleverly mislaid it that looking back, the transition seemed smooth.

This tall man was handsome, like Thomas. And he was usually funny and easygoing, but unlike Thomas, he was sometimes morose. He didn't look like a white man but neither did he look black. He never went to church with them, but they did things as a family. He was always around, and he had lots of money. He took them to Dairy Queen for ice cream cones or for leisurely rides in his shiny new car. Their mother was happy again and Ada grew used to him being around, and in a surprisingly short time, Ada decided that she liked him a lot.

Ella dated him for a couple of years before she married him and became Mrs. Jacob Wright. The family moved into a three-bedroom ranch-style house on Tacoma Street. It was a nice place, with a full basement, on the east side of town. The basement was fixed up and it looked almost as good as the upstairs did. There was a bathroom down there, and a bar with a large beveled mirror that covered one complete wall.

This was the first time Ada had lived in a house that her family wasn't renting, and although she wasn't quite sure why, she knew this was a step up for her family. She was proud of the modern-looking home their new father provided for them. The back yard was fenced in and there was a grape arbor there. The neighborhood was nice, and although Ada had never given much thought to such things before, it now occurred to her that this was the kind of home that she could be happy to bring her friends to.

Ella's children called their step-dad Jacob Daddy because although they came to love Jacob, they never forgot their Thomas, and they knew that Jacob could never replace him. Ella couldn't say their real father's name without a whine in her voice, and the two fought whenever they met up with each other. The children didn't see Thomas as much as they wanted to, and they missed him. Still, in time, Jacob was also father to Ada. Once again her family was complete. And somehow, no one seemed to remember that this man— Jacob Daddy—was the same man who stepped aside, leaving Thomas to strangle their mother nearly to death just a few short years before.

August

It was suppertime. Anthony and August were home, but the girls were in Willington Park, across the street from their house. August was busy trying to fix his bike. The chain had come off again. Since late afternoon, when the girls ran the short distance across the street into the park—which they considered their own private playground—he had been hard at work repairing his bicycle.

Every morning that summer, even before the girls were out of their beds, August, who turned 14 that year, was up and dressed, getting ready to deliver the papers on his route. He was proud of his job and that he was earning money. He had plans for his wages. His mother had promised to match his savings penny for penny, and his dream was to own the shiny new bicycle he saw at K-Mart. Meanwhile, he was forced to spend time most days reattaching the chain on his rickety old one.

The girls should have been home by five, but some of the neighborhood kids had coaxed them into a continual 'one more turn' on the swings. Swinging was one of Ada's favorite pasttimes. Flying high into the sky on those long summer days, Ada could be completely absorbed in the thrill of play, where nothing, no darkness, could intrude. As she and her sister swung they sang the little song they learned at school. They called it *the swinging song:*

How would you like to go up in a swing…up in a swing so high…? Over the treetops and chimneys tall…up in the clear blue sky…How I like to go sailing high…like a bird on the wing…How would you like to come swing with me…? Swinging way up in the sky…

They swung happily, with their long braids flying behind them, while they sang at the top of their lungs. Often they lost track of time. The hours would melt away and then too soon the day would be gone.

They'd race home in near panic, developing excuses to ward off the punishment that was certain to greet their arrival.

Today was no different. August was still working on his bike when his mother sent him to find his sisters and bring them home for dinner. He was frustrated by the interruption and bargained for more time to finish. When his request wasn't granted, he was quick to connect the chain. Then he rode across the park to find his little sisters. The message from their mother sent the girls racing for home. They took the shortcut across the plush, green grass. But August took the long way back. His bike was making slow progress on the grassy terrain, so he circumvented the park and directed his bike out into the street.

Time passed, and their mother had just started to fuss when they heard the sirens. Even before they opened the front door to see the commotion at the corner of their street, Ada knew something horrible had happened. A crowd of their friends and neighbors were filling the block, and a boy—a friend of August's—was rushing toward the house. It was his frantic screams that drew them to their feet.

The next time Ada saw her brother he was lying face down, broken and twisted, in the street. His head had been crushed, and there was an expanding dark puddle surrounding him. In dazed fascination, Ada watched as the blood drained from her brother's body. This liquid was not bright red in color, like blood she had seen on other occasions. This was black, and there was too much of it.

She had never seen death before. She only thought of death when she thought of Great-aunt Augustine, whom she had never known, or when she looked at the strange old picture of her Aunt Helen who had also died long before Ada was born. Aunt Helen never seemed real to her. She was just a serene young woman—an apparition from an old photograph, who hadn't truly existed. And Aunt Augustine was almost a hundred years old. It was natural for her to die. Death was something that happened to old people, and to people who lived a long time ago, but not to her brother. It never crossed her mind that this terrible thing could happen to someone she loved.

Ada prayed harder than ever before. She prayed that August would not die, that he would not join her aunts in that ominous place where dead people go.

As she watched and prayed, the specter of her brother's prone body on the hot pavement dimmed. She closed her eyes, became weightless, and then drifted away from the horrible image that sickened her and weakened her knees.

Ada opened her eyes again. With relief she realized she was safe in her bed, in the room she shared with her sister. Diffused light from the bathroom across the hall filtered through the cracked door and into the room. Angela was asleep. The house was still.

She struggled to remember the terrible, intangible thing that had troubled her. It was a horrible dream, Ada assured herself, and although she wasn't quite convinced, she drifted back to sleep.

A Family Portrait

Ada thought August was dead when she saw him lying broken in the street, but he lived for three days after that. She overheard the grownups talking. They spoke in sad, hushed tones about the will of God, made preparations for food, and orchestrated funeral plans. No one spoke directly to her, so she gathered what bits of information she could and digested the pertinent details.

Her mother had been inconsolable, and her friends—mostly women from The First Baptist Church—were like a protective wall that surrounded her. Ada wanted to ask them questions, but language eluded her, so she kept quiet and listened to words that weren't intended for her ears.

Ada heard her mother say, "If those girls had been where they were supposed to be, August would still be alive." Ada seized those words and tucked them away for safekeeping.

She willed herself to better times. Times when August had been happy, doing the everyday things that kept him a safe and constant part of her world. She never imagined her big brother would not be with her, so she had taken for granted the little things that August did that made him special. She tried to remember now how nice his smile was, and the gentle look of his dark eyes, and how handsome he was when he was dressed in his shirt and tie and ready for Sunday school.

Ada had always loved her brothers and her sister, but now that August was gone, and she could never again hear his voice or tell him how much she cared, now that it was too late, she realized she loved him more than she could bear.

Someone said that August was in a coma. That meant that he was in a "very deep sleep, a sleep without dreams," Ada was told. She grabbed hold of that thought, too, and held on for dear life. It gave

Ada hope, and since she had been bargaining with God for August's life, she was not prepared for the news that her brother was dead. The announcement saddened her, but it angered her, as well. She learned later that the young man who killed her brother was the drunken son of a rich white doctor. That detail made her angrier still.

The days surrounding her brother's death folded themselves into unreachable little pockets of time, which disappeared into the nether regions of Ada's brain. She tucked away the anger too, not knowing quite where to direct it, but the deep sense of guilt that she felt couldn't be parceled away. Instead, it morphed into phobias that followed her throughout her childhood and would plague her the rest of her life.

Ada remembered a picture of the four children that was taken a few months before her brother died. It was an Olan Mills photo in a nice frame and it sat proudly on a curio in their mother's living room. She remembered the day the picture was taken. They had all dressed in their nicest clothes.

August and Anthony were neat in their light blue shirts, navy ties, and dark blue trousers, and the girls were wearing matching blue dresses. Ada liked it when she dressed like her sister, and when people told them they could pass for twins. Ada thought it was true, except that Angela was half a head taller than she was.

She and Angela had gotten their hair pressed that day, and they both wore it down in the back with spiral curls falling over their shoulders. The front was pulled away from their faces, and then up into a big loose bun that just peeked over the tops of their heads. Their straight, clipped bangs, Ada believed, gave them an air of sophistication. She had felt proud of herself, and she'd thought how pretty her sister was. And how her little brother, Anthony, appeared mischievous and cute, which he was, and how studious and handsome August looked.

When Ada looked at the picture now, her eyes were drawn to August's face, like his was the only one that mattered. She would study that face in the years to come, as if committing this image to memory would capture the emotions August felt on the day it was taken. She remembered him laughing and tickling her, making her smile for the camera. She saw him with the crooked smile and the kind, expressive eyes that were in no way accusing. His thoughts of her were gentle.

He stood behind her in the photograph, with his hand resting lightly on her shoulder, and now she peered into his eyes, willing him to say, "It's OK, Ada. It's all right. It's not your fault."

And she then would not have to be afraid.

Roman

Later that year, the year August died, Ada decided there was something wrong with her mother. Ella was more cross than usual.

She had cried for a long time after August died, but after a while the tears stopped. Now she was crying again, it seemed, for no reason. And she was tired all the time.

Jacob Daddy was different, too. He and Ella exchanged knowing looks, like they were sharing secrets. As was her custom, Ada listened for pieces of information. She knew they were trying to speak in code. Whenever she entered the room the dialogue either ended or changed. It irked her. She had just about decided to talk to Angela (Angela was two years older; almost thirteen now, and she always knew things) when her parents broke the news: Ella was pregnant!

They all embraced the announcement, but no one more than Ada. To Ada, this was no mere pregnancy; it was a miracle. And though she hadn't quite worked it out, she knew that somehow, this birth would be magic. It was a second chance; a birth to negate a death.

She and her siblings had been a unit. There were four of them, two girls and two boys. They were perfect, right down to their matching names, all of which started with the same letter of the alphabet.

When August died, the balance was broken. No longer a set, they were uneven. The dissonance worried Ada; it troubled her more than she realized.

The new baby would make them *even* again. Ada decided she needed to name this baby. And of course his name would begin with the letter 'A'. That would make things the way they were before. It was important to her.

This baby could never replace August. That wasn't her intent. But Ada would make him *fit*, and she prayed the baby would be a boy.

In the end, it was Ella who named her son. She named him Roman Scott. "Come and meet your baby brother. This is Roman," Ella said, when she presented her new son to his sisters and his brother. Ada bristled, and for a while she couldn't say the boy's name. But Roman was beautiful and easy to love. None of them thought of him as a stepbrother. In every way that counted, he was one of them.

Still, Ada thought she should have been allowed to name him. She hadn't been, and since no satisfactory reason for this slight was given, Ada determined it was yet another of her mother's spiteful schemes to punish her.

Ella

Ella was conscious of the scars on her legs, but Ada didn't see them when she looked at her mom, and she hadn't noticed her mother's limp until it was brought to her attention. Her mother was pretty and stylish and smart. Ada loved sneaking into her mom's closet to look at the nice things there. Ella wore pretty two-piece suits that made her look like Jackie Kennedy. She had lots of costume jewelry and little pillbox hats, and colorful silk scarves that Ada believed to be worth a fortune.

Her teeth were iridescent white, her lips were always red, and when she smiled her eyes sparkled.

All of Ella's children had her eyes. Anthony's especially glistened like stars whenever he stared in awe, or when he thought something was funny. And when Ada was complimented on her eyes, which were large, intense, and dark brown in color, she knew she had her mother to thank.

Whether Ella's long hair was swept up into a beehive or worn down, turned under at the ends and resting on top of her shoulders, Ada had to admit that no one's mother was better looking than hers.

She was small in stature, but there was nothing small about her presence. Although Jacob dwarfed her and Thomas stood head and shoulders above her as well, it was Ella who always wore the pants in her family.

Until Thomas' outburst on the night their marriage ended, Ella's word was law. Thomas had always been the negotiator, always suing for peace. Her outbursts were still volatile and frequent, but Jacob would simply exit the room when she wanted to fight, leaving her frustrated and irate that he'd refuse to fuel the fire. When his absence threatened to extinguish the flames, Ella refueled them. She could throw a perfectly good tantrum whether anyone listened or not.

Ada remembered long hours she spent trying to make herself inconspicuous, so her mother would not notice her until her anger subsided. She remembered feeling frightened and sad for Anthony, when he'd caused their mother to spiral into a tirade that might last for hours and would certainly include a harsh beating with a belt or a switch or the whip-like cord from an iron. She remembered huddling with her brothers and her sister in one of their rooms, or on the front porch if that was safer, while their mother ranted and screamed into the air, until she wore herself down and the tantrum ended as abruptly as it started.

She remembered them asking each other, "What's wrong with mom?" and the empty shrugs that meant nobody knew. It was a way of life. They learned to get out of the way before their mother could 'blow.' They joked about it. "Mom's about to have a hissy," they would half-tease. Or, "She's on the war path," one of them would warn. They made funny faces when they cautioned each other, but they kept their distance until the coast was clear. Sometimes though, there was no escaping Ella's anger, and then there was nothing funny about it.

People tiptoed around Ada's mother, afraid to set her off. In an instant she could change, erupting into spasms of emotion that couldn't be predicted or accounted for. Her temper was legend and everyone had an Ella story. But the years of tantrums that labeled her 'tyrant' also served to mask a lifetime of untended hurt and pain that festered within her. And how could her children know that this woman who both allowed and injected so much pain into their lives, was herself a victim of an inscrutable pain from which she had yet to recover?

A Hard Head

By the time she was 12, it was clear that Ada was a strange kid. She did outlandish things, but more than that, outlandish things constantly happened to her. She was a contradiction. She was klutzy and absent-minded, and poised and old for her years. She could be giddy one minute, on the brink of tears the next, and then suddenly ready to fight.

At home, Ada displayed behaviors that her mother couldn't control. The whippings that had worked in the past were becoming less effective. Ella told Ada, "You have a hard head, and a hard head makes a soft behind." Ada knew what her mother meant, but she was prepared to endure the pain. The beatings proved that she'd driven her mother to distraction. If that was the price she had to pay for the privilege, the price was not too high.

During this time, another quirk developed. Ada started to pad her body with layers of clothing. At first Ella thought it was funny, but when the practice persisted and she couldn't force her to stop, she blew a hissy. The padding consisted of numerous pairs of shorts worn under her clothes to give the appearance of curves that didn't exist. She smoothed out the disguise with a long-line girdle that she'd pilfered from her mother's lingerie drawer. Her thin legs and arms extending from the obviously padded torso confirmed for Ella what she'd suspected for some time: her daughter had become a wack job.

Ella considered the outrageous behavior a reflection on her—a bad one. Ada wore the padding for days on end before laundering them. Ella attempted all manner of persuasion, but Ada refused to abandon the habit. When all else failed, a desperate Ella resorted to shaming the girl. She ridiculed her before friends and relatives, divulging the secret beneath her daughter's clothes and saying how musty Ada smelled with all of her unwashed padding.

This tactic also failed. Ada became angrier and more stubborn. Ella didn't know it, but the layers of clothing served a double purpose for her child. The obvious result was they added thickness to her form, giving her curves, and making her body more similar to her sister's. But more than that—and not even Ada was conscious of this—the layers meant protection for her. They shielded her body from unwanted physical contact. So the layering continued, the periods between washings increased, and Ada reveled in her mother's dismay.

Another war erupted each night. It took place in the room Ada shared with her sister. Ada was afraid of the dark and refused to sleep in a dark room. The battle wasn't between the sisters because Angela didn't care whether the light was on or not. The problem was Ella. Every month when the electric bill came, she brandished it above her head while she fumed and cursed the air. "Do you think we grow money on trees? You think I can run out the back door and pick money off of the bushes? Do you think I just dig holes and pull money out of the ground?"

Her mother would screech until her voice was gone. So every night, the battle raged. Ada always won. Cocooned within her soft cotton blanket, with only her eyes exposed, she'd wait for her mother to switch off the light. No matter how many times Ella turned the light off, in the morning, when she came into her daughter's room, the light was on again.

When bad things happened, Ada and Anthony were the usual suspects, whether there was evidence against them or not. Truthfully, Ada did cause a lot of trouble. But Ella, not being God, wasn't all-knowing, so Ada bristled at the fact that she was usually the first one accused. She was indignant for Anthony, too, because he followed close behind her in the number-two spot.

Ada vented anger by writing letters to her mother. These came in the form of prose and verse. They were hate poems, and although they weren't addressed or signed, it was obvious they were written for Ella and that Ada was the author. At an early age Ada began to show a talent for writing. She composed songs and wrote stories and received high marks and praise in her writing classes. She put these talents to use—explaining in vivid detail why she hated her mother. She expressed the hope that her mother would die, and even suggested the methods of her demise. Ella would find the poems where her daughter placed them. Sometimes she'd read them aloud, laughing to show Ada she hadn't inflicted pain. But she was pained that her daughter wanted to hurt and humiliate her. The gulf between them deepened.

Ella had two favorite sayings: "A liar will steal and a thief will lie," and, "There are two things I hate…a liar and a thief!" The words gave Ada powerful weapons to use against her mother.

Because Ella hated a thief, Ada decided it was great fun to take things from her mother. It increased her pleasure knowing Ella was aware of the thievery, and was powerless to stop it. When she was accused of stealing something, sometimes Ada lied. "No, I didn't take it," she would say, especially if it was obvious that she had. Then she'd wait for the sermon on liars and thieves. But usually when she stole things, with a smug look, she'd admit to the crime.

In the years to come, Ella would plead with Ada not to steal. When begging fell on deaf ears, Ella threatened her daughter with juvenile detention. "So, send me to Juvie. They can't stop me," Ada would boast. "You can't stop me and the police can't stop me. Nobody can stop me." Ada was miserable and she decided her mother should be, too.

School for Ada wasn't much better. There were problems with her behavior and with her academics. Her teachers conceded that she was bright. But she was inconsistent. She often couldn't do simple math problems or remember her times tables, so she counted on her fingers. Yet out of the blue, Ada would ace a math test that she should have failed. She had strange packets of knowledge that came out of nowhere, but at other times, data that should have been easy to recall was elusive. She daydreamed a lot. In the middle of class she often drifted away. She sometimes grew quiet and stared into space, as if in a trance or lost in deep thought. At other times, she was disruptive, willful and undisciplined. Her teachers praised her good disposition, or threw up their hands at her lack of restraint. She could be mature or childish, and her teachers thought certain of her behaviors were just plain weird.

Everybody agreed something was going on. Her moods, her disposition, and her behaviors could spin on a dime, as if there was more than one Ada. But she wouldn't talk, and no one could figure out how to help the troubled child.

During the first year of middle school, Ada developed the practice of writing upside down. She turned her papers upside down and leaned low across her desk until she almost covered it. From this awkward position, she wrote upside down.

Several of her teachers threw fits. They could see no reason for it. And she performed the ritual with such pomp and flair that she drew the other children's attention and caused a commotion in class. The report soon reached Ella, and she blew a gasket, too. But Ada stuck to her guns. No amount of reasoning on the part of teachers or school counselors could produce the desired effect. Ella punished her daughter, but without result, and so finally, she gave up. And Ada, who was proud of her small victory, continued the practice.

For science class, Ada developed another routine. She made it a point to take her seat each day, and then, without delay, she'd retrieve the treasure trove of makeup from the small cosmetics bag she always carried. With great care, she positioned the makeup on her desk. Then for the entire class period, she would admire herself in the mirror of her compact while applying makeup periodically throughout the hour.

Since ada was not allowed to wear makeup (her mother said she was too young) and since her mother so often called Ada vain, Ada decided to steal the makeup from her mother's purse. And for her, it was nothing more than a bonus that her mother's foundation matched her own skin tone; she would have taken it anyway.

Mr. Baker, the science teacher, would scold her in his quiet, puzzled voice. "This is not a cosmetics class, Ada," he would say, as he'd take the makeup from her. Little did he know, he was enabling. The fact that he persisted in confiscating her makeup necessitated her continuing to steal the cosmetics on a regular basis. But even when his vexation peaked and he implored her to adjust her behavior, Ada wouldn't. Once, when her teacher begged her to explain why she felt it was necessary to apply makeup during his class, she was at a loss.

She couldn't explain, even to herself, the reason for her conduct. Ada loved science and she respected Mr. Baker. And she could tell that even when he was irritated with her, he liked her, too. So it pricked her conscience when she caused him frustration.

Sometimes he'd keep her after class. He'd sit on the edge of his desk to have one of his serious talks with her and Ada would think how nice he was. *I wish he was my dad and I lived in his house,* she would tell herself.

But those were dreams that would never come true. She could never answer his questions. Not unless, she decided, he asked her the right one. There was something however that Ada was desperate to tell her teacher. She came close to talking to him on a couple of occasions. She remembered thinking once, *If only he would ask. I wish he would ask.* But he never did.

Still, when her tests were examined, Ada always got high marks, and her teacher was at a loss to explain how she could excel in a class she consistently ignored. And Ada hoped Mr. Baker would be proud and that he'd continue to like her.

But Ella was a different matter. Ada devised schemes to annoy her mother. This cosmetics theft was just such a scheme. The madder Ella got, the more Ada liked it. It was at some point before her eleventh birthday that Ada officially declared war. By now, she had many weapons in her arsenal and she perfected her use of them. The battle persisted for nearly three years. Her primary target was her mom, and though her allies were for the most part unseen, Ada was not fighting alone.

Finding God

After years of conflict, a miracle occurred: Ada found her way back to God. No one could say what caused the change, or precisely when it happened, but gradually the anger subsided, as if a truce had been called, and then, once again there was peace in Ella's house.

Theirs had always been a religious family. Even in her troubled years Ada accompanied her family to church, and during services she behaved like a good Christian. She could not be so irreverent as to disrespect God's house. But all bets were off once services ended. Usually Ada started cutting up even before they were home. Ella knew her daughter's piety was a charade, so contrived that it barely pricked the skin. But then out of nowhere, Ada *did* change, and the badness, it appeared, was behind her. Ella saw it as a tribute to God, an answer to her own passionate prayers, and as evidence of the Rev. Harris' powerful sermonizing. Ada got baptized. Ella couldn't have known the significance of that baptism for Ada. Ada was 14, the age August was when he died. August died unbaptized. Although Ella was not aware, Ada had burned with questions when August died.

She had sought out Reverend Harris and they walked in the park across from Ella's house. This was the day of her brother's funeral, shortly after the service. The girl had come home, and changed out of her Sunday clothes. She put on a pair of shorts with a matching ruffled top. The outfit was new, and she sensed it had been bought to appease her. They walked a short distance away from her house and stopped at the swing set. This was the scene of Ada's *transgression*, and it unnerved her to be there. She had not gone to the park since August died. It held damning memories for her. It resurrected her guilt, reminding her of the last time she'd seen her brother alive, and had spoken to him.

She had watched her brother start back across the park that day before she went racing home. She wished she had told him goodbye. She had not. Now she positioned herself on one of the swings, but she had not come there for play. She dug her feet into the soft ground beneath her so the swing could not move. Nagging questions consumed her thoughts.

"What happens to people when they die?" she asked the preacher who had known her since the day she was born.

In obvious discomfort, Reverend Harris cleared his throat. He paused a moment before he explained. "Ada, you know that when people are good, they go to heaven," he told her, and he drew in a fortifying breath before he went on. "But when people are bad…when they are wicked, they go to hell." Ada knew all about heaven and hell. She knew that bad people went to hell and burned forever, but the idea of that didn't bother her because no one she knew was bad enough to go to there. She didn't know any wicked people.

"So, August is in heaven," she stated. It wasn't a question. Because her brother was good Ada knew he was in heaven. What she wanted to know was: *what was heaven like?* She wondered how soon a person went to heaven after he died. Did he go there right away? And what was August doing there? Most importantly, Ada wanted to know if August could hear them and see them now. She wondered if he heard her when she talked to him, which she often did. She wondered what her brother was feeling. And if he understood how sorry she was that he was dead, how sorry she was that she caused it.

Since August's death, Ada had been afraid, though she wasn't quite sure why. She wasn't *really* afraid of August, not of *her* August, as she had known him—the way he had been before his death. *Her* August was quiet and gentle and even-tempered. She knew he loved her and would never hurt her. Even when she irritated him, he couldn't stay mad at her for long.

Ada remembered once, though, when August was supposed to be watching her and she had broken something. It was something important that belonged to her mom. She wasn't supposed to be meddling with it, and more than once, August had told her so. She messed with it anyway, and it broke. It was an accident, but August had yelled at her.

When Ella found out, she yelled, too, and then she whipped Ada with
a long, skinny switch, the worst kind. She had to admit though, she
really deserved it…but it bothered her that August got in trouble, too.
He didn't get whipped; he got grounded. He couldn't watch TV or ride
his bike for a week. He loved riding his bike more than anything. He
was mad and he stayed mad at her for a long time. And Ada felt guilty.
August seldom got into trouble, because he almost never did anything
to warrant it. Even when she said "sorry" (and he knew she meant it),
August was ticked. After a while, he came around. But Ada had been
sad when he was angry with her. She never wanted to upset him that
much again.

Now Ada wondered if people changed when they died. And if so, how
did they change? Ada could not be sure. She wanted answers to those
questions. She had heard Reverend Harris preach about dying. He said
that people give up their bodies when they die, so they can get into
heaven. They get angels' bodies, and great white wings, and they fly
away to glory.

Well, if August went straight to heaven and he was there now, then
Ada knew he was happy.

Everyone said heaven was a happy place, a better place. The streets
were paved with gold, and everyone there played on golden harps.
And you got to see Jesus and to be with God. So if he were in heaven,
then he'd have no reason to be mad at her. Or at least, she knew, he
wouldn't be able to stay mad for very long.

Reverend Harris was still carrying his big leather Bible. He had
been reading from the worn old book earlier, during services at the
church. He didn't open it now, but he massaged the fancy letters on
its face with the palm of one leathery hand. His face contorted, and
his brow—always creased—now folded into an even more cavernous
line, like somebody fighting a stomachache. The lettering in elegant
gold print read 'Holy Bible.' And the preacher stared so intently at
those words that Ada was looking there, as well. Ada had not noticed
before how old the minister was, but now she found herself studying
him, too. She decided that he was one of the oldest people she knew,
even older than Big Mama and Big Daddy; and older than Grandma
Reynolds, who Ella declared was older than God.

Reverend Harris continued fingering the ancient book like it was a talisman. Ada believed everything in that book. She wanted to hear again how great heaven was, and how happy August would be living there. She wanted him to read to her from the book. The Reverend looked at her solemnly, and when he spoke, his words, like his eyes, were filled with regret. "Ada," he said her name like he was testing his voice. His hesitance made her uneasy. "You know that August wasn't baptized when he died." Ada hadn't thought about that. None of them had gotten baptized yet.

She didn't respond, so the preacher continued, "The Bible says that in order to get into heaven you have to be baptized, Ada. It's like a rule." She regarded him with widened eyes. "You have to be born again and August wasn't born again. He wasn't born again, and he hadn't gotten baptized." Ada stared incredulously at the preacher's mouth while her mind dissected his words. She didn't care about the rule. It shouldn't apply to her brother. She narrowed her eyes into accusatory slits.

"So what are you saying? What does that mean?" Ada demanded. "August is not in hell!" She flung the words. The preacher noted the angst in her voice and measured his next words carefully. "Ada, sometimes it's hard for us to understand God's will, but when we remember that the Lord is a just God, we are able to accept his will, and that's what it means to have faith."

Then the preacher explained that God had created a place between heaven and hell. He told her this was a place where people could go when they died without being baptized. It wasn't as bad as hell, but you suffered there a while. Babies went there automatically, he said, and anyone who died before they were baptized. He explained that 12 years of age was *the age of consent*. That's when people become old enough to make the decision to accept Jesus. None of this made any sense to the child, and her expression told him so.

"Jesus was 12 when he went to the temple to teach the scribes. That's when he reached the age of consent," he tried to convince her. "Remember when Jesus worried his parents by disappearing from them during the Passover?"

Ada remembered the story. She loved the Bible stories and she always paid close attention at Sunday school. But she ignored the question now.

"That's when Jesus first knew God was his father." The Reverend reminded her, "Remember when they came looking for him, Jesus told Mary and Joseph that they should have known he would be in the house of his father. So when Jesus was 12 years old, he knew who his true father was, and that's when he agreed to do God's will. He was old enough then."

The old man regarded the top of Ada's bowed head. He couldn't see her tears, but her shoulders shook slightly and she sniffed several times, and he knew she was crying. "I know this is hard to understand, Ada. August was a good boy. But at 14, he *was* old enough to be baptized. And unfortunately he wasn't. He couldn't go straight into heaven, Ada." Ada remained silent. "But he isn't in hell, Ada. He's in purgatory."

Ada asked the question she was compelled to ask, knowing the answer would deepen her pain: "What's it like in purgatory? Do people *burn* in purgatory?" Ada had squeezed her eyes shut, as if closing them tight would lessen the sting. She wanted the preacher to answer her, "No, it's a place where people go to sleep and rest." She wanted him to say, "No, Ada, he's just asleep. In a deep sleep without dreams"…that it was like the coma she learned about just before August had died. But that wasn't the answer he gave. He evaded the question, saying instead: "This is not an eternal punishment, Ada. And you need to remember that our prayers can shorten the time it takes to redeem a soul from purgatory. And Ada, there are many people praying for your brother."

Redeem a soul. What does that mean? It was too much. Ada stopped listening. Without a word, she got to her feet and started back across the grass toward her mother's house. He watched her stiff little back as she walked away from him. The preacher shared the young girl's distress. But he knew there was no way to console her. When Ada asked to talk to him, he had dreaded the conversation. They had spoken on several occasions before, and her insight always impressed him. Ada was a bright and sensitive little girl. He knew her brother's death deeply troubled her.

The preacher had accepted the notion that God's ways are above man's. But that concept was hard for a child of 10, even one as perceptive as Ada. "We can't question God's will," he told Ada. "There are many

things that are hard for us to understand, and there are *some* things
we aren't meant to understand at all." He directed these words to her
back. When she was older he hoped she'd be able to accept that truth.
But for now there was no comforting her. He couldn't find the words.

His own thoughts were troubled as he matched his steps to the young
girl's. He placed one hand on her shoulder, hoping to express with a
touch what his words had failed to convey. In silence, they walked the
short distance back to the house. She walked with slow, determined
steps. She ignored the tears that flowed down her cheeks; she didn't
try to wipe them away. She didn't want to draw attention to them.
And she didn't speak again to the Reverend Harris. She didn't tell him
how his words tore at her heart. Her brother wasn't in heaven. He was
suffering somewhere, in a place like hell. There was no way she could
get him out.

And Ada remembered her mother's pained words. "If you had been
where you were supposed to be, your brother would still be alive." Her
mother had spoken in grief, but still the words rang true.

Ada felt helpless and sad. She crossed the street to her house. There
were people on her front porch. They were friends, mostly from
church. The air was filled with the smell of food. She had smelled the
aromas all day. People were still getting out of their cars and making
their way to her house. Their street was lined with cars, like someone
was having a party. Ada could hear voices from inside the house.
Some of the voices were festive, like they didn't know someone had
died. Her brother was in purgatory, a place as bad as hell. A place
where you suffer and burn until God says you can get out.

And her house overflowed with relatives and friends. They were
having a party while her brother was dead. *I wish they would all go
home.*

Ada entered the house and she closed the screen door behind her.
She entered the crowded front room. Several people looked up. They
smiled benevolent smiles and extended well-meaning greetings. Some
showed concern, softly calling her name when they saw her tears. Ada
didn't respond.

She maneuvered her way through the sea of people, her eyes glued
to the floor. She needed to get to her room. She was being rude, she
knew it, but she didn't care. Tears still streamed down her face, and

she felt she was on display. She wanted to disappear; to be alone to interpret her thoughts and to calm her mind. There was no clarity to her thoughts. They were fleeting and scattered, swirling out of control.

If she was alone, in the safety of her room, maybe she could hold on to an idea long enough to make it make sense.

She had just reached her bedroom when someone, very close to her ear, whispered her name. Ada didn't answer. For a brief moment, she wondered who had called her. She wondered what they wanted. She dismissed the voice. She suddenly felt tired….

Now the voice was in her head. She strained to listen…"Just go to sleep now," was all it said. And then it turned to mist and evaporated like dew drops on a sun-drenched day. Ada succumbed to the familiar sensation of weightlessness. She closed her eyes and drifted away.

Baptized

Late one night, the last night of summer revival service, Adalia stood up and accepted the Lord Jesus as her own personal savior. Ella never looked a gift horse in the mouth. So when her younger daughter was persuaded to repent at the tail end of that revival program, Ella was as surprised as anyone, but she was proud and happy. In her heart and out loud, Ella said, "Thank the good Lord," and she meant it! She had worried about Ada's eternal soul, and she was happy to have her daughter back and to have peace in her life again.

Ella never understood the turmoil that brewed between the girl and herself. She prayed about it. She implored God to reveal the cause of the problem with her daughter. She had her theories. She knew that Ada envied her older sister. In her view, the jealousy was without cause, but Ella decided it was the root of Ada's problems. Ada tormented her sister whenever she could. She wore Angela's clothes to school, even though they were too big for her. And she wore Angela's shoes, although they were too small and they pinched her feet.

When she discovered that some new article of clothing had been worn and discarded, or that her favorite shoes had been stretched out of shape and would no longer fit her, Angela would dissolve into angry tears. Ada developed a callus from forcing her too-big feet into her sister's shoes.

No one understood why she loved to torment her sister the way she did. Once, a desperate Ella gave Angela permission to 'beat the crap' out of her sister. That didn't work, either. Nothing did. No persuasion, coercion, or threatening tone dissuaded Ada from torturing her sister. "Ada, why do you persist in irritating your sister so?" Ella often demanded, but the question went unanswered. It never occurred to the frustrated mother that her daughter *had* no answer. "Because I want to," was all the girl would say. "When I *don't* want to anymore, I'll stop."

The truth is, Ada had decided that Angela was her mother's favorite. That was an offense the older girl had to pay for. And since punishing Angela also heaped coals upon Ella's head, the benefit was twofold. For her, it was a win/win situation.

Ella was aware of the accusation Ada threw at her; the charge that she played favorites. It was ridiculous. She reminded Ada and anyone else who would listen, "I gave birth to all of my children. I carried them all. I had the same labor pains every time I lay down to give birth. How could I love one child more than another?"

In theory it made sense, but Ada refused to buy it, so the battle continued until that sweltering summer night when Ada stood up in church and told the congregation, "I want to be a Christian." With bated breath, Ella waited for the day of the baptism, and she wasn't entirely convinced until Ada came up out of the baptismal pool. As far as miracles go, this feat wasn't on par with the virgin birth, but for Ella, it ranked right up there.

Peter Collins

Ada was 15 when she met Peter Collins. She was 16 when she married him and gave birth to his child. The night they met, First Baptist Church was having an ice cream social. The Young Adult Choir had sponsored it, and they hired a jazz trio for entertainment. This was a first; it'd never happened before, and the conservative little church was rife with opinion regarding the matter.

Ada loved music, and she was beside herself at the thought that a real live band, a group of professional musicians, was coming to their church. She spent most of her allowance each week on records–LPs and 45s. She especially loved the Motown girl groups, and she knew all of the lyrics to their songs. She knew her voice was good, and she dreamed that one day she'd be a famous singer, like Gladys Knight, Diana Ross or Martha Reeves.

Ada and her sister and two other girls from school formed a singing group. The girls were really her sister's friends. They were two years older than Ada, like her sister was, and she was flattered she was allowed to sing with them. She knew what that meant: it meant acceptance. Ada had always been Angela's little sister. When Ada started high school Angela was already a sophomore. Angela was cool and popular.

It wasn't just that she was cute. Angela was built. Boys liked her. They didn't see her as a little girl because she didn't look like one. Instead of sharp, protruding bones, Angela had soft, round curves. She didn't need to stuff her bra with socks like Ada did; she had real breasts. She was tall and shapely. Her features were perfect, and her fawn-colored skin was flawless. She didn't have to fight with her mom to wear makeup; she and Ella *shared* makeup tips. Angela was even allowed to borrow Ella's clothes, and they looked good on her.

To Ada, it was plain that she didn't measure up to her sister or to
her sister's friends. So when she was with them, she felt like she was
tolerated but not really wanted. And it wasn't that Angela mistreated
her sister. She didn't. But everyone knew that when Ada tagged along,
it was as an unofficial chaperone. Ella knew there was less chance that
the girls would get into trouble with Ada nearby.

Ada's real value was that she could always be counted on to tattle.
"Ada couldn't keep a secret in a bucket," Ella would say, and mostly it
was true. It was in her nature to blab. Ada could spill the beans even
before she knew there were beans to spill. Still, the major conflicts
between the two girls were over. Ada no longer tormented her sister.
The jealousy she'd felt when she was younger had been replaced with
something bordering veneration. She was proud of her pretty sister
who was so well liked and popular. She looked up to her, and she
relished being called Angela's little sister. It gave her a kind of a status
that she couldn't achieve on her own.

She and Angela grew close. They had become friends. Still, the two-
year difference in their ages might as well have been ten. Ada was
younger than her 15 years while Angela was mature for her age, and
that caused the only rift between them. But when Ada opened her
mouth to sing, her talent transcended her youthfulness.

She was writing lyrics and composing songs in grade school. By ear,
she picked out the melodies that filled her brain on an old piano their
mother bought. She performed her compositions for anyone who
listened, basking in the high praise of family and friends who had
become her captive audience.

Her mother scolded her constantly for humming at the dinner table.
It was considered bad manners. Ada appreciated the importance of
etiquette, so this was a habit she wasn't proud of. She tried to stop but
she was unaware that she was humming most of the time. There were
always melodies in her head, struggling to get out. And they would
inevitably find their way past her closed lips and out of her mouth.
It wasn't something she was mindful of. Like a force of nature, like
breathing, the occurrences were natural. But others became aware.
In middle school, she caught the attention of the music teacher, Mrs.
Carson. Ada and her sister had both been accepted as members of the

Madrigals. That was the prestigious name of Joyce Kilmer School's advanced choir.

The two girls entertained Ella and Jacob (and themselves) with songs from the musical *Sound of Music*, which they knew from beginning to end, just as their teacher had taught it to them. They divided their sweet voices into perfect two-part harmonies and sang for hours on end. Music was a pleasant diversion for Angela, but for Ada, it was more than that. It was more a passion than a pastime.

She could lose herself in a song. She escaped, could hide in a melody, just as she escaped into the words she produced with the aid of paper and pen. At church, Ada found a new outlet for her passion; she sang with the Young Adult Choir. At 14, she was asked to audition with them. She was happy to be considered old enough and good enough. When she was accepted, and graduated from the Youth Choir (she called it the baby choir) what Ada felt was pure bliss.

She often was asked to sing lead. She loved the reaction she got when she belted out a song. The big voice coming out of her small body always surprised people. She loved the idea that her voice could electrify the congregation, and began to realize there was power in it. When she sang, the church would erupt into an absolute frenzy. People would be filled with the Holy Ghost, and Ada had to work to remind herself she was *supposed* to be singing to honor the Lord, and not to make herself look good.

And now Peter Collins was at her church. He and two other boys had been hired to play. She and her sister chose good seats on the benches near the front of the church, along with the other members of the choir. They weren't singing on that night. They were spectators, and Ada found herself vainly wishing the boys would be hearing her sing. But they weren't a part of the program. The event had been vigorously announced by word of mouth and with colorfully penned ads, which read: "You're Invited! It's our annual Ice Cream Social. Join us for an enjoyable evening of gospel and jazz…Followed by ice cream, punch, and cake."

The catchy flyers were professionally printed and had been hand circulated for several weeks prior to the event. The young ladies in the church (most of them sang in the choir) had at first discussed whether they *could* find 'enjoyment' in any kind of music that didn't have vocals, but after catching sight of the musicians, they locked themselves in a new debate. The new discussion centered on which of the three boys was the cutest. Their scrutiny wasn't unnoticed.

From time to time, the guys would throw the girls a casual glance, causing them to feign indifference. But when Peter looked up and caught her eye, Ada's nervousness showed. It embarrassed her to be caught looking at him. Cocking one brow, he surveyed her, piercing her with a studious gaze that appeared to see everything all at once. She later learned this was his signature look. It added to his charisma and appeal.

His face was, for the most part, unreadable, but Ada sensed a confidence in him that bordered on arrogance. She was intrigued. Even under the best of circumstances, Ada lacked confidence. With her pretty sister beside her and the other girls from the choir there as well, the competition wasn't merely stiff; it was ludicrous. She had about as much chance with Peter Collins as an ice cube in hell.

Besides that, there was something about him, some vague, whispered badness, and a quiet coolness in his eyes that spoke of danger. It warned her, *this boy really isn't a nice person.*

Ada ignored the premonition. She shouldn't have. She fell into the spell of the magnetic young man at the piano, and was hooked. With lethal attraction, her fate was sealed and on that day a disastrous new chapter began in her life.

Memories

By the time Ada met Peter, although she wasn't completely aware of it, parts of 10 years had vanished from her life. As though she'd been sleeping and dreaming, she strolled through adolescence in a daze. She recounted her life in highlights and excerpts, like trailers from a movie. She remembered that Jacob married her mom, but the actual ceremony was lost in a fog. Her brother's death was embossed on her brain, but its aftermath was surreal.

Somewhere along the stream of time she and Ella grew closer. They managed to develop the typical mother-daughter relationship, one with all of the usual problems attached. Angela's friends were Ada's friends now, too. And she and her sister were friends. They shared makeup tips and fashion tips; they wore each other's clothes, and gossiped about boys. Angela was her protector, the big sister who looked out for her.

For the most part Ada's life was good, except that key parts were missing, which bothered her. There were snapshots to prove her presence in the world, but often she felt more like a visitor in it. Her family would tell stories of places they'd been and things they'd seen, but Ada was liable to not remember. People were always forcing their memories on her, and she learned to pretend that they were her own. It was easier that way.

"Come on Ada, you were there," she'd be coaxed. "You have to remember." But she would not. She tried not to question the strange lapses of time that plagued her or to agonize over them. And usually, they didn't derail her. She just told herself: *This is the way I am. I've always been this way and I probably always will be.* But sometimes the quirkiness bothered her. She'd feel foolish or embarrassed by something she couldn't remember, and she'd laugh about it to mask her unease. At 14, when she made her *great change*, she became good-natured. She learned to mock herself. People liked her. She became genuinely kind-hearted, and fun to be around.

Most people didn't recall her turbulent pre-teen years, her reign of terror. Those who did remember just chalked it up to growing pains, and so she was absolved. Her friends, those who knew her well, overlooked the kinks in her personality, and accepted the inconveniences they caused. They covered for her when they could and ignored the weirdness when they could not. Strangers who witnessed her odd behaviors simply thought she was eccentric. She was obviously intelligent, so they forgave many of her foibles. And since she never had to face them again, the opinions of strangers weren't of real consequence to her, anyway.

Her oddities took many forms. She might promise to meet a friend somewhere, and when she failed to show up, she'd insist that either she had never made any plans, or that she had completely forgotten them. She'd be so contrite, it would be hard to stay angry with her. She routinely forgot people, places, times, and events. She lost *things—misplaced them*—all the time. She *got* lost all the time. She might seem to not remember a person she should know, or claim never to have been to some place she had been. She lost track of time and was never on time. Simple directions confused her unless they were explicit and meticulously written down. Even then, there was no guarantee she could follow them. One day she would claim to love a particular food, or a color…or a movie she had been to; the next day, without warning, her predilections would change.

 She could snub a good friend or acquaintance and later apologize, insisting it was an oversight. Sometimes, it appeared she was lying about her role (or her lack of involvement) in some situation or circumstance, but by reputation, she was moral and honest, so it was difficult to reconcile these conflicting aspects of her character. It was generally accepted that, no matter how guilty she might appear to be, she was somehow innocent in *motive* if not in deed.

These were the flaws that weakened Ada, and inside, where no one could see, she felt highly at risk. She had the constant sensation of walking a tightrope or hugging the edge of a precipice. She never felt she was on level ground. She tried to hide it, but the stress of this nagging fear made her feel fragile, and this frailty made her easy prey. She couldn't have known it, but Peter Collins sensed this frailty the moment they met. Like a consummate predator, he sized her up. He studied her until he smelled her fear and fully exposed her weakness, and this weakness more than anything else attracted Peter to her.

The Courtship

When the music ended, Peter and his band joined their hosts for refreshments. There was ice cream and cookies and cake, and supervised socializing. Some of the older members of the church, who disapproved of the arrangements to begin with, were present to make sure the evening's events remained wholesome. Ada, her sister, and several other girls from the choir were seated at long wooden tables covered with white paper cloths. The rented tables and folding chairs were special, provided especially for the occasion.

Ada snatched up a ringside seat to watch Peter and his friends perform. She was fascinated on so many levels. She felt like she was at a concert, or at least, this was the way she imagined a live concert would be. This experience was a first for her. She wasn't allowed to date yet— she couldn't even talk to boys yet—not officially, anyway. She was impressed by the music the guys played. They sounded like a recording, as good as anything she heard on the radio; as good as the records she listened to endlessly. Their sound was like R&B but with a soulful, jazzy feel. She knew jazz, from listening to her Uncle McNeil's recordings. He played Wes Montgomery and Nancy Wilson and Nat King Cole for her, and she liked them. She even listened to 'Old Blue Eyes,' Frank Sinatra. When he played his LPs for her, her uncle told her, chidingly: "Now your music education is complete. This is real music."

What she was hearing in church made it hard for her to stay in her seat. She wanted to sing along with the catchy melodies, and she wanted to dance. The music caused Ada to daydream. She and Angela and two of their friends, Garvena and Janice, had formed a group. They called themselves Tempest Four. She wasn't sure where the name came from, but she thought they were good. They hadn't rehearsed for a while, because they couldn't find a band to play for them, but the dream hadn't died. Ada still saw bright lights, and fame, and a record deal in their future.

She could see herself on stage. She would be the lead singer. She saw
herself touring with a band, with admiring fans calling her name. She
would write and sing her own music. She and Angela would pluck her
family from middle-class black suburbia. Ada would be happy. Her
mom would be proud.

The trance was broken when the three young musicians finished their
performance and sat down across from her. She thought she would
die. She was seated at the end of one of the tables. She didn't look up.
Her vocal chords were frozen and she knew she couldn't speak, but it
didn't matter. The boys, she knew, had to be there because of Angela
or one of the other girls at the table. They wouldn't want to talk to her.
Boys always flocked to Angela and her friends. She was too skinny
to draw anyone's attention and too awkward to keep it if she did. She
concentrated on the small plastic fork that had had been pointed in the
direction of her mouth. The utensil held a piece of gooey white cake that
all at once was too big for her mouth. The confection no longer appealed
to her. She just wanted to put the fork down and leave the table, but
that would look weird. For the sake of appearances, she jammed the
cake into her mouth, and found that it tasted like sawdust. Ada gulped
twice to force it past the knot that had formed in her throat. But the knot
moved to her stomach, and prevented the food from settling there. Ada
was afraid the cake would come up. She could taste its bitter aftermath
in the back of her throat, and she wanted to gag. Extreme nerves always
affected her this way.

She had never been this close to a boy before, and she wondered if the
sanctity of the church annulled her mother's rules about being with
boys. Her mother had lots of rules about boys. Her girls could receive
phone calls from boys when they turned 15, but they couldn't go out on
dates. When they were 16 they could go out on the weekends, but their
curfew was 11 o'clock, and no one messed with Ella's curfew!

"When can we stay out till 12:00?" they used to ask her. "When you're
married," she would answer.

Nothing at all happened during the week. Schoolwork came first and
was a priority in Ella's house. As a result, all of the kids got excellent
grades. Because Angela and Ada both consistently made the honor roll,
Ella had amended a rule. She allowed boys to come to the house on

weekends to visit both girls, even though Ada was only 15. But they still had to be chaperoned. And Ada still couldn't go out with boys.

Angela had a string of boyfriends. Acquiring them required very little effort on her part. She was 17 now, a senior, and had been dating for a year. Ada loved to watch her sister get ready for dates. Then she'd listen enviously to the details of the date at the end of the night. Boys nearly fell over themselves trying to get next to her. But Angela's tall, good-looking boyfriends never seemed to notice Ada. They were always nice to her, teasing and friendly, but they saw her as a kid. It was pitiful. Her mother's rules were wasted on her, since no one was interested anyway.

Peter's deep voice registered through her thoughts, and tore her away from her daydream again. *He's way cool*, she mused. "Too cool to cough," her sister would say.

It was amazing how his words mixed smoothly with the banter that flowed up and down the table, and still his voice managed to stand out. He'd fit in anywhere, she decided. She wanted to look at him, but didn't dare. Instead, she continued to stare at the ice cream that had turned to mush on her soggy paper plate. She didn't glance up until she heard her name. "Ada!" It was Angela who called her name. "I was just telling the guys about our singing group."

Peter was looking at Ada, and a queer little smile lurked at the corners of his lips. She ignored his gaze, and focused on Angela instead, hoping she looked less stupid than she felt. Her sister made a face that said, "Hey girl, I'm trying to help you out here," and she knew it was true. When Ada told her sister earlier she thought Peter was cute, Angela told her, "Go for it."

"Do *you* think he's cute?" Ada had asked her sister. "He's all right," she said, but the answer lacked enthusiasm, and Ada was glad. She didn't want Angela to like Peter. She didn't need the competition. *If I were Catholic*, she thought, *I'd be praying to the saint of lost causes right now.* Instead, she thanked God that Angela was out of the running.

Ada realized that conversation was still flowing around her, but she wasn't part of it. She tried to listen, catching bits and pieces of it…but her mind was mired in its own thoughts. She did know that when the boys sat down, they'd circled Angela like Indians around a wagon train. Her own name had gotten *some* wear and tear, but when the dust settled, the tall, studious-looking bass player (his name was Kenny) had

Angela's phone number. Marilyn Johnson was talking to the drummer, whose name was Jimmy, while Ada sat there like a bump on a log. She felt like the consolation prize.

She heard her name and realized Peter was looking at her. He had asked her a question but she'd been daydreaming again.

What was the question, she asked herself. *Oh, yeah*: "So you guys have a singing group?" he had asked. She scrambled for an answer. All she came up with was, "Yeah, well, we had a group but we couldn't find anybody to play for us."

"The guys might be willing to play for us," Angela said. She was still trying to help.

"Yeah, that'd be cool."Ada answered. It was all she could manage to say.

When she spoke she moved forward in her seat and bumped the rickety table hard with her knee. At the same time, with one little jerk of her elbow she knocked the plastic spoon from the sodden plate of melted ice cream and cake, and overturned the cup of punch she had abandoned soon after Peter sat down. It formed a sticky puddle on the table, and then dripped onto the floor. A bright red pool of it splashed over her legs and puddled around her feet. She was surprised how much punch that Styrofoam cup held. The distraction drowned out her answer. "OK, now he knows I'm stupid," she murmured to herself.

"Here, take this." Peter leaned across the table to hand her a small stack of paper napkins, which she used to try to wipe the punch from her legs. He was speaking directly to her, and his voice sounded amused. Ada was mortified, but she knew she had to answer him. The conversation went like this:

"Man, I can't believe I did that. What a mess. Thanks."

"Don't sweat it. It's no big deal. I'll get you some more punch."

"No, that's OK, I was finished, anyhow. But thanks."

"Seriously, it's not a problem. I was gonna get myself some more, anyway," he said.

Ada was trying to sound nonchalant, but she didn't pull it off. She was having trouble putting sentences together and she was afraid he was laughing at her. "And, I'd love to hear you guys sing," Peter added. He had said that as he came to his feet and moved toward the corner of the room where the refreshments were served. Ada didn't answer. She was too nervous. When he came back to the table he had brought her a glass of punch anyway, and he had a small paper bowl with a rock-hard Neapolitan ice cream square in it. She wished he hadn't. She was much too jittery to eat or drink. She watched the ice cream melt.

Within a week, Peter had called her on the phone. Within a month, he was a fixture at their house. She found it hard to believe he was interested in her. She couldn't believe that her mother allowed it. This boy was almost three years older than her, practically a man. But for some reason Ella liked him. Ada kept pinching herself.

Peter seemed too good to be true. He wasn't quite 18, but already he had a real job, working for an electronics company and earning a lot of money. Everything about him was *cool*, including his sports car, a fire-engine-red '65 Dodge Charger. It had no scratches, no rust, and no dents. "It's cleaner than the board of health," she bragged to her friends, who were suitably green with envy. He washed his car at least twice a week, and it always had a fresh coat of wax. Whenever he drove up, she was thrilled. He gunned the motor, announcing his arrival, when he pulled up in front of her house, and the neighborhood girls went mad. He looked good in that car.

She still wasn't allowed to leave the house with him, not until she turned 16. But they sat on the living room couch, kissing (Ella didn't know about the kissing), holding hands and talking in quiet voices. It was official. He was her boyfriend, the first real one she had. He called her his 'main squeeze,' which meant she belonged to him.

He came over every weekend and stayed until 11 o'clock. He'd laugh and joke with Ella for a while, but Jacob always made himself scarce and never had much to say. In time, Ella would disappear but Ada's little brothers stayed underfoot, forcing Peter to bribe them for privacy. For a couple of bucks, they would leave Peter alone with their sister.

At 10:30, the countdown began. Ella would call out the time, letting the teenagers know that the clock was ticking. They dated for almost a year before Ada turned 16 and won the right to go out with Peter. When Peter started taking computer classes at the local university, she couldn't get over how smart he was. Already, he could fix just about anything: radios, TVs, clocks, anything electronic. But in the matter-of-fact manner she loved, he informed her: "Computers are the wave of the future, and that's where my future lies." Ada burst with pride.

Meanwhile, Angela had gone off to Ball State. She was a freshman there, studying to be a teacher, and she had a steady boyfriend of her own. When she brought him home to meet the family, Ada knew it was serious. He was several years older than Angela, but Ella liked him, too. His name was Gary Williams, and he was earning a degree in business. That scored high marks with Ella. He was making something of himself, and Ella deemed him a good catch for her daughter. When Peter and Gary met, Ada was proud that her boyfriend could hold his own with a college guy.

Peter had talents Ella and Ada weren't aware of. For one thing, he could wiretap phones and bug houses. When they discovered this talent years later, Ella laughed, and ascribed it to the mad genius gene. She wasn't unduly concerned. "There's a thin line between genius and insanity. You can't get to be as smart as Peter without having a few kinks in the armor," she said. It turned out that Peter had more kinks than they knew.

Despite a full load of classes, Peter still worked full-time for a major electronics firm. It was already obvious he was going places. When he started taking the computer classes the notion was confirmed.

Ella boasted on him. "Very few whites and no blacks at all could get a job like his without a degree in electronics. And now he's learning computers, too!" She was pleased with the choices her girls had made. She saw their successes as her own personal accomplishments. Their good decisions reflected well on her. Ada was happy that her mother was proud. *She* was pretty proud, too. She still couldn't see what Peter saw in her, but whatever it was… Ada wanted to make sure that it never changed. He held her like he thought she might break; treated her like a princess; and he made her feel precious and loved. It was something she'd never experienced before.

He told her she was beautiful and smart, and that he loved her innocence. He bought her little presents that made her feel special, and when they were together, he made it plain that she belonged to him.

Peter could be jealous, but Ada liked that, too. She liked the idea that he cared enough to feel possessive of her. She couldn't imagine he believed she'd be interested in anyone else, (there could never be anyone else) or that he could be insecure where other boys were concerned. He'd lost his temper once when a boy just looked at her. He grabbed her by the arm and jerked it so hard that it hurt, and for a moment, it scared her. But when he apologized and pulled her up against him, his voice was filled with regret, and there were tears in his eyes. "I'm sorry, Ada. You know I would never hurt you, baby. It's just that I hate the idea of some other guy looking at you. You belong to me, Ada. I can't live without you and I don't wanna share." And then he said: "I love you, Ada."

'I love you, Ada.' Those were magic words. That's when she really knew he cared. He had cried real tears when he thought he hurt her; when he thought there was a chance he could lose her. For Ada, this knowledge was profound. She never had really felt loved. Now, this perfect guy *cared* about her. He was strong. He was smart. And he cared.

Ada learned something that day. She learned she could forgive Peter, even if he hurt her. She could forgive him because he cared. Peter learned something too… and for him, another piece of the puzzle fell into place. He *tasted* the need in her, the greedy need for affection. It was palpable, and it flowed from the core of her being. He knew that she liked feeling small in his arms, like a child in the arms of a caring dad. That bit of info would be useful. He had deliberately hurt her that day, just enough, just enough to *see*. He was testing the waters.

When he grabbed her by her arm, her feet lifted easily from the ground. It actually surprised him. He knew she was slight, but oh, the feeling he got when she flew up in his hands like a leaf in high wind. Her big eyes grew wider and he read the emotions written there. She was confused at first, because she didn't know how she'd upset him.

The truth was, she hadn't done anything, and that was the beauty of it. *She hadn't caused his anger at all.* His rage, in fact, had been make-believe. He manufactured it. He could do so at will, whenever he wanted to startle Ada with some act of domination. Peter knew that the element of surprise was a useful tool when dealing with women. He'd had girlfriends before. Even when Ada was convinced that he was only with her, Peter had girls on the side. She would find out soon enough; he could never belong to anyone. So he wasn't jealous, and the outbursts of temper were simply a means of controlling her.

He replayed the scene in his mind, stringing together the components. He played little games with her, *orchestrated* to show how strong he was. He pulled up his sleeves and flexed his hard muscles for her and her stupid little brothers. She would 'oooh' and 'aaah' like a schoolgirl when she felt his sinewy arms. When she wrestled him, of course he would win. But she pretended to be surprised, and would protest. But she *liked* it when he beat her. She thought it made her look cute. Sometimes just looking at her sickened him, and yet he realized that her need to be dominated could be useful to him. So when she widened her eyes in fear, he smiled inside. He would patiently cultivate that fear, harvesting a full, healthy crop of it.

Another emotion that clouded her eyes was sadness. Like a whisper she strained to hear, it drifted in softly, but it was darker than gloom, and thicker than fog. Its effect on her was potent, intoxicating. Like wine to a wino, it addled her brain. It came quickly on the wings of her fear. He recognized it and congratulated his own skill, priding himself on this great knack he had for reading people. He still had to learn where her weaknesses came from. And then all the pieces would fall into place. But this was enough for now.

Peter decided Ada was a keeper. She could be worked with. She was young and easy to mold. She seemed to want a daddy. He was happy to give her one.

So he held her while she cried, and delivered the speech he'd rehearsed so well. He looked into her eyes *and he cried on cue,* while he mentally recited his findings: *She needs to think that I care...I can hurt her because she cares...She is easily convinced that I care.* He felt almost giddy with pride. For Peter Collins, this was a productive day.

Home Run

Ada was working Peter's last nerve. By now, he had wasted more than four months on her, and still he hadn't gotten past first base. She kept making up stupid excuses, and it was a real struggle for him to keep his cool. He knew he could just take it from her. Then he could dump her. She was so easily frightened, he was sure he could get what he wanted and still keep her quiet. But he wanted her to *give in to him*, because he decided he wasn't through with her yet.

Peter had to admit that he liked being with her as much as she liked being with him. He didn't see this as a bad thing but it was news to him, this recognition that *she* brought something of value to the relationship. She fed his ego, made him feel good about himself. She made him feel strong and in control, and he *liked* having her around.

He would tell her, "You're my woman." She'd grin a silly grin and melt like warm butter in his hands, and he liked it. He gave her little tasks to do, just to keep her in line. "Ada, make yourself useful," he'd tell her. "Go out to the car and get me my jacket." And she would scurry off like a scared rabbit to bring him a jacket he didn't really want or need. Or he'd say, "Make yourself useful and get me a drink." She'd do it.

The control he had over her was addictive. He couldn't get enough of it but he had to be cool. He didn't want to become too attached, to need her.

He wanted to tell her, "Ada, make yourself useful and give me some." He knew he couldn't say that just yet. He was wearing her down. She let him use his finger on her, and for the time being that was enough. His friends, *his boys*, believed he was the man. He bragged to them about his little church girl. "Yeah man, she's my woman," he told them. "I could have her now if I wanted. I'm just taking my time. If you play your cards right, you can get 'em to do anything you want 'em to do. But don't worry. I got her nose wide open."

By that, he meant she had fallen hard for him. The guys believed him because he was smooth. It was obvious that her nose was open. Peter kept his friends up to date with play-by-plays of his progress with Ada. And they cheered him on.

"Hey man, that's cold!" they would say. But the words were meant as a compliment. Peter knew how to keep his women in line. He was the model they studied.

When they finally had sex, Peter couldn't believe it himself. He'd been sweet-talking her like usual, kissing and groping her, and begging for more. She was pushing at his hands like she always did; fighting him off, and then…and then all of a sudden it seemed…he was inside her.

"Peter. That hurts! What are you doing?" Her voice had registered, but barely.

He answered her. "It's OK, Ada. I love you. You know I love you? I'd never hurt you. You won't get pregnant, baby. You can trust me, Ada. You know you can trust me."

She continued protesting and pushing at his hands. "We can't, Peter," she wailed, and her voice was desperate. He promised her, "Ada, I won't spill in you; I can take it out in time."

The words were instinctive; they never consulted his brain. Her eyes were closed. He had a vague awareness that she was crying, that he was hurting her, but he didn't stop. Then she was quiet and still, and he was inside her. She wasn't fighting him anymore. She wasn't pushing at his hands or trying to make him stop.

He didn't know, though it wouldn't have mattered, that Ada had turned her mind off and drifted away. Her body was still available, and he was consumed with need. When he violently shuddered and pulled himself out of her, Ada was just nominally aware.

He wasn't concerned that she might become pregnant. He *had* pulled himself free before he could spill. He was satisfied. He looked at Ada. She appeared groggy or dazed, like she'd just awakened from a deep sleep. Peter liked to study her face. He used it as a lesson plan. It taught him so much, but still, there was a lot to learn about her. This was phase two. He'd gotten her to 'put out,' although even he questioned whether she'd been fully present.

She didn't look at him. Mechanically, she sat up and straightened her clothes. Her parents (their mistake) trusted him enough to leave them alone in the darkened living room. They turned in early, instructing Peter that the curfew was still 11 o'clock. Her pesky little brothers hadn't interrupted them once. They had been asleep for over an hour. But still, there was always a chance that they could be caught, and the knowledge added a nervous excitement.

Peter watched Ada's back as she navigated the dark hall to the bathroom. She hadn't spoken to him, and he wondered if she was mad. Didn't matter. He knew he could straighten her out. He smiled a smug smile to congratulate himself.

He couldn't wait to tell his 'boys.'

Knocked Up

When Ada first suspected, she couldn't process the information. It couldn't be true. But it was. She had missed two periods and the third one was late. Ada was always the first to admit how naive she was, but even she knew what that meant.

The first missed period slipped by her. When she missed her second period, she started to worry. Now, Ada was late for the third month and she was panicked. She kept asking herself when this could have happened, and how. But she didn't have an answer. Ada felt stupid and sick and miserable. And she didn't know what to do. She wanted to talk to Angela, but Angela was away at school. She couldn't tell any of her friends. She didn't want to see pity or disapproval in their eyes.

Her reputation would be ruined. Now she was one of *those* girls, a bad girl who got into trouble. She'd have to go to a home for unwed mothers, for sure. Ella would kill her. Then she'd have a fit, and then she'd kick her out. No, there was no one she could tell.

For the previous month, she'd been hiding Kotex under her mattress. She made a big production of announcing her period. She whined and complained that she was dying from cramps and couldn't go to school.

She used up several packages of pads, and begged for money to buy more. She was biding her time until Angela came home. Angela was coming for a visit in a couple of weeks; she'd help her figure it out. Or at least she'd be there when she told her mom.

Ada thought about ways she could lose the baby. She could never have an abortion; that would be murder. But if she fell down a flight of stairs, or got hit hard in the stomach, she might abort.

She'd heard once that if you ate a lot of hot stuff, like if you drank two or three bottles of hot sauce, you could lose a baby. And someone had told her about a girl who untwisted a wire coat hanger and used it on herself. She knew she'd never do that. She couldn't do any of those things.

She hadn't started to get a belly yet, so no one suspected. She found herself thinking maybe she was just very late, but she knew that wasn't true. She was pregnant. And then there was the problem of Peter. She tried to guess his reaction. Would he be as mystified as she was? Would he dump her? Did she even care if he did?

Ada watched as her dreams circled the drain. She had planned to be a journalist. Mrs. Carne, her journalism teacher, said she had talent. The woman encouraged her. Ada was a staff writer for the school's paper, the *Gazette,* with her own byline. She also wrote for the teen section of the *Indianapolis Star,* the biggest newspaper in the city. And she was learning the mechanics of the newspaper business. Ada loved writing. She loved everything about it. Her life had been right on track. Now, she was 16 years old, still in high school, and pregnant with her boyfriend's baby.

Just thinking about it depressed her. She couldn't control the tears. She was always crying these days. And she was sick as a dog. She needed to talk to Angela. Her sister was practically a woman and would know what to do. She wanted her sister to come home.

Ada fell asleep each night scripting out Peter's reaction. She couldn't decide how she felt about him. A big part of her was mad at him. He tricked her. Against her better judgment she had trusted him and he got her pregnant. Ada had always pretended to be wise when her friends talked to her about sex. They all had boyfriends, and although none of them had gone all the way, they all pretended to know all about it. "It feels soooooo good," one of her friends told her, with a voice of authority. "But you gotta make sure you use something,"she was cautioned. Ada still had questions. She wanted to ask, "Use something, *like what?* What would he use?" But she didn't ask. She didn't want her friends to think she was dumb.

She thought of the times they had made out. It hadn't felt good. Not good at all. She'd always been disappointed. He'd plaster her with those wet, slobbery kisses that never really turned her on. He'd pressure her to the point of frustration, pestering her for sex. And when his hands became too familiar, she'd find herself outside her body…*drifting*…she'd get lost in the familiar *nothingingness* that peppered her life. Still, she was sure she would never have given in, and yet, she was pregnant. Bits and pieces of vague conversations drifted back to her. Peter had said something about *pulling it out.* Pulling *what out?* Ada was confused. *He was just using his finger.*

They were on her mother's couch, the brand new French provincial one that was shrink-wrapped in plastic to keep it clean. Both of them were hot and sweaty, and his wet mouth on her flesh, which adhered to the sticky plastic, made her want to take a bath. His fingers were more ambitious than usual, and she whispered in a startled voice: "Peter, stop it! What are you doing?" She was asking *that* question constantly; he was forever fumbling around, irritating her. But that night, he was relentless; and he really had started to hurt her. That's when he assured her, "Ada, relax. Just relax, Ada. It's OK. I won't spill anything in you. I'll pull it out in time. You won't get pregnant."

She wanted him to stop, but he wouldn't. "No, Peter. Peter, what are you doing?" she demanded again before vanishing into the fog. The memory briefly enlightened her before it became extinct. Still, parts of her needed to believe that it wasn't his fault. That maybe he didn't know they had gone *all the way.* But that was hard to believe. Peter was experienced and should have been looking out for her.

He was her first boyfriend, she trusted him, and he tricked her. Was it on purpose? He said he could pull it out in time and she wouldn't get pregnant. Her thoughts teetered, back and forth like the seesaw she rode in Willington Park when she was a kid; round and round like a horse on a carousel. She couldn't make up her mind. She fell asleep wondering…did he trick me…? But deep inside, she thought she knew.

The Dilemma

Are you sure?" Peter asked her. His eyes, which were usually narrowed into slits, were now wide with surprise. He managed to lose all his cool points. He appeared to be as dumbfounded as she was. Ada had never seen him ruffled before; his discomfort increased her distress.

"Yes, I'm sure, Peter," she answered him. "I missed two periods and I'm late again. This is the third month in a row."

They were sitting on her mother's couch. The elegant style of it, the refinement of its color (a muted ballerina pink), the ornately curved lines of its decorative wood moldings, belied the vile things they had done there.

She didn't try to hide her irritation. Ada had worked it all out in her mind. She was angry that he allowed this to happen to her. As far as she was concerned, it was entirely his fault. She hadn't wanted to have sex with him. All she wanted was to be *held*. She wanted sweet words and handholding and his protective arm around her waist. She just wanted to know that he cared, but he badgered her and tricked her. She was glad he was scared. *He should be scared.* He should be every bit as scared as she was.

"Is it mine?" Peter's first question exasperated Ada, but this one *floored* her, and her mouth flew wide open in protest. "Of course it's yours," she wailed. "You know it's yours. You're my boyfriend. You're the only boy I've done *anything* with."

"I didn't say it wasn't mine, Ada." Now Peter sounded dejected. "I'm just trying to figure out how the heck this happened."

"You promised we weren't really doing anything, Peter, so *you* tell *me* how it happened."

He ignored her question. Instead he asked: "So what do you wanna do?" His voice had an edge, like he was fighting for control. This conversation wasn't going the way she planned. She felt angrier, more fragile, and more frightened by the minute. She couldn't decide which emotion to indulge.

"Does your mother know?" Peter asked. His voice was frail, and he looked stricken, like with a bad case of the flu. For the first time, he wasn't the strong, in-control boy she was used to.

"I don't know what I'm gonna do, Peter." she told him, and she softened her voice just a little. "And no, Momma doesn't know, yet. I couldn't tell her."

"You're gonna have to marry me," Peter informed her, and his bravado returned, like it was a done deal. She decided he must be *nuts*.

"I'm 16 years old, Peter. I'm not getting married. I guess I'll have the baby and give it up for adoption. But I'm not getting married, and I'm not having an abortion, either." Peter absorbed her words, and his squinty eyes narrowed even more.

"We're gonna have to tell our parents," he said.

Ada took in a deep breath. "I'm not having an abortion," she repeated.

"Nobody said anything about an abortion!"

"No, but you know you were thinking about it!"

"Oh, so now you're a mind reader. You can tell what I'm thinking?"

Ada felt a familiar rumbling inside, and a phantom voice said, *"We don't care what you're thinking."* She labored to shut out the voice.

"Look, I'm just saying, I can take care of you and the baby, Ada, so if you want to get married, we can get married. I don't want any kid of mine growing up without a father. Let me talk to my mom and dad first. Then we'll talk to your mom together. We'll figure it out."

When they first sat down, Ada had scooted to the far end of the couch, placing as much distance between them as she could. Peter scooted closer now and pulled her to next to him. He was calmer now, and more in control, and Ada relaxed a little. She wanted him to hold her. She didn't try to pull away.

He hadn't blown a gasket, but it hurt that he accused her of being with some other boy. That was the same as calling her a slut, and she didn't appreciate *that* one bit. And she told him so: "I'm not a slut, Peter! So you know this is your baby." Her voice softened, and it was filled with hurt. Peter did know. He'd only raised the question out of frustration. He'd had a really hard time getting Ada to give in to him, and he'd worked on her night and day for months. Besides, he made sure that no one else got close enough to be competition. So he did know. This was his child.

"I know it's mine, Ada," he finally said. "We can do whatever you want. But we need to decide. We have to be ready to tell our parents something."

Peter hadn't been prepared. Ada's news gave him the shock of his life. A baby! The idea had never occurred to him, and he felt stupid for letting it happen. He wasn't lying when he told her he could pull it out before he spilled. He didn't intend to cum in her; he couldn't believe that he had. He was sure he'd pulled it out in time.

His first inclination was to get mad and he knew he'd have to be mad at himself. Ada obviously didn't have a clue. She didn't want to get married. That surprised him. Was it just that she didn't want to marry him, or did she not want to get married, period? Any girl would jump at the chance to marry him, and he almost told her that.

Didn't matter, though. Peter made a decision. This was his baby. Nobody was giving it away and nobody else was going to raise it. He would talk to his mom and dad first, and then to Jacob and Ella. He'd make sure they all knew what his intentions were.

Peter held her stiff body against him, on her mother's fancy pink couch, as he peered into the darkness, and he smiled his sinister smile…because…there was a wedding in his future.

Angela's News

Everyone was proud when Angela went off to school. As the oldest, she was the first to go. Her grades had been excellent. She had studied hard and won scholarships to help with the costs.

It was a big day when Angela graduated from high school. Ada was as excited as Angela was about the commencement ceremonies. When Angela marched across the stage to get her diploma, Ada cheered louder than anyone. She would miss her sister but it would feel good being able to say that Angela was away at school.

They'd all gone to Ball State to help Angela move into her dorm, and they sent care packages to help keep her from being homesick. Ada hadn't begrudged her sister anything. She knew her day would come.

Anthony was a bit of a disciplinary problem, but Ella was sure she could straighten him out. Ada was never a problem academically. In two years Ada would follow in her sister's footsteps, and two years after that, Anthony would.

Little Roman was almost six. Thanks to Jacob's good income, he'd be attending a private school when he started next year in first grade. He'd be the first of Ella's kids to do so. She wanted the best for her children and she was doing all she could to help them achieve their goals. But the kids were growing up and she especially missed her older daughter.

Ella was glad when Angela announced she was coming home for a weekend visit. Her boyfriend, Gary, was driving her. By midweek, Ella was busy preparing Angela's favorite foods. She made plenty, so there'd be leftovers for the youngsters to take back to campus with them. She even made homemade ice cream, Ada's favorite. Ada was more concerned about what was *already* in her stomach. At that moment, ice cream was the last thing on her mind. Angela and Gary had seated themselves on the couch. Ella sat in a Queen Anne chair across from them. For a minute, the conversation was breezy, but Ada, who listened from inside her bedroom, detected the emptiness in it. She stretched herself out on her bed. The door to her room was ajar. Ada strained to listen—not for content; rather she was waiting for the conversation to end. Ada got off of the bed and walked to the door. She strained harder, but could no longer make out what they were saying. The conversation had grown suspiciously subdued, and Ada's interest was piqued.

"So, what are you going to do?" Ella asked. For a moment, there was silence. Ella repeated herself. It was something she did not like to do.

Gary answered, "I'm gonna marry her," he said. "I love her, and we're getting married."

Gary managed to utter the words but couldn't drive the anxiety from his voice. Ada stopped listening and walked back to her bed. She understood what the words meant. Angela, herself, was in trouble. There was no way she could help Ada. Ada wanted to pray but doubted God would be listening. She fell asleep that night, without saying her prayers.

The Wedding Day

On may 7, 1970, both of Ella's girls got married. Ada walked down the aisle in an expensive pale green dress—an A-line with large, lime green buttons running down the front. It was form-fitting, and if Ada had been in possession of curves, the dress might have shown them off. Instead, it simply hung on her, judiciously fulfilling its function in life.

Her hair did look pretty. It was cut into a shoulder-length bob. Short, blunt bangs fringed her forehead. Her lips were painted a soft rose color, and her eyes were carefully accentuated with a pastel tint that matched her dress. Ada's lashes were naturally long, framing her large eyes, and they were darkened, and lengthened even more with thick coats of eyeliner and black mascara.

The ensemble was completed by stockings that wanted to slide down her long thin legs, and bone-colored pumps that made her feel she was balancing on stilts. She should have looked very grown up, but she didn't. She looked small and scared and still awkward the way young girls are before they learn what to do with their arms and legs.

The aisle was the narrow hallway leading from her mother's bedroom and into the front room of their house. She'd gotten pregnant in that room, on the couch that now seated some of the people who were guests for her wedding.

Angela had preceded her down the aisle, and she did look grown up and beautiful in her off-white dress. Both grooms were dressed in nice dark suits. Gary looked nervous, but there was love in his eyes when he looked at his future bride, and Angela beamed a radiant smile as she came down the hall to stand beside him.

Only a few guests had been invited. Due to the circumstances, there had been little fanfare accompanying the hushed announcement that both of Ella's girls were getting married.

To friends and family, the predicament was announced as follows: "Angela and Gary are in love. They decided they couldn't wait to be together. They want to get married right away. We're gonna have a small ceremony at the house; just a few friends and family." And like an afterthought, it was quickly added: "Oh, and Ada got herself pregnant. She's gotta get married. So we're gonna make it a double wedding."

As Ada walked toward Peter she felt like it was a death march, like she'd read about, when the Jews were sent to their deaths in the Nazi concentration camps. She had begged and pleaded all week, hoping for a reprieve. But Ella scolded her, saying she was being dramatic, and ought to be on stage.

She had been sick all week, and moody. No amount of cheerfulness on Angela's part could make her feel better. The fact that her sister was in love and had found a boy who loved her, only made Ada feel worse, more wretched.

She was being forced to marry a boy who didn't love her, to have a baby, drop out of school, and move in with Peter and his parents. And she knew they didn't like her. They blamed her for trapping their son and ruining his future. They never said it, but she knew they felt that way.

But she was the one whose future was ruined. They had ruined her future. They'd ganged up on her. They wanted her to get married and keep the baby. *She was the one who was trapped*, and there was nothing she could do.

A black trail of coal-colored tears ran down her face and didn't stop until long after the last guest had gone home.

She did manage to say, "I do." But the phrase had been stuck in her throat, so everyone sighed visibly when the words escaped, in a sob, from her mouth.

The basement was festive. There were party streamers that declared: *'MAY 7TH, 1970…OUR WEDDING DAY.'* And the fancy paper plates with matching silver-trimmed cups and napkins were the expensive kind that wouldn't dissolve under the weight of the mounds of celebratory foods Ella had prepared. Silver and white balloons cascaded from the ceiling and bounced up against the doors, and a huge three-tiered cake, crowned by two matching brides and two matching grooms, graced the large rented table in the middle of the room. The menu that day was extensive. There was roast beef and roast pork and fried fish and baked fowl, and greens and green beans, and mashed potatoes and candied yams, and sweet potato pies and caramel cakes, and cookies, and peanuts and candies in little china dishes.

After consuming their fair share of the wedding feast, followed by ice cream and punch and wedding cake, Angela and Gary left. They had honeymoon plans; they both were able to take a few days off from school. But Ada couldn't remember details. She didn't see them leave. For her, the day had flown by in a rush of confusion. She felt like she'd been *in and out* all day, just checking on the progress of things. There were highlights, but no continuous train of thought.

And then suddenly she was a married woman. Her mother said so when Ada begged her again to let her stay. "Please, Momma! I got married like you wanted. Now can I please just stay here? Peter can still come to see me on the weekends like always. Please, Momma," she begged.

The answer was an emphatic "no."

"You're married now, Ada." Ella said. "Your place is with your husband. You're gonna have your own family now. You have to go home with him. We'll let you get settled, and we'll come to see you in a few weeks."

And that was that. She was barely 16, pregnant and married. She picked up her overnight case and followed Peter Collins out the door. She climbed into the shiny red sports car she used to be so proud of.

The big house on 42nd Street (where she had lived when Thomas was the only father she knew) was a distant memory now. It had nearly been lost in the vast warehouse of her brain. Now it was this house, the one across from the park, that she thought of as home. This is where she wanted to stay.

Ella walked the newlyweds out to the car. At the curb she swung an arm high above her head in a gesture of goodbye. Ella still stood in the front yard waving when Peter Collins drove Ada away from her home. And the girl couldn't see through the tears in her eyes that her mother was crying, too.

The Honeymoon

da was still wearing her pretty, green dress when they pulled into Bakersfield Manor. Such an ambitious name, Ada thought, for a flophouse that lured johns and hookers with hourly rates for sex and depravity. Ada Collins had never seen such a place before. She'd never even imagined that such horrible places existed. But now here she was *in a flophouse*, on her first night as Peter's wife.

She clutched her light blue overnight bag to her chest like she thought it might save her. It was stuffed with toiletries which were intended, but failed, to make her feel womanly and romantic.

The sheer pink nightgown she'd brought with her had been Ella's. When her mother gave it to her, she held it up to her neck and appraised herself in the big mirror over Ella's bed. She looked ridiculous. She protested, "I look like Lucille Ball wearing Marilyn Monroe's party dress."

Silky pink slippers, a gift from Angela, matched the gown, but they made Ada's feet feel conspicuous and big. She thought of the fancy attire in her bag and felt even more out of place in view of the squalor of the transient hotel.

The girl at the desk looked at the young couple with marked indifference when they stepped into the lobby. When the young woman glanced at Peter, her eyes widened in a slight show of recognition. Ada wondered if he'd been to this horrible place before. With a slight bob of her head she acknowledged Peter. Then her eyes swept Ada from head to toe. The inspection had taken one fraction of a second but Ada felt as if she'd been placed on display.

She needn't have worried. The woman saw just one more fast-tailed little girl who was stupid enough to give it away to any boy with a tongue smooth enough to cause her to open her legs. She had no way of knowing that the young couple was married, and this was their honeymoon. Anyway, it wasn't her concern. Her concern was the paycheck that fed the four babies she had earned from similar encounters with worthless boys when she was a stupid kid.

Besides, there was another girl standing at the desk with a guy in an old played-out suit, and the desk clerk was more interested in them. That couple had drawn Ada's attention, too. The girl was in hysterics. She was young like Ada; only a year or two older, and she was every bit as scared.

"Come on, retard! We only have an hour, and the clock's tickin'." The young man's words were harsh and his tone was harsher.

The girl was named Priscilla, and she was terrified, but her protests were unintelligible, and within a moment's time, Ada knew she slow. *Mentally handicapped*, Ada, corrected herself, because she had read the term in a book, and she agreed that it sounded kinder.

The mentally handicapped kids in Ada's school seemed so innocent and sweet. They were trusting and naïve and Ada felt sorry for them. She'd even stood up for them a couple of times when the jokes got to be cruel. That had cost her some cool points, but she didn't care.

Priscilla's situation was impossible. The boy with her was an obvious thug. Although he wasn't a big guy, he looked tough. He was long-limbed with lean, sinewy muscles. He looked like someone always eager to fight, like he had something to prove and was anxious to prove it.

He didn't just have rough edges; he was rough all over. And you could tell he didn't care what people thought. Priscilla, didn't want to be with him; that was clear. It was also clear that it wasn't her choice. "I wanna go home," Priscilla was crying in earnest. "I changed my mind." She wailed, "Take me back home!"

"Come on, retard." The boy had her by the arm, and he spit the words out like venom, through clenched teeth. "I'm through playing with your stupid behind. Come on. Let's go!"

Priscilla tried to wrench her arm free from the man. She wasn't fat, but she was tall and stout and solidly built. Still, she was no match for him. Her short brown hair had once been subdued with Dippity Doo, but it had rebelled and now stuck up in wild spikes all over her head.

She had the kind of face you couldn't pick out of a line-up. What *was* noticeable about her was her demeanor. There was innocence in her that mocked her size, and her speech indicated her mind had stopped developing long before her body did.

Her 'friend' was near the end of his patience. He wanted to hit her, but with great effort he restrained himself. "I'm not gonna tell you again, Priscilla," he spat through clenched teeth.

His voice registered low but was potent. Ada felt its force though it wasn't directed at her, and Priscilla lowered her voice in response to it. She still cowered and whimpered, but her objections, now quieter, were falling on deaf ears.

Paula, the young woman at the desk, at least had the decency to look uncomfortable. She wondered where Priscilla's family was, and how she'd hooked up with this punk.But her small twinge of conscience was squashed by the coldness in the young man's eyes.

The man had paid for a room and he was entitled to one. As long as he wasn't really violent she couldn't afford to get involved. They didn't pay her enough money for that. So she'd thrown one questioning glance at Peter and then quickly looked away.

Peter hadn't spoken to Ada, or touched her, or even looked in her direction since they entered the hotel. He'd been absorbed in the drama before them, and for an instant, Ada had been distracted too, so distracted that she'd forgotten her own dire circumstance.

But this was just for one brief moment. Looking at Peter now and reading his face brought home to her the dilemma she was in. She was just as helpless as Priscilla was and there was no one to help her.

The cold-eyed young man with Priscilla didn't intimidate Peter. What Ada saw when she looked at her new husband was much more unnerving than apathy. She saw approval and morbid fascination in Peter's eyes. Peter had a look of camaraderie that told the thug, 'handle your business' and that caused the blood to chill in her veins.

The only compassionate soul in the hotel lobby that night belonged to Ada, and she was powerless to act. The young man had seized Priscilla and shook her hard. "If you don't come on, I'm gonna scramble the few little brains you have left in your stupid head, girl. Come on, here! Move your nasty butt! Let's go. Let's go!" And then he shoved her. She was still whimpering when he marched her in the direction of a long, dark corridor. That corridor housed damp, stale-smelling rooms fit only for whores and one-night stands.

Peter once more acknowledged the man as he pushed his young victim before him. Peter lifted one side of his mouth at him in a crooked smile of kinship.

Ada felt camaraderie that night, too. She'd met the retarded girl's eyes as she was marshaled past her. She was sick for herself and for the girl.

Strange Fruit

William (Big Bill) Collins had lived in the house on Prospect Street for many years. He lived there with his wife Bettie and with the son and daughter their union produced. Bettie was his second wife. She was a *good church-going woman* who liked to stress above all things the importance of trusting in God. She tried to instill that virtue in her offspring, but she knew she'd failed with her son when he, the older of their two children, announced that his girlfriend, Ada, was carrying his child. This new development meant Peter would have to alter his life. He'd have to postpone college. Arrangements would be needed to accommodate the new circumstances that were thrust upon her son.

As was often the case, Bettie felt she was being plagued with the trials of Job. The predicament caused her to wring her hands; she came just short of questioning God. But being a Christian woman, it was her duty to open her home to Peter's new wife and their unborn child.

Bettie would dispense with the recriminations she was dying to lay at the young girl's feet. This was just one more cross she'd have to bear. *I'll find my reward and my peace in the heavenly glory,* she assured herself.

The Collinses' daughter, Jessica, was about the same age as Ada. Bettie would try to think of Ada as a daughter, too. The girls would be friends.

The newlyweds lived in Peter's room from the time they moved into the house. There was plenty of space there for the crib and for the small changing table that were purchased for the baby. The walls were treated to a fresh coat of egg-shell–colored paint, and Ada was allowed to bring her big mahogany hope chest to set at the base of her new bed. Ella, who procured it second-hand, had given the chest to Ada. And she had to explain to her what a hope chest was. "I got a good deal on it," her mother told her when she came to visit, and the chest was dropped off. "But this is an expensive old chest, probably an antique. You take good care of it."

She treasured the chest, filling it with only her most precious possessions. You could lock and unlock it with a key, which Ada kept hidden for safekeeping. And she attached great significance to it, wishing it would bring her the hope its name implied.

Soon the whole house showed signs that a new life would be entering the world. Once the initial shock wore off, the Collinses embraced the idea that they'd be grandparents. They became anxious to bring this new baby boy or girl into their home.

William Collins had entered his second marriage late in life. And although she had never been married before, Bettie was older, too. Nearly two years into the marriage, when Peter was born, Bettie was already 40, and her husband was more than a decade older than that. Their family welcomed the arrival of their only other child, a daughter named Jessie, when Peter was two years old.

With a boy and a girl, their family was complete, they were secure in their finances, and they were about to be grandparents.

They tried to picture their son as a father. He had a lot of settling down and growing up to do. His recklessness was the blight that flawed their otherwise brilliant son. Big Bill had tried to set a good example. He'd taken the boy under his wing and tried to school him, but his efforts met with limited success. In financial matters, William had done all right. He was a shrewd businessman who owned properties all over town. Their home was paid for and there was money in the bank.

Affable, well respected, and well liked, William was considered to be a fair-minded and levelheaded man. Not much was known about his home life, but he had friends in important places, and was influential himself behind the scenes in local Indiana politics.

William's son was known in the area, too, but his reputation wasn't as stellar. He was known to be bright and self-confident, but his confidence bordered on cockiness. He inherited his father's keen business sense, and had a head for numbers, but he was stubborn and wouldn't take instruction. A lot of his problems stemmed from a loathing for anyone and anything white. He hated authority, which he typically spelled 'whitey.'

Peter came to the conclusion early on, that 'whitey' (better known as 'the man') was hell-bent on running his life. Especially when race was involved, his temper got the best of him. William had pulled strings in the past to rescue Peter from his temper and to intervene on his behalf. Both he and his wife agonized over their son's indiscretions. Peter drove his fancy red car the way he lived his life: way too fast, and with reckless abandon. As a result, William paid a stack of speeding tickets and constantly circumvented legal issues on his son's behalf.

Peter was hot-headed, and had had more than his fair share of fights, verbal and otherwise, with kids in the neighborhood. Once, he and a couple of the thugs he ran with had attacked a group of boys. Peter hit one of the guys with a tire iron from the trunk of his car. It was all due to some minor infraction that, William knew, his son had blown way out of proportion. Bettie outwardly blamed the boys Peter hung out with and she blamed the boys Peter was fighting. They were some young white kids who were up to no good, Bettie was sure. But in her heart she knew Peter's temper was responsible. In any case, the police had been called, serious charges were filed, and William, again, had to intercede on his son's behalf. That incident, in particular, frightened them. They were getting older; they wouldn't be around forever. And they knew firsthand how fierce Peter could be when his temper was out of control. He never actually hit his dad or his mom, but there were a few times when William had feared he might. They worked hard to avoid pushing Peter beyond the breaking point.

William had heart-to-heart talks with his son. He warned him that he'd come to a bad end if his temper weren't controlled. And Bettie was on her knees constantly, with prayers as loud as they were heartfelt, that went something like this: "Please dear Lord, open my poor boy's eyes to the path he should take. Please God, remove the bitterness of his heart and the vexation of his spirit." And then, once she was satisfied that her supplications had hit their mark, she'd 'leave it in the hands of Jesus.' The beleaguered couple loved their son. At heart, he was a good boy, the fruit of their old age, and they had both vowed to protect him however they could. And so Bettie prayed, William paid and Peter continued to seethe.

Moving Day

Ada moved into Peter's house the day after they were married. She was shy and ill at ease. She looked around the great old house with its high ceilings and large drafty rooms. It was cold and daunting. This was Peter's home. She felt it would never be hers.

Mr. Collins asked her to call him 'Dad,' or 'Pop,' but she couldn't. He told her: "There's no difference between you and my own flesh and blood, Ada. I don't see you as a daughter-in- law. I see you as my daughter."

Ada thought maybe he meant it. He went out of his way to make her feel at home. But from the start there was something about him and his strange-acting wife—and something about that house—that set her nerves on edge. She decided not to let her guard down. There was more to these people than met the eye.

Ada still stung from her first night with Peter at that nightmarish hotel, and she blamed *everybody* for her ordeal. She blamed her mother for allowing him to take her there, and for making her get married in the first place. And Jacob was silent when he could have intervened. He should have insisted that his stepdaughter go someplace nice on her honeymoon. He had money. He could have sent them to one of the fancy hotels downtown.

Mostly, though, Ada blamed Peter, but she could never tell him how she felt. The boy she'd been with last night was Peter unmasked, and he completely frightened her. All of his pretenses were gone. He made sure she understood the full import of their first night together. Without soft words of comfort; with no declarations of love; without apologies or explanations; or an inkling of concern, he had dragged her into the foul-smelling hotel room and pounced on her.

Ada revived the memory and constructed a wall of resentment around it. At the same time, she unveiled a *conspiracy theory*, identified the major players in it, and assigned various degrees of resentment to each one of them, because all of them, her immediate family and his, were culpable—had either permitted her ill treatment, or caused it. The only innocent party was Angela, who had been unaware of her plight.

But it wasn't so much that Ada disliked Mr. Collins, it was more a matter of knowing he couldn't be trusted to do the right thing. He hadn't stood up for her, and he could never be her father. He was decent enough on the surface, but something was wrong inside. And this she determined even before she learned the disgusting hotel she'd honeymooned in was one of the businesses owned by Big Bill Collins.

When Ada learned that Mr. Collins' owned the transient hotel, her opinion of him plummeted. How could he make it his business to run such a despicable establishment? How could his wife, *the consummate Christian*, allow her husband to operate such a place? How could they, in good conscience, send her there on the night she married their son? No, she decided. She couldn't bring herself to call him Dad; she never thought of him that way, and it caused a measure of discomfort between them.

Despite his protests, Ada called her father-in-law 'Mr. Collins' until the day he died, which was eight years later, when his heart gave out while he played with her child on the high-priced Oriental rug on his living room floor.

Bettie Collins

Bettie Collins was seldom seen and seldom heard and that suited Ada just fine. For the most part, the pious old lady (in secret, that's what Ada called her) stayed in her bed. Ada sometimes went a whole day without seeing her.

Old lady Collins was puzzlement to the young girl. Ada doubted very much that her mother-in-law owned a nice pair of slacks or an everyday dress or a pair of street shoes. She never saw her in any of them. Bettie's normal attire consisted of a sturdy bra, a thin cotton slip (white) and a well-worn pair of faded pink house shoes. A salt-and-pepper wig that was perched impudently on the top of her head always covered her hair.

When her snowy-white hair showed, it was in braids, like a child's would be. But it was nice hair with a soft, fine texture, and there was enough of it to cause Ada to wonder why it was never displayed.

From the time she woke up in the morning until the lights went out at the end of the day, six days a week, it seemed that Bettie was in her room, and in her bed. In truth, Ada couldn't say what time Bettie woke up. She could never tell whether the old lady was asleep or awake. The only sounds that slipped from Bettie's room came from the television, which was always turned on.

The drone of the TV failed to quiet the blaring silence that trumpeted through the house. Bettie rarely cooked and she never cleaned. Her husband and her daughter did most of the housework. Ada was convinced that this husband and wife had their roles reversed.

Ada made sure she kept Peter's room clean. He could never criticize her housekeeping. Bettie Collins' only talents were quoting Scripture and watching her stories on TV. When Ada did hear footsteps in the otherwise quiet house…the signal of Bettie's approach, Ada steered clear of her. Mostly, Ada stayed in her room, too. She'd hibernate there from the time Peter left in the morning until he returned to the house at the end of the day. Then she was obliged to come out to spend time with him while he visited with his family.

At the end of the long week, Bettie Collins would make a miraculous resurgence to life. Like a butterfly leaving its cocoon, she'd emerge from her room fully dressed, early each Sunday morning.

With her purse on her arm and her bible in hand, she'd suddenly appear, looking put together and fine and prepared to go to church. This was a weekend routine that Bettie never altered. Ada was amazed. Actually, the old lady was a nice looking woman. In fact, she looked enough like her son (who Ada still considered to be handsome) to cause Ada to joke: she looks like an old Peter Collins in a wig.

It was hard for her to reconcile these very disparate images of Bettie Collins. After church services (which Mr. Collins rarely attended) he prepared a big Sunday dinner, which was served in the formal dining room at the massive supper table, a sturdy construction of ornate-looking deep mahogany wood. It was a beautiful structure. It reminded Ada of pictures she'd seen of far-away places and times long ago.

Bettie always sat at the head of the table, which somehow seemed appropriate, and Mr. Collins sat to her immediate right.

These Sunday dinners were festive times in the Collins household and in spite of herself Ada grew to look forward to them. There was always a large dish of bubbling-hot macaroni and cheese, which for Mr. Collins was a staple, and which Ada also loved, and either candied potatoes or whipped Idaho spuds, which would be covered in rich brown gravy. There was a crock-pot filled with mustard, turnip and collard greens all mixed together and swimming in the smoky juices of a salty ham bone. And no matter what other meat was present (there would be at least one other meat—usually a juicy pork roast or a tender roast beef) a succulent ham, whose aroma filled the whole house, occupied a place of honor at the center of the table.

In the beginning, Ada avoided these gatherings like the plague. She'd hold out in her room, resisting the temptation to dine. She'd feign a headache or a toothache, or just pretend not to be hungry yet. But the aromas almost always cajoled her, until in the end, hunger overpowered anxiety. Then she'd take her place at the table, beside her sister-in-law, with whom she felt the most at ease, and shyly dig into the foods that enticed her. But Ada's weekdays were spent in solitude.

With Bettie sequestered away in her room, the house was quiet. Peter worked his day job and went to school at night, and Jessie was at school all day. She was a sophomore like Ada had been. Her last class wasn't over until 3:00 p.m. and her bus delivered her home a full hour after that.

Jessie would exchange a quick greeting with Ada, and then she'd race to the kitchen for a snack. They never skimped on groceries, so there were always large quantities and assortments of food in the house. After her treat (usually some form of chocolate) Jessie headed for her mother's room for a short chat.

Ada anticipated Jessie's return from school each day. She missed her own sister, and since the two girls were close in age, she started to see Jessie as a surrogate. When Jessie was home, she served as a buffer between Ada and Peter, *and* she cushioned Ada from the rest of his family, whom she didn't feel close to. Even so, Ada found she was jealous of the affection Jessie received from her parents. She knew it wasn't Jessie's fault, but their constant devotion to their daughter reminded Ada that she'd never felt loved by her own mom, and that her father had been shut out of her life from an early age.

And Jessie was spoiled—also not her fault. She was the baby, and the only daughter born to older parents who doted on her and indulged her (Ada thought) in excessive ways. Jessie and Peter spent most weekends (either Friday or Saturday nights) at All Skates. They'd been hanging out there for years. It was the rink where the cool black kids roller-skated and hung out. Ada was invited but she didn't fit in. Ada never learned to skate.

Sometimes she went to watch her husband and his sister. She was always impressed by their smoothness as they glided around the rink. Peter and his sister had been skating since they were kids, and they looked like pros, dancing and stepping and skating all at the same time.

Jessie and Peter offered to teach Ada to skate, and in the beginning, she tried, but Ada was pregnant and she was afraid to join them out on the floor. In time, her stomach got big and she thought she stood out like a sore thumb. Even after the baby was born, when pregnancy wasn't an excuse any more, Ada wouldn't skate with Peter and Jessie.

She still didn't fit in. She was clumsy, she wasn't cool, and she was still afraid she would fall.

Ada remained torn in her view of William Collins. He was a walking, talking contradiction. He *was* likeable, and she thought that deep down he was probably a good person. But he had flaws she couldn't ignore, because they impacted her, and the better she got to know him, the more clearly she saw the failings and the more her bewilderment grew.

He got home from work each day close to the time that Jessie came home. He carried a briefcase full of papers, and she knew that he owned several businesses. But other than the infamous Bakersfield, where she had honeymooned, Ada had no idea what his businesses were. In actuality, she had no concept of what it meant to own or run a business, anyway. She had no point of reference. Everyone she knew worked for someone else. As her Big Mama would say, "Very few whites and no blacks at all" owned their own businesses. So she was impressed in spite of herself that this strange man could provide for his family so well as a businessman. He was a short, stout, gruff-looking little man who smoked a fat cigar that was always clamped between his teeth. He was intelligent. Ada knew that because he understood things that went on in the world.

He liked to talk politics and had an opinion on world events. He always wore a suit and tie, and he kind of strutted when he walked. Ada didn't think he swaggered on purpose. He naturally seemed to walk that way; like a little penguin or a duck. But William's gruffness dissolved when he opened his mouth.

His eyes sparked mischief, but not the truly bad kind. Rather, he had the look of a naughty boy who was busy plotting pranks. And when he looked at her, it was with kindness in his eyes. He had the gentle, placid eyes of a decent man. But she also saw in his eyes a twinge of guilt.

If he hadn't been Peter's father…if circumstances had been different… Ada could have liked him. But William had sins (they were sins of omission) that she couldn't ignore; she couldn't forgive him, and she couldn't negate his guilt.

Ada carefully tended her feelings. She nursed her hurts, giving them all the room they needed to grow and plenty of fresh air to breathe. She hated living in Peter's house. She felt unloved and unwanted, yet Peter had trapped and imprisoned her. She was on his turf, and the advantage was all his. His temper had evolved with frightening intensity, and since that first night at the hotel he never attempted to hide it.

She was his wife now, living in his house, and Peter controlled his house. Angela was away at school and had no idea of how things were for Ada. If she had known, she would have fixed things. Angela would have cared.

If Angela were around she'd have had more than a fighting chance. So she missed her sister and thought of her longingly. But when she thought about Ella and Jacob, hurt and anger battled within her. If they had cared, she wouldn't be in this mess to begin with. So when Ella came to visit, which was rare, her emotions were a jumble. Depression and resentment joined forces, and she felt homesick, like a prisoner on visiting day.

Her mother and her two favorite aunts (her mother's sisters) usually came together. They brought care packages and news from home. And when they were ready to leave, Ada felt that little pieces of herself were being broken off and carted away. Her eyes would fill with tears and she'd feel abandoned again.

Jacob never came to see her at all. Her relationship with her stepdad, the man who had spiraled her into the path of chaos to begin with, the man who started having sex with her just as she was learning to recite her ABCs and to write her name (and who continued to do so until her first period came)…her relationship with this man was a strange one. His role in her life was obscure. In fact, *she wouldn't recall her abuse* at his hand until long after she was grown, when he was a sickly old man. It would be years after that before she'd be able to process the information.

This tall silent silhouette of a man who hardly ever made his presence known was again the ineffectual, shadowy figure he'd been at her first recollection of him. She didn't love him. She didn't hate him. She didn't know the man at all.

Peter's family confounded her as much as her own family did. They were nice to her. They told her this was her home, and she was a part of their family. But she saw how they treated each other. They were close; they looked out for one another. The Collinses loved their children. It was plain in the way they dealt with them. When Jessie and Peter squabbled, the parents would find a way to reconcile them so that neither their son nor daughter would be hurt. They tried to be fair with them, to help them to dissolve any riffs between them.

The rules didn't apply when Peter mistreated Ada. And they knew he mistreated her. He would push her or shove her and they wouldn't get involved. He yelled at her with a fierceness that caused her to tremble, but they wouldn't be drawn in. When the violence escalated, and shoves turned into backhanded licks, which soon became punches, they stood mute. They watched as their son propelled his young wife into walls. They watched when his face bulged with rage and hers distorted with fear. They were quiet while she feared for herself and the baby she carried; a baby she now wanted more than life itself. They ignored her cries for help and made themselves scarce, so they gave tacit approval to the abuse. But then later, when the storm had passed, they'd come to her sheepishly. They'd look at her with guilty eyes but they'd never mention the abuse. Bettie would pull Ada aside with concern. She would summon Ada from inside the heavy curtains that cordoned her off from the outside world. Ada would move at a snail's pace, dreading an audience with the old woman. She'd seat herself on the edge of the matriarch's bed, in compliance with the old woman's command, and prepare herself for unwanted advice. "Honey, try not to make Peter mad," Bettie counseled, with misery in her voice. "You know he has a temper. You know how mad he can get. You have to be more careful. You just have to try harder, Ada. Try not to make him mad." Ada would bite her tongue in an effort not to answer. And then the old woman would assure her: "I pray for you every day, Ada," she'd say. "Not a day goes by that I don't open my eyes with a prayer for you. And at night I close my eyes the same way."

Ada didn't doubt it. The old woman was indisputably fond of prayer. She wondered though, if the good Lord got as tired of hearing Bettie's voice as she did. "I pray the Almighty will keep you, Ada. I pray for you and for Peter, too. I am constant in prayer about Peter's temper… that he'll learn to control his temper! You don't know how that boy vexes me!"

Here, Ada thought: "*Peter* doesn't know how he vexes you, either." But like so many others, she kept that thought to herself.

The old woman continued: "And don't think I don't talk to Peter about his temper! I talk to him. I just keep on talking and praying for both of you… that the good Lord will intervene and touch Peter's heart. And I pray for the child you carry. But Ada, you have to try harder not to make him mad. I stay on my knees for you, Ada, praying the good Lord gives you strength and wisdom and faith. But you have to pray too, Ada." Bettie always ended her sermon the same way: "Meanwhile, Ada, just throw this burden on Jesus. Give all this worry to Jesus," she would say. "Just give it to Jesus." She recited this like a mantra, these pearls of wisdom. And while Ada tended her swollen and bruised face, she pondered the words and her resentment grew by leaps and bounds. The duplicity wasn't lost on her.

The old lady would dismiss Ada from her bedroom lair, her conscience salved and intact. She'd return to her prayers, her daytime soaps, and the crossword puzzles she so loved to solve, leaving the young girl to lick her wounds.

Well, she didn't always quote it, but Ada knew her Bible, too. She remembered the false friends who comforted Job. They came to him during his trials, but he saw them for what they were. They were self-righteous hypocrites who offered no comfort at all. She knew the story and its parallel. So Bettie Collins could keep her prayers. Ada could do her own praying.

Erin Joy

Ada lived with the Collinses for almost two years before she and Peter moved into their own house. It was their first home and Ada was surprised that the idea of it excited her. They had a child now, an adorable baby girl whose full name was Erin Joy Collins. They named her Erin after the main character from one of Jessie's favorite soaps. Ada wasn't sure where the middle name, Joy, came from. It just popped into her head, and it seemed to fit.

Erin's effect on the Collins house was amazing. The big old house came to life the moment she was born, like it was placed under a spell. It became warmer and brighter, and more filled with laughter and joy. And another effect: Ada came out of her seclusion. She had to. As soon as Erin learned to crawl, she began exploring.

The baby saw the entire house as her playground, and she refused to confine herself to any one room. No place was off limit to her. She even ventured, unannounced and uninvited…and without repercussions… into the dark dungeon of her grandmother's bedroom.

She was the most beautiful baby. Strangers stopped Ada on the street to admire the child. As she grew, and started to wobble around on her chubby legs, she became even more adorable. She was comical and impish, with plump cheeks that begged to be pinched. And she had the fattest, deepest dimples (they were absolute holes in her cheeks) that Ada had ever seen.

Her skin, which was as smooth as silk, was a rich deep chocolatey color. Ada called her 'my little Hershey's kiss.' Her enormous brown eyes were expressive. They laughed when she laughed and cried when she did.

She was born with a head full of satiny-smooth hair that quickly sprang into wild crazy curls, and then into fuzzy thick braids that bounced off her shoulders and whose ends were secured with barrettes to make them behave. When she began to talk, she was precocious, like her mother had been at her age. Both sides of Erin's family were under her spell.

Ada was overwhelmed at the feelings that surfaced when she brought her daughter home from the hospital. She couldn't imagine that she had once entertained the thought of *getting rid of* the baby. The thought haunted her. She had expected to love her baby, but she was surprised at the depth of feeling that emerged. She wrote a long poem heralding Erin's birth. And she preserved a portion of it on a small decoupage plank of wood (which Ada carved) that hung above her baby's crib. She carefully hand-printed the words to the poem. She found just the right stationery. She glued the paper with the written words onto a smooth piece of wood and shellacked it with several shiny coats of varnish. The poem was a testament to her love:

The sun was beaming in the sky.

And Gabriel blew his horn.

The world stood still expectantly when Erin Joy was born.

A tiny bit of happiness; a life so fresh and new.

She fills our lives with blessedness and makes our dreams come true.

Erin's aunt Jessie and her grandpa Collins were always vying for the young child's attention. Erin was close to all of them, and they doted on her and spoiled her rotten. Jessie was always snatching the baby up and racing off with her. Their excursions resulted in ridiculous amounts of candy and toys and articles of clothing that really were fit for a little princess. Jessie bought strings of pearls and shiny patent leather shoes, and frilly dresses that were full and stiff with petticoats. Jessie once turned up with a tiny fur coat (it was satiny soft rabbit fur, dyed white) trimmed with iridescent pink buttons that were shaped like bows. She had paid nearly a hundred dollars for it—a small fortune at the time, and Ada, although mortified and outwardly appalled, was secretly pleased and amused.

Erin's grandpa was no better. The minute he came home from work he'd gruffly call the child to him. They'd wrestle on the floor, and play games of hide and seek, with Erin searching for lost treasures hidden in the pockets of his slacks or suit coat. Whatever she wanted was hers.

Mr. Collins would disappear, with Ada's daughter in tow, for hours at a time. They'd return with piled-high ice cream cones or other snacks and pastries to spoil her dinner. And Ada would fuss, but in truth, she loved seeing her baby indulged.

The old lady still kept to herself, but even she seemed to perk up when the impish little girl was near. She would call for Erin (before Erin learned to walk) and Jessie or William, or sometimes Ada herself, would bring the baby to the old woman's bed. She'd cuddle there with the child, or Erin would explore the mysterious room where her grandma spent so much of her time.

The old lady's displays were more subtle, her proclamations more subdued, but it was evident she loved the child, too. Ada wasn't jealous. It gave her pleasure to watch Erin's eyes dance with glee when she was presented with some unexpected new prize. Her deep dimples would peep out from inside her cheeks and Ada would dissolve in the love she felt for her daughter.

Most unexpected of all was Erin's effect on her father. Once Peter was accustomed to the idea of having a child, he maintained that he wanted a boy. But the instant he laid eyes on his daughter, that changed, and Erin became the light of his life.

Because of the baby, in many ways, Peter was a different man. When he looked at his pretty, little girl, his squinty eyes softened, and when Ada searched them for deceit, she couldn't find it there. Peter was genuinely proud of his daughter. He bragged about how smart his daughter was. He carried her picture (and Ada's) in his wallet. He secured her in her child seat in the back of his souped-up sports car and paraded her in front of his friends, playing the proud father. He started to drive more carefully. He drove slower, observing the speed limit, for the sake of his precious cargo. He admonished his friends (both Bettie and Ada called them his *hooligan friends*) for smoking or cussing around the baby. He even forbade his dad to light his beloved cigars when Erin was in sight.

Peter nicknamed his little girl 'Grasshopper.' He called her 'Hopper,' for short. He came up with the name while watching an episode of one of his favorite TV shows, "Kung Fu." He had two reasons, he said, for calling her that: Number one, because of the little chirping noises she made when she first started to talk, and secondly (and more to the point), because, like Kwai Chang Caine (the character David Carradine played on the show) who never surpassed Master Khan (his teacher), Erin would always be learning from her dad.

"I am the master; you are the student, Grasshopper," he informed her. "When you can snatch the pebble from my palm…then you will be ready to leave, Grasshopper. When you can snatch the stone from my hand, the student will have surpassed the teacher." She wouldn't know what her father meant, but she would diligently try and predictably fail to retrieve the stone from his outstretched hand before he closed it again into a tight fist. It was a game they played, but the game was less serious for her than for him. Peter called her by that name (Grasshopper) for the rest of her life, and it defined the relationship he wanted with his daughter: all-knowing master versus deferential student. It was a relationship he never obtained.

You Can't Go Home

Peter was doing well at the electronics company where he was employed, but he decided on a career change. He announced he was 'branching off into computers.'

He was working full-time, had an associate degree, and was taking night classes to obtain a bachelor's degree. His natural aptitude for electronics carried over, and soon he was at the top of his classes in computer science. "Computers are the wave of the future," he'd told her, and Ada was pleased that Peter would discuss his plans with her. He talked with her about problems and opportunities at work. He even mellowed toward his superiors—outwardly, at least. He explained his strategy: "You have to play the game. That's the only way to get ahead in the white man's world." It was a lesson his father had learned, and he tirelessly preached it to his son until the logic clicked and stuck.

This new relationship they shared, and the notion that he seemed to now want her trust and approval, was alien to her. Ada was confused, but she listened raptly to his plans and was fascinated at the scope of his ideas, and his innate intelligence. Ada trusted little else about him, but she did trust both his intellect and his common sense. He had his wits about him, and she believed in his ability to care for them financially.

It was on the heels of this news of his career change that Peter announced the plan to move his little family into a house of their own. He'd actually purchased a house. It wasn't a rented property, but a house they would own. The old saying that Big Mama applied to any great exploit achieved by black folks pertained once more: 'Very few whites and no blacks at all'…she'd say…and she'd follow the phrase with the appropriate feat.

Well, Ada thought, *it's true. Very few whites and no blacks at all owned their own homes, especially right out of high school.*

Peter's father co-signed for him, but the house was theirs (or it would be in 30 years or so). It was impressive, and Ada felt proud in spite of herself, that they were doing so well in such short a period of time. Peter was making good on his promise to make something of himself. They were homeowners. Ada felt validated. It never occurred to her to be concerned that her name was not on the deed to the house.

She had complained to her mom a few times, saying only that Peter was mean to her; that he had a temper. And Ella had seen actual evidence of his temper on a couple of occasions. Once, Ada appeared on Ella's doorstep in tears. She had the entire print of Peter's hand across the side of her face. She announced she was leaving her husband and wanted to move back home. Ella had heard that song before. Ada was distraught, and begged her mom to let her come home. Ella would not allow it. A day or so later, she knew, Peter would show up, the kids would make up, and Ada would go traipsing off with her husband again.

Ella knew Ada had a way of exaggerating. Things probably weren't nearly as bad as she let on. "All young couples fight," she told her daughter and herself. Ella knew firsthand how exasperating the girl could be. She had a mouth on her that wouldn't quit, and a stubborn streak a mile long. So although Ada begged her mother to let her stay, Ella sent her daughter packing, sent her back to her husband. And Ada never asked to move back home again.

A month later, when their baby girl arrived, Ada became content and Peter's temper cooled down. Having a baby was good for them. Ella could tell. Becoming a father had done wonders for Peter's disposition. He loved that little girl. She mellowed him.

Ella had been wise to make Ada marry the young man, and it had been wise to make her go home to him. He'd just needed time to grow up. *He's still a kid*, Ella told herself; *you have to make allowances*. And now she congratulated herself. She had been right.

Security Blanket
for Fading Dreams

The house the kids bought wasn't large and it wasn't new, but it was well built and 'had a lot of potential.' It was an older home in a neighborhood that had seen better days. Peter called it a fixer-upper, but he described it with an exuberance that caused his eyes to widen and shine.

They decorated the house together. They bought linens and housewares and paint. Peter asked for her input on furnishings and color schemes. They scavenged secondhand stores and yard sales for knick-knacks and wall hangings to accessorize the place.

Ada started to feel like a young wife for the first time in her married life. The feeling scared her, but she listened as he detailed his plans for their future. She felt pleased when he asked her opinions. And although she tried to resist, she found herself growing hopeful about her future and her life with him. There were still small voices inside her head. And they still whispered quietly, causing confusion and fear. She sometimes felt delirious; tossed by waves of thought, like a small boat adrift in a turbulent sea. It frightened her, this idea that not even her own her mind could be trusted to tell her what was real. She had been suspicious of almost everyone, and especially Peter. She examined the evidence that was placed before her and came to a conclusion. The evidence looked like this:

He liked to make her feel small.

He liked to make her cry.

He humiliated and embarrassed her in public.

He manipulated her and played games with her mind.

He hit her.

These facts told her his intentions weren't good. He didn't love her. He never had. This was a horrible thing to know, but oddly, there was *comfort in the knowing*. Acknowledginghis motives protected her. It told her where she stood and how to defend herself. And long before the baby came, she settled the riddle in her mind. She decided not to trust him. She would not let herself be fooled. But that was before the baby was born.

Ada latched onto the truth that was dangled before her… that once she had verified his real feelings… it was snatched away, and replaced again with doubt.

And it wasn't just that he was buying a home for them that relaxed her reserve. It was the pride in his voice when he told her about it; when he showed it to her and their child. He was happy and he was proud of himself, but it was more than that. It seemed that he needed her to be happy, too; that he'd done this thing for them.

Why? she wondered. *Why should it matter to him that she was happy. Could it really be that he cared?* Ada resisted the idea, but was born to be a wife and mother. She loved keeping house. She loved having friends over, cooking meals, and entertaining and hosting them. But, the thought that Peter cared was a dangerous notion. It unsettled her mind again. She tried pushing the idea away, and she damned herself for thinking it. But she thought it nonetheless.

Peter moved his young family several times in those early years of their marriage. Each time they moved it was a step up. They moved from their first house on College Avenue to a nicer place on Station Street. Later they bought both sides of a double, a large two-family dwelling, that Peter converted into a one-family flat. For a while they lived within minutes of Ella's house, and Ada visited her mom and her little brothers frequently. Eventually though, Peter's company offered him a promotion, which meant relocating to another part of the state. He proudly accepted, and moved his family south of Indianapolis to Columbus, Indiana.

By now, they had two little girls, one as precious as the other, and a cherubic little boy who was arguably the cutest baby alive at the time. Peter gave his name to his son. They called him Peter 2—or Little Pete—to distinguish him from his dad. That same year, Peter received the promotion of a lifetime and was given a position in upper

management. For the militant young man from the south side of
Indianapolis, this was a great accomplishment! The company relocated
him again, this time out of the state—to West Bloomfield, Michigan, an
affluent suburb of Detroit.

Relocating was never a problem for Ada. With each move, she gained
greater confidence. She never had trouble making friends. She looked
at each move as a fresh start; a chance to abandon a flawed life. No
matter how hard she tried her problems persisted, following her from
place to place. On the surface, she was calm, but there were always
undercurrents that threatened to capsize her.

She was, more or less, a lady of leisure. Peter didn't want her to work
outside the home and Ada had never really wanted a job, anyway. She
never felt confident enough to do anything. For a short time when she
was still very young, she agreed to clean rooms for her father-in-law
at his hotel. He had mentioned to her that he needed help, and Ada
was surprised when Peter said 'yes' to the idea. She liked the thought
of earning her own money, but the hotel was vulgar and knowing the
kind of business that was carried on there was too much for her.

"It's a straight-up whorehouse, Peter, and I really don't want to work
there," she said. She wanted to say that memories assailed her the
minute she walked through the door, and that there was a stench to
the place that sent her reeling. She called it immoral, and it goaded
her that Peter would want his wife to work at such a place, changing
the filthy sheets of people who used the rooms for sordid one-night
stands.

Peter talked her into it. Actually, it was his demand. He told her that
he needed the help. Money had never been an issue before, and Ada
had a hard time believing it suddenly became one. After just a few
months she rebelled and quit the job, telling Peter she couldn't in
good conscience keep working there, but she remained hurt that Peter
thought so little of her that he had encouraged her to do it in the first
place.

Ada started attending night school classes at Manuel High when
Erin was less than a year old, and that same year she earned her high
school diploma. It wasn't easy. These were the early days, and still
they were turbulent times for her and Peter. His temper was still bad,
but not consistent. "I don't know," she once told her sister. "Maybe

that makes it worse." Ada had to admit that he seemed to be fighting harder to control it, but still there were erratic outbursts that left her shaky and unsure of herself. Even when his attacks weren't physical, when he wasn't hitting her, she was intimidated by his presence. His attitude caused her to revisit her first opinion of him. He didn't love her and couldn't be trusted.

Her sister was well on her way to earning her bachelor's degree. When Ada held her high school diploma in her hand, she was proud. Her mom had promised her a crisp new one-hundred-dollar bill as incentive, and when she held the currency in her hand she felt a sense of accomplishment. It wasn't the money that made her glow; Ada always had money she'd gotten from Peter. It was the note of approval in Ella's voice, and the look of pride in her eyes, when she handed the money to her daughter that caused the girl to beam. These were things that signified the approval Ada had always coveted.

Ada wanted to continue her education, and this diploma was the first step. She wondered if a career in journalism would be within reach. But Peter was still in school, and even though she knew they were doing OK, he always insisted there was no money for Ada's education. Maybe later, he always told her, when Erin was older and his job was more secure. But two babies later, college was still on the back burner. Eventually the idea was shelved altogether.

Peter assured her he'd always take care of her. He promised that she didn't need to worry about paying bills or having a job. So far, it was true. He did take care of her material needs. He earned a good wage, managed it well, and was generous with her. She tried to convince herself he always would be.

At the end of each week when he brought home his pay, Peter would hand her two brand new hundred-dollar bills. It always caused Ada's eyes to light up. The money was to buy groceries and whatever else was needed for the house. But there was always money left over, and she could spend it however she liked.

Peter still played gigs most weekends and those jobs paid good money, as well. It was nothing for Peter to hand over the entire amount he'd earned from playing the keyboard, at the end of the evening. So, although Ada had problems, money was never one of them. The money appeased her, so that college became a distant dream, but she was so busy indulging herself that she barely noticed as it faded from view.

In time, though, a new development emerged regarding Ada's relationship to money. She became obsessed with it; began hoarding it. Eventually, she'd amassed an impressive nest egg that Peter knew nothing about. He was her only means of support, he made sure of it, but Ada was secure in the knowledge that she had a reserve of cash to fall back on *just in case*. So Ada saved. She tucked bills into the pleats of the living room drapes and stuffed them into the fat pillows of the couch and the cushions of chairs. They were frozen in containers that used to hold juice, and taped to the bottoms of dresser drawers.

Outside the house, Ada had family members and friends deposit money for her into their accounts, and open other accounts for her, secret ones, that were not in her name, but were available for her use.

It would be years before Ada would have a checking account of her own or learn to balance a bankbook. All of the bank accounts, their houses and their cars, and all of their bills, everything they owned, was, and always had been, in Peter's name. She didn't know how to write a check or balance a checkbook, but Ada had money—lots of it.

By the time they moved from Indiana, she had more than $15,000 stashed away in secret places. It made her feel as secure as the cottony blanket with the soft satin trim that covered her childhood bed.

Voices

An unusal thing happened from time to time without any warning. Ada might be walking when she'd stop suddenly and turn, throwing a glance over her shoulder. She'd stop in her tracks, in mid-thought, mid-sentence or mid-step, and she'd stand still and listen very hard, straining her ears.

She heard or thought she heard a faint voice, or sometimes voices. She never was certain so she'd stand motionless, concentrating for a long moment tuning her ears, trying to hear. Sometimes she swore she heard her name. Then she'd question whether the voice had come from inside her head or out, or if there had really been any sound at all.

She'd blame it on an overactive imagination, or decide she was tired and just needed more sleep, and she'd try to go on about her business. But for a while, the sensation would linger causing mild anarchy inside her head.

There was sometimes the strange feeling that something was missing; that there was something she should be remembering, something she should know. It toyed with her sanity. Ada felt that sensation several times one particular morning. Ada had tried to shake the feeling all day, but it persisted and eventually became so relentless that her mind was etched with the memory of it. It became one of those curious things that were key in defining the anomaly of her life.

Later that day her friend Kathy called her and begged, "Wanna come out and play?" This, of course, meant shopping which was their favorite pastime. They got an early start, dropped off Little Pete with a sitter then stopped for coffee and donuts. They needed to fuel their stomachs before they hit the mall.

They spent the morning gabbing as though they hadn't seen each other in weeks. In fact, they saw each other nearly every day. If they did skip spending some part of a day together, they were sure to speak on the phone.

They had all day to shop. As they browsed they cracked themselves up, over everything in general and nothing in particular and periodically both of them would dissolve into uncontrolled fits of laughter.

Their laughter attracted the attention of other shoppers, who responded with amused glances and cackles of their own. They were being silly in the way that Ada couldn't afford to be when Peter was around. He would have called them *raucous* and *undignified*, and he wouldn't have been amused. His disapproval was always like a poison that killed her sense of humor.

"Cool it, Ada." That was all he needed to say. He'd raise one brow threateningly and look hard at her through his slanted eyes, and she'd know he was serious. He didn't need to raise his voice or his hand. Whatever it was that had made her laugh before would no longer be funny, and her good mood would fade along with her laughter.

Ada was still at the mall with kathy, when she first thought she heard her name. It wasn't as if someone were speaking to her. It was rather that, in conversation, someone had *mentioned* her name. Ada was being discussed, and the voice was familiar. She'd heard it before. Even before she turned to look, instinct told her no one was there; that the action was all in her head. Her instinct was right. She glanced over her shoulder to find that only Kathy was at her side, and she was absorbed in a display of small gold hoops that were marked 75 percent off. Kathy hadn't spoken to her. Ada shook off the troubling sensation.

Just before leaving the mall, Kathy and Ada both spotted a price-reduced, 14-karat rose-gold chain. At 80 percent off, the store was 'practically giving it away.' They play-fought over the chain until Ada mischievously snatched it from Kathy's hand. Kathy protested, but she was stifling a smile, and when she threatened Ada with physical harm, the sales girl was amused. "Maybe you better let her have it," she joked, directing the taunt at Ada. "She probably knows all your dirty little secrets!" Kathy grinned at the clerk and bobbed her head emphatically, assuring the girl it was true. She thought it was.

Ada could sometimes be quiet and reflective, giving kathy the feeling that her friend was millions of miles away and completely distracted.

Every now and then they laughed about it, and Kathy made jokes when Ada seemed *spaced* and lost in thought, asking: "So, did ya have a nice trip, Ada? Did you bring me something back?"

Ada would resurface and often, at those times, she'd appear distracted and a little confused. It was a running joke between them, but a good-natured one, and Ada was never offended. Kathy was sure the two of them knew each other so well that there were no secrets between them. But she was wrong. Ada had secrets that no one was aware of.

Magic Tricks

Just the night before, Ada had been in tears. She had cried herself to sleep because Peter had hit her, but years would pass before anyone knew. The parts of her brain that remembered conferred with the parts of it that did not. Peter had slapped her hard with the back of his hand and sent her flying into a wall. She bumped her head on the hard surface and heard an ugly thud.

Before she could recover from the shock of it, he delivered a second blow. He hit her with a closed fist, this time on the side of her head. Instantly, she heard a ringing in her ears and then quite distinctly, she saw stars. The blow knocked her to the floor, and the suddenness of it left her dazed and confused like the split second following the impact of a car crash before the reality of it sets in.

It had been a while, several months, since the last time he'd erupted that way. What's more, he had developed an uncanny ability to charm her between outbursts. He could be every bit as good as he was bad. So Ada had let her guard down, and he caught her by surprise.

Even though his outbursts were less frequent, and not as severe as they had been at the start of their marriage, they were no less terrifying. She realized that she was just as afraid of Peter as she'd ever been. She couldn't explain, even to herself, how he had wormed his way back into her affections.

She squeezed her eyes shut, reliving the nightmare, and her mind went haywire. Events weren't occurring in real time. She watched herself in slow motion with the hushed commentary of announcers giving a play-by-play depiction of the action. Her brain was a twisted mosaic. It continued to function, but erratically. The content was there but the emotion was absent and her thoughts were numbed.

He had appeared out of nowhere. He did that often. She'd see him first in the corner of her eye, then he'd be in full frontal view and she'd know he'd been watching her, and she'd quiz herself as to how that could happen.

She had been at the stove that night, baking. She was making a lemon pie, his favorite. She got the recipe from her Aunt Lillian; she perfected it, and was proud of how well she had learned to cook. She whipped the meringue until it saluted and stood in stiff peaks in her large mixing bowl.

The crust was made from butter cookies, moistened with melted butter and crumbled into an aluminum pie pan. The lemon filling was made from Jell-O pudding, with two teaspoons of lemon extract for added tartness, and a few extra teaspoons of sugar for the contrast in sweetness. The result was spectacular. The last time she made one Peter gave her his equivalent of high praise. "It's decent," he told her. Ada knew that in Peter-speak 'decent' translated to 'very good,' plus, he smiled when he said it, so Ada was pleased.

She was smiling to herself, absentmindedly humming a tune, and adjusting the peaks and valleys on the marvelous creation when Peter appeared. She caught a swift movement that startled her, but before she could cringe, she was on the floor.

When Ada pictured it now, that swiftness of his hand as it flew against her face, it revived an emotion, and she shuddered as the feeling stirred and came to life. Peter hadn't spoken a word. He just strode in with his own brand of justice for some anonymous infraction. By now, Ada knew it didn't really matter whether the breach was real or imagined. With little or no warning, his anger would come. Sometimes a blow accompanied a booming, out-of-control voice. Other times the attack came out of dead silence. Always, though, there were cold, menacing eyes.

And usually, there was no explanation. Peter didn't have to explain himself. When he was mad at her, he expected her to know why. This scenario caused a vicious chain of events that went like this: She'd ask Peter what was wrong; he'd accuse her of 'playing dumb' (which made him madder still), which made Ada more afraid, which destroyed her ability to speak, and caused him further rage. She learned early on just to apologize, profusely and profoundly, for whatever Peter accused her of saying or doing. She learned that it was useless to deny guilt. Peter had an uncanny power. His ability, his trick, was to make himself grow. His essence, his presence, and even his voice were tangible, emergent things. Like magic, like a force he threw around her, like a magician's cape, his presence astonished her.

She felt its effect long after he was gone. It followed her like a ghost, and influenced her thoughts and her mood. He practiced this trick and mastered it. Ada mastered a trick of her own. When she sensed that Peter was angry, she could make herself small. She could transform herself into the tiniest of targets.

Her trick was to disappear, to shrink inside herself until the danger was gone. A safe, secure corner of a secret world would beckon her and she'd go there. She'd find her way through a maze of time and thought, and she'd rest there until the storm had passed and it was safe to come out again. From this safe distance, there would sometimes be glimpses and flashes of thought. And pictures, like scenes from a child's View-Master, flashed quickly before her eyes, like someone kept changing the view.

And voices, mostly calming, but occasionally damning, would be speaking her name. Usually she pushed past the voices and the patches of jumbled thought, and fell fast asleep in a veil of emptiness.

In this place, she was safe, away from trauma. She could stay there for days at a time. That's where she had gone the night before, when Peter came at her with his voice and his fists.

The Peter who came to her later was a different Peter; one who soothed her, who said he loved her… and was sorry. But his apology fell on deadened ears. Someone muted the sound and dimmed the lights until all color was gone from her world. So the parts of her that Peter could see and control were still within his reach, but her mind was unattainable.

Peter knew none of this when he pulled her into his arms that night. She came unresisting, and when he held her even after she'd fallen asleep, he was unaware that it was only her body he was holding. She slept late the next morning, and awoke with just remnants of the incident the night before. She was surprised that she didn't feel too bad, that there were not serious effects from last night's episode with Peter. She chided herself for her choice of words.

She had euphemisms for words and ideas she found too difficult to say. For Ada, saying, 'Peter hit me' would be almost as painful as an actual blow, and Ada had long ago learned to avoid words that brought her pain. So rather than 'fights,' she and Peter had 'incidents' and 'episodes.' He never 'beat her'; he 'got upset with her' or 'he lost his temper.'

When she climbed into bed the night before, she scooted as close as she could to the edge. She lay very still. She hardly dared to breathe when Peter lay down beside her. She thought how his touch made her flesh crawl and his mouth on hers made her want to gag. She was afraid she would be sick, but instead, she began adding numbers in her head until her mind was anesthetized and Peter's image was gone…and she was, too.

He awakened the next morning before she did. When she did come awake, she didn't get out of bed. He told her not to; he told her to sleep in, that she needed her rest. He'd get breakfast for the girls and himself, he said, and he'd drop them both off at school. Little Pete, he told her, was still asleep. He was being nice to her. She knew the routine. Ada turned over in bed, closed her eyes, and ignored him until the girls came in for their goodbye kisses. "Your mommy doesn't feel well," he told his daughters, answering the unspoken question in their eyes. Both girls hugged their mom for a long time before they turned and left the room.

Erin threw her mother one long last look, and Ada was drawn to the little girl's eyes. She had her lunch box in one hand and her school bag, stuffed with papers, was on her back. She grabbed hold of her baby sister's hand, and Lydia was bouncing wildly, the way five-year-olds do, but there was no spring in Erin's step as she turned on her heel and guided her sister to their father's car.

"We'll see you tonight, Ada," Peter said. He was still standing by the bed, and she felt him looking down at her.

"OK," Ada answered. Her eyes were shut. It was hard for her to look at him.

She snuggled deeper inside the covers, pretending to fall asleep, but the curious bickering inside her head interfered with the ruse. "He hit us again last night. She let him hit us," said an angry voice.

"Yeah, but what could she do?" a kinder voice asked.

"We better do something. He's using us for a punching bag!"

"Yeah, he beats her like a drum and then he plays her like a fiddle," an older voice said in singsong fashion.

The voices hurt, caused a peculiar sort of pain, but she reminded herself they were only words and they couldn't touch her. And besides, the words didn't apply to her. He didn't beat her. If she didn't think in those terms, she'd be OK.

She was living a good life. Her mother was saying so all the time. She was young to have so much. She had a nice house and a new car, and beautiful children, who were absolute rays of sunshine.

Peter's voice brought her back to the present. He called her name and Ada realized he'd been speaking to her. Still, she didn't answer, so Peter bent over the bed and leaned in close. It struck her that his cologne smelled good, and the incongruity of the fact that anything about him at all should be pleasant wasn't lost on her. He pecked her cheek and then his lips touched her neck. She kept her eyes closed and carefully measured her breaths, still feigning sleep. "We'll talk tonight," Peter said, and then he said, "I love you, Ada," and like always, when he said those words, she was surprised.

It unnerved her hearing those words from him. She wanted to ask him not to say them. He didn't love her and she knew it. She didn't answer. She kept pretending to be asleep as he moved away from her and toward the bedroom door. She listened until his footsteps faded. Then the front door opened and closed, he started his car, and he and his daughters drove away.

When she was satisfied that the coast was clear she jumped out of bed. She peeped in on her sleeping son and then checked herself out in her bathroom mirror. There was a knot on the back of her head that she felt with her hand, and the inside of her lip was cut, but her face wasn't swollen or bruised. There was stiffness and pain in parts of her body, and her head hurt, but there were no visible signs of the episode from the night before.

But there *was* a strange, undefined tightness in her chest, a dull throbbing that fatigued her and caused her to want to sleep. She didn't try to resist the urge. She climbed back into bed and drifted off. She was still asleep when Kathy called her. She had been happy for Kathy's invitation to shop. Spending Peter's money always made her feel better.

All at once, Kathy's voice intruded into what most people would have labeled a daydream. Kathy had her locked in a huge embrace and was thanking her profusely. Ada was only marginally aware that she'd purchased the chain they'd been fighting over, and placed it in her purse.

As they were leaving the mall, they paused, trying to remember where they'd parked the car. It was after they found their bearings, and pointed themselves in the right direction, that Ada dug in her purse and produced the little bag containing the necklace, and handed it to Kathy. That's when Kathy hugged her.

"Don't say I never gave ya nothing!" Ada smiled.

"Yeah, well my brilliant strategy all along was for *you* to buy the necklace and then give it to *me* as a gift." They were still giggling when they drove out of the mall parking lot.

By 1981, Ada had changed. She was no longer the frightened girl who'd been pushed from the nest at 16 and forced into a cold, grown-up world where she felt frightened and all alone. She was a young woman, capable of navigating the world. She had children of her own, who depended on her.

Little Pete looked as if his father had spit him out. And as he grew, he developed the mannerisms that identified him with the Collins clan. In fact, all of Peter's kids were small images of him.

"Yeah, well the Collins gene is strong," Peter would brag. And when people commented that Ada had done nothing more than *carry* the babies, she would scoff. But in secret, she was glad that Peter was happy to claim his kids; that there was no doubt they belonged to him.

Ada was especially close to the older of her two daughters. It wasn't that she loved Erin more; it was just that the bond between them was somehow different, stronger. Maybe because Ada had been so young when Erin was born, it was like they'd actually grown up together. And Erin in was an *old soul*. Sometimes she startled her elders with her perceptions. She became a little mother to her siblings. She loved them fiercely, and was protective of them.

Lydia, a middle child in every way, was an unpredictable little girl who blew hot and cold. She was wearing glasses by the time she was four years old. Her already huge eyes were magnified until they were twice their size behind the thick lenses, making her look like the wise old owl in one of her favorite stories. She was a pretty child, and was every bit as intelligent as she looked. She was precocious, but like her sister, she could never truly be called bad.

Little Pete was Erin's baby. She was eight years old when he was born. She'd insisted on taking care of him then and considered it her job ever since. He had a head full of the biggest, fattest curls imaginable. Ada thought proudly how each of her kids was as beautiful as the one before. From infancy, Ada stimulated their minds. She talked to them and sang to them, and read to them from storybooks. She told them bible stories and taught them morals as soon as they were old enough to listen. She was determined to get them off on the right track, and to teach by example and not with words alone. She was proud of her family, all of whom were good looking and smart. Most of all, she was proud that they were good kids, well-behaved and well-disciplined. Strangers commented on it when they were in public.

They lived well. Peter traveled all over the United States, receiving training and attending seminars. Often, his wife and kids went with him, and Ada was thrilled. She thought they lived like kings. When they traveled for business, they ate in fancy restaurants, and the company picked up the tab. While Peter worked, Ada spent her days shopping in big cities like Washington or Boston or New York. Or she lazed around in their nice hotel rooms, ordering room service and watching TV until Peter came home at the end of the day. Then they were off to see the sights.

They moved in different circles now. They hobnobbed and rubbed noses with Peter's bosses and their wives, who were all older than them, and white. The people Peter once vowed to hate were now his running buddies, his friends. Ada knew her husband's prejudices had merely gone underground, but still, she was impressed that he could hide them well enough to make the advances he needed to make in life. Another surprise: he gave her the credit for helping to temper him, calming him, he said, when he was stressed by the job. So Ada adapted to her new circumstances. She learned to walk the walk and talk, and to dress and present herself as professionally as the other wives did.

Her natural intelligence was an asset. When she helped Peter write his presentations and speeches, her cleverness with words came into play, and Peter acknowledged her contributions.

She liked people, and they responded in kind. She wasn't biased or constrained by pre-conceived notions, and she was easy to talk to. Although she lacked a college education (which was a sore point with her) she was well-read and current on world events, and was able to fit in easily. Once she'd recognized these things and allowed herself to feel a measure of self-worth, she started to come into her own.

There were still serious problems in her life. The chasm between Ada and her mom still existed, and it bothered her. She wished she were closer to her mom; she wanted to feel the love and approval she'd been missing her entire life. But all things considered, she believed their relationship was better than it had ever been.

Her mother respected her more, but Ada didn't have false illusions. She and her mother would never be friends. There would always be problems between them, and the best way of coping was to leave the past in the past and move on. She knew who her mother was and she warned herself not to expect more.

Ella could still be fierce, and if she was angry she wasn't one to be played with. When her temper flared she could spin on a dime and spew venom. More often than not Ada was on the receiving end of it. Knowing the precursors, Ada made herself scarce at the first sign of trouble.

She tried to remember details of growing up in her mother's house, but her memory was so faulty that she was often frustrated by the effort. Time flew by so fast, and she had a hard time capturing all but the very essence of it. She remembered sadness, confusion and pain. She remembered the hatred and bitterness and fear, but it was a struggle to connect those feelings to something solid and concrete. And *consciously* the feelings weren't connected to her mom. They came out of nowhere and stayed for a while before dissolving like mist at sea.

Ada hardly saw Jacob Daddy anymore; he was an afterthought in her life, an aura in her mother's house, and then one day, without fanfare or preamble, he was gone. She couldn't remember when she first noticed his absence, this man who had replaced her dad. She only knew that one day, her mother was alone again, and Jacob Daddy, the man Ella called 'the love of her life' had quietly moved on with his.

Ella married several more times. These marriages were a non-issue in Ada's life; they didn't affect her at all. The thing that did concern Ada—what she concentrated on—was gauging Ella's moods, and then conducting herself accordingly.

She learned from Ella's example the kind of a mom she would never be. She wouldn't be distant, unapproachable or cold. She wouldn't raise her voice at her kids or beat them in anger. She would listen to them when they spoke. She'd indulge them, allowing their foolishness. She would always encourage their dreams.

Ada loved her kids. They were her world, and there was nothing she wouldn't do for them. They would always know how much she cared, and that her love for them was constant and would never change. But somewhere in the stream of time, something did change in Ada's world.

Somewhere along the line, to her detriment and quite against her better judgment, Ada fell in love with her husband.

Columbus

The house in Columbus was cozy, inviting and warm. Ada felt secure here, with her family intact and her world under control. They had the problems common to all families but for the first time in her life Ada was relatively at peace. It was a false peace.

In a very short while, the façade would crumble. Ada's world would fall apart, because in that cozy house in Columbus, childhood memories that had both haunted and eluded her for a lifetime, resurfaced.

The first ripple accompanied visitors from home. Ada was excited; her family was coming to call. She felt good about her pretty house. It had actually been a model home before Peter bought it. There were three bedrooms in a circular floor plan. With its large dine-in kitchen, cozy fireplace in the living room, and the spacious family room, the house suggested affluence.

Leaving behind the big city and moving to this small southern Indiana town where she was totally unknown had given her a complete new identity in life. It was a fresh start, and Ada felt she was leaving her past behind. She had devised a way of reasoning that allowed for that notion. Here, in this new town, she could be who she wanted to be. She would travel without the emotional baggage that had burdened her most of her life.

Here, no one knew of the physical abuse that embarrassed her so, or the crushing lack of self-esteem that stunted her emotional growth. Here, the gaping holes in her memory were unseen and unknown. Her doubts and fears could be discarded. She would leave them behind, and the face she presented to this new world would be accepted as the authentic and true one.

She was happy and a little smug as she prepared for her first houseguests. She was anxious to show off her new home. Most of her family, her brothers, her two favorite aunts, and her mother, were coming to wish her well in this new phase of her life.

Her sister hadn't been able to come, but she called and sent a gift. This was a housewarming, but Ada couldn't have known that along with the gifts they bore, her family was bringing unsolicited childhood memories—painful ones—to her peaceful new home; that along with their genuine love and good wishes there would be pitiless flashes back to an era that Ada had cast from her brain.

She had hoped that Columbus would be a beginning; and it was a beginning of sorts—a time when strong alliances were formed, and deep within, unseen forces, determined ones, climbed from the abyss and rallied helping Ada to manage her life.

Not All, But Enough

It was midday, on a Saturday, when Ella and her clan pulled up to Ada's house. They were overwhelmed with excitement, happy to be spending time with Peter, Ada and the kids.

By now, Angela was living in Texas. She was divorced from Gary, but she was doing well. She married a successful accountant and was living and teaching elementary school in a suburb of Houston. Ada missed her big sister terribly and she was disappointed she wasn't able to make the trip.

Anthony and Roman were proud of both of their sisters. And they loved their little nieces and nephews, who were really more like younger siblings to them. They were a close-knit family, and family gatherings were important to them, so they had a routine for occasions when one of them was unable to attend a family function.

Someone present would telephone the absent relative and then pass the telephone around until everyone had gotten a chance to talk. That plan was in force during that first visit to Ada's house, so Angela was able share in the festivities by phone.

As usual, Ada prepared well for the occasion and the house smelled of all of their favorite foods. Both Peter and Ada enjoyed entertaining. They anticipated every contingency and were always prepared, so when people came to their house they felt welcomed and at ease.

This visit was no different. Everyone ate until they were stuffed. The instant their food digested even the slightest bit, they would eat again. Peter was always in charge of sightseeing tours, so they'd load up in two cars and start off on excursions for parts unknown. Then, they'd return to play board games and eat yet again.

They told family stories that caused them all to laugh, and they'd talk until time flew away and dusk began to creep past the curtains and into the house.

It was during one of these marathon sessions of storytelling that Ada suddenly came to her feet. She had been right in the middle of the commotion, lazing comfortably on the floor of the family room, propped up against the bottom of the cushioned couch. Without a word, she disappeared into her bedroom. When she came back, she carried a magazine that had been carefully folded and tucked into a lingerie drawer of her dresser.

No one noticed when she left. When she returned, instead of reclaiming her place on the family room floor, she sat across from her mother at the dining room table. Ella acknowledged her daughter with a slight smile.

Both of Ada's aunts were at that table, too. They were busy polishing off the final pieces of Ada's sweet potato pie, which had been winning rave reviews all evening.

Ada didn't look at either of them. She looked at her mother as she placed the magazine, face up, on the table and then slid it a short distance to rest in front of her. And the whole time, she studied her mother's eyes, searching for…for what? She didn't know.

She had received the magazine in the mail several weeks before. It was a subscription she'd had for over a year. She always enjoyed the articles. They often fascinated or intrigued her, but none of them had ever affected her like this particular one did.

On the cover was a man, a big man, all in dark shadows, who peered ominously from behind the frightened figure of a little girl with large, haunting eyes. She held a ragdoll by one dangling arm, and the caption, which chilled Ada's blood, read: "Sexual Abuse…the Lasting Effects."

When Ada got the magazine from the mailbox, she had stared at those words. She tried to make sense of them, and to understand why they seared her so. The message really didn't register in any way, and yet it registered in every way.

Her brain had begun to swell, and then to hurt, and she felt the very real danger of being swallowed alive. A deepening dark mist enveloped her, and she noted, absently, that her hands were shaking. She didn't know why. In the next moment she was surprised to realize that she was holding her breath and seemed incapable of letting it go.

At first she conversed with herself…she inwardly reasoned, telling herself to calm down and to simply exhale.

And then when it became clear to her that she actually had forgotten how, the message became a desperate and fierce command.

"Breathe, Ada. Breathe!"

Ada berated herself until finally she complied, and though it had taken some time, she eventually calmed herself. But still, for long moments afterward, she had an uncomfortable tightness in her chest, and a familiar, frightening breathlessness, like something was resting on her chest, like something heavy was crushing the air from her lungs. She had folded the magazine and tucked it away. For a time, she managed to put the troubling episode out of her mind.

She didn't recall it again until Ella's visit, when Ada's beautiful house was full of family and life and memories of good times.

That's when suddenly, she came to her feet, without thought, and like an android she drifted to the bedroom to reclaim the object of her distress.

When she returned and pushed the magazine across the table, Ella received it as covertly as it was intended. A silent alarm had gone off, but no one else noticed or was involved. It was a message shared only between the two of them. Ella glanced at the article and her brow creased in a quick flicker of comprehension before she silently pushed it away.

Neither of them spoke, but the words came loud and clear. And Ella understood. With her eyes, Ada had said, in no uncertain terms, "I remember. Not all, but enough."

Dreams

While they were still living in Columbus, Ada began having strange dreams. The content of them was often disturbing, but it was more than that. Even if the dreams seemed benign, the effect they had on her was profound. Sometimes, when she awoke from one, her thoughts were troubled, scattered, and unsettled. Sometimes, she woke up confused, and she would scramble to investigate her surroundings.

She might throw open the door to a closet to see if a sharp new outfit she'd dreamt about really existed. Or she'd check the pockets of a coat, looking for something she dreamt she'd placed there. Sometimes she'd find herself looking for ticket stubs from a movie she'd only seen in a dream, or she'd dissect a conversation she remembered from her sleep. She'd check and recheck the clock to convince herself of the time, and then still she'd consult the calendar to apprise herself of the date. Her dreams could be uncannily real. But stranger than that, even when she was fairly certain she was *awake*, she'd wonder if she were dreaming. *Is this a new phenomenon, or am I just noticing it more?*

She didn't know, but if she thought too hard about it, she got headachy, then foggy and fatigued. These sensations were warning signs, signs that told her she needed to *stop*. Ada learned to obey the signs. But the problem was impossible to ignore, especially when there was so much evidence that things simply weren't right.

Ada remembered something that had happened years ago. An expensive pantsuit somehow appeared in her closet. It was a suit she would never have bought for herself, or worn, but somehow she knew it was hers. She agonized over that suit. It wasn't that the suit wasn't nice; it was very nice, and she liked it *OK*, but not for herself. Maybe for somebody else.

It was too old for her, too conservative, and it cost more money than she would have paid. Still, it was in her closet. Ada had had a dream about that very suit. In her dream, she had gone to the mall. She'd been window-shopping when she saw the suit. She tried it on, and bought it. She brought it home and hung it in the back of her bedroom closet. She found it exactly where she dreamed it would be. There was no reasonable explanation for how it got there.

It was brand new. The receipt was tucked into a front pocket of the jeans she'd been wearing the day before, where she knew it would be. The receipt said, "All sales final. No credits, no exchanges, and no refunds." The suit became a symbol for her, a symbol of the bizarre, unnamable *something* that was wrong in her life.

She was stuck with a suit she didn't really like, didn't want and couldn't really afford, and if her life had depended on it she couldn't explain why.

She'd been in this dilemma before. She wanted to investigate. She started to ask Peter about it. She told herself, *maybe it was a gift.* She knew better. It had not been a gift. If she raised questions, she knew she'd end up with more questions. She didn't have any answers, so she did what she did best. She shrugged it off. The next time Ada visited her mother, the suit became a present for her.

Ella loved it. "It's beautiful, Ada," Ella told her daughter. "And it fits perfectly."

Ada liked it when she made her mother smile. She pushed her dream and her concerns about the suit to the back of her mind.

Actually, Ella got lots of presents that way. Although she felt slightly guilty about the re-gifting, Ada basked in any praise she got when she made Ella happy. After all these years, Ada still craved her mother's attention and she courted her affection. She liked to buy her presents or to write poems that extolled her love or praised her virtues as a mother. It hadn't always been that way. Ada still remembered the near hatred she once felt for Ella. When she thought of it now, it was a memory of a completely different place and time.

More than that, she felt that she'd been an entirely different person then. She had been hateful and angry much of the time; a person she could barely remember now; someone she didn't know. She doubted that she and her mother could ever be as close as she wanted them to be, but their relationship at present was pretty good.

As long as she stayed focused on today, on the here and now, the tension that still existed between them was manageable. She couldn't afford to revive the old feelings. It was risky to think about childhood or growing up in Ella's house. There was something ominous there, and so memories came with a price. Time passed. Ada was a grown woman with a family of her own.

Materially, her husband gave her everything she needed and most of what she wanted. He wasn't as volatile as he had once been, but he was distant, and absorbed in his work. Ada had her children, and she had good friends. She stayed busy and she told herself she was happy. Yet she continued to feel pushed from the nest too soon. And it hurt. It still lodged in her throat like a dry piece of toast.

Since the night of the housewarming in Columbus, Ada had been unsettled. She and her mom had never discussed the secret that lay between them, but it was there and she felt that they shared it. Since that time, recollections came frequently and they always made Ada sad. Without warning and from out of nowhere, feelings would envelop her, and she couldn't push them away.

The memories were ancient ones, but they always felt fresh and new. Ada was left breathless and winded, breathing too hard like she'd been running a race.

In one potent memory, Ada was in the basement of her mother's house and the walls were closing in. She was 16 years old again—a young 16—and she was very much afraid. She was in the basement because Ella had called a meeting "to talk some sense into Ada." She was outnumbered. All of them were there, all of the grownups in her life.

Jacob sat mute with unreadable, odd-colored eyes that stared straight through her. Peter was there, too, looking responsible and mature. She looked foolish by comparison. Both of his parents had come, looking grievously wounded, like some personal injury had been done to them. In fact, everyone looked so pained, so assaulted, that Ada nearly forgot that she was the one in trouble.

Trouble. That was the term they used for it in those days, at least in polite circles. But her mom had put it another way. "You spread your legs for that boy." Ella nearly screamed the words. "You got yourself pregnant and you've ruined your life."

Ada felt like a whore. The impact of her situation hit her full force. The words stung and then coursed through her veins like snake's venom. She'd tried to explain, to defend herself. But her words sounded foolish, even to her own ears: "But Mama, we didn't do anything. We didn't do anything! Peter said we were just fooling around."

The words fell on deaf ears and her fate was decided that night. She would marry Peter Collins. She wished she had listened to the voices all along. Some of the voices had been harsh, others agitated, even angry; and instinctively, she knew the anger was directed her way.

"We warned you." Those voices told her. New voices spoke sadly now from deep within. She should have listened when they told her not to believe. She should have listened to the people inside her head.

The Troops

Ada was almost 40 years old when she finally met the troops. They stepped out from the shadows one by one, with extended hands, and presented themselves, and all at once, as the truly bizarre nature of her life came into focus, she pondered the frightening question of whether she'd be able to salvage her mind.

And for the first time, as she looked back at the chaos of her life, it was with a measure of understanding and a burgeoning sense of pride. She would learn to be lenient with herself, and more forgiving, because she'd walked through perilous fields of battle and so far, she'd managed to survive.

Peter moved his family to West Bloomfield, Michigan, in 1981 when Erin was eleven. Lydia was a wide-eyed kindergartener and Little Pete was still a pudgy three-year-old. When Digital had transferred him in the summer of that year, he left his young family behind in Columbus and went there on his own. For several months Peter lived out of a hotel room, commuting back to Columbus on weekends. Some weeks Ada took the trip back up north with him. She loved to travel. She saw these trips as a vacation and an escapade.

When summer came, Ada and the kids joined Peter at the Farmington Hills Holiday Inn. The hotel was their home for several months while they house-hunted in earnest. The kids had a ball; they lived like kings off the fat of the land, with video games and room service, and long hours splashing in the Olympic-sized hotel swimming pool.

They finally settled on a picturesque house near the end of the proverbial long, winding road. Ada considered it the prettiest house on the block and she worried that they couldn't afford it.

They also looked at a house in Southfield, a Detroit suburb. It was less expensive, but in Ada's estimation, it was just as beautiful. The

Southfield house was large, too, and had also been well cared for. It sat on a gargantuan lot that disappeared into endless acres of tall, thick-trunked trees.

Erin didn't like the Southfield house, or its setting. "It's way too country," she complained, mostly to her dad. "There's hardly any streetlights, and it's pitch dark out here at night. I'll be scared at night in all of these trees."

It *was* rural, but Ada liked that about it. And she liked that there was a good mix of blacks and whites, and that the schools were exceptional. It was a whole lot of house for the money. Ada knew it was an excellent value and Peter knew it, too. But the West Bloomfield house was practically new; it had been recently constructed, had only one previous owner, a confirmed bachelor, and he had taken excellent care of it.

This large house sat on a plot of well-manicured, plush green grass. The acreage wasn't as great, but the back yard was ample and pretty, and the way it sloped gently into a large common area that was shared by several neighboring houses, it reminded Ada of a finely maintained park. There were flowering bushes and shrubs, and several fruit trees already were in bloom.

Ada had to admit that this area would be a perfect place to raise kids. There was plenty of room for a basketball hoop and a shiny new swing set. Already there were flower gardens with beds of tulips, lilies, and begonias, and several rose bushes flaunted magnificent red and white blooms. There was even a modest vegetable garden beginning to sprout produce that Ada was anxious to tend.

The township was predominately white and Jewish, but that didn't worry Ada. Columbus had been almost entirely white, and she had adapted. It sounded cliché, but some of her closest friends *were* white.

Ada's religion had taught her not to be biased, and although her family had always preferred to associate mainly within their own race, that sentiment never rubbed off on Ada. As long as a person treated her well, Ada wasn't much concerned with the color of his skin.

Ada's neighbors in Columbus represented a different segment of the Caucasian population. That city had a small town feel. People there appeared to be more curious than prejudiced. There was a lower level of sophistication there, but Ada didn't see that as a bad thing. For the most part, people there were down to earth and friendly.

West Bloomfield, they soon learned, was one of wealthiest communities in the country. It had an air of affluence and prestige that made Ada apprehensive. She was used to living among whites, and she had no problem with people of wealth, but she didn't want to live *in a community of snobs.* That was what concerned her.

Erin fell in love with the house, so when Ada balked, Erin sidestepped her mother's authority and went to her dad. "Get me up in here," she begged him…and finally he complied. "OK, Hopper," he told her. "It might be a little steep for your old dad, but I'll see what I can do."

Ada was vetoed, and within a month's time, they were in their new home. Ada ignored her reservations and settled in. It was an exciting time and she wasn't really unhappy. Peter was 32 was Ada 29 and they were living the American dream. They were young to have established themselves, so well. They looked like a conventional married couple, and Ada no longer felt like she was playing house. They had arrived.

Peter had poured on the charm during the long months he'd spent away from home, and Ada, who was sociable, made friends each time she visited him. So by the time he moved his family there, he and Ada already had many good friends in the area. The transition was painless. Ada was quick to make ties within her religious community. In no time at all she was anchored and at home in her new environment. But while she was busy adding the finishing touches to their beautiful home, her life began falling apart in earnest. Within a few years, her world lay in shambles around her. Years of abuse, verbal and otherwise, joined forces with odd childhood trauma, and these had taken their toll. This was a condition that she had failed to recognize. Peter's manipulation was so masterful that to Ada it was largely unseen. She failed to notice that her husband was driving the sanity from her mind. To many of her friends it was obvious, just as it had been to most of her friends in Columbus. People there worried about her, and they worried about her now in this new place.

She remembered one incident that occurred not long after their move to Bloomfield. He had swerved the car to an abrupt stop in a quicksilver moment of anger that had nearly caused her heart to stop. They were going to a party at some friends' house when Peter got lost. They'd driven in circles for almost an hour before Ada suggested they stop for directions. Peter exploded. Ada had seen him explode often before, yet she was never prepared for the suddenness of it. He stopped the car with a fierceness that left her shaken and breathless. "What did you say to me?" he demanded without looking at her. Ada knew full well he'd heard her. She was afraid to answer him…and she was afraid not to answer. "I just said maybe we should stop and ask for directions." Her voice was weak. She hated the sound of it and was sure Peter did, too. "Did I ask you for an opinion?" His voice was too calm. He still didn't look at her. He didn't need to. The question alone was villainous. It hung in the air like a specter between them. It was dusk, and the car was dark. The lights that illuminated the street managed only to cast gloomy shadows through the glass.

"Ada, if nothing else ever sticks in your head, you need to remember this: if I have an opinion, and you have an opinion…and yours is different from mine, you keep your opinion to yourself." Ada didn't answer. She didn't know how.

"Did you hear me?" he demanded. "Yes." That was all she could manage. She felt as if very strong hands had spanned the circle of her neck and were wringing the air from it. The chill she fought off had nothing to do with the frigid weather outside the car.

"What did I say, Ada? Tell me what I said." His voice was flat, deceptively emotionless.

"You said if I have an opinion that's different from yours, I should keep my opinion to myself." She answered the question by rote, and another little piece of her died. Ada studied his profile from the corner of her eye. She decided again that she hated him. And she said the words, in an act of defiance, to herself, *'I hate you. I hate you. I hate you. I hate you.'*

She repeated the phrase over and over until she realized she wasn't saying the words alone. Peter put the car back into gear and drove in silence. He never looked at Ada. He simply started the car and maneuvered it back into the flow of traffic. He delivered them to their friends' house and when they entered, it was arm in arm. Ada plastered a waxen smile tightly across her face. There were still words ringing in her head, but they'd changed slightly. Now they said, "*We* hate you. *We* hate you. *We* hate you." Ada nodded to herself in acceptance. She absorbed the silent words that ricocheted in her brain. But she never forgot *his* words, and the quiet rebellion began.

Eroding Oz

Peter's control over Ada had been complete because for so many years he controlled her mind. But with the passage of time, erosion set in and his control began to crumble. The first cracks began when friends of *his* became friends of *theirs*, and then became friends of *hers*.

When some of their friends first started to whisper to Ada that Peter's manner toward her was abusive, she resisted the idea. She'd laugh it away, defend him or she'd make excuses, the way she always had. But in her heart, their words rang true and she couldn't completely dismiss them. She felt criticized, and it embarrassed her that people noticed she allowed him to treat her the way he did.

These were people she liked and respected. Some of them were women who worked with Peter. She knew their concern was genuine. She trusted them, and their opinions mattered to her. Ada had never been a working woman. She wasn't like her sister, who was educated, or her two brothers who were successful in business. She felt inadequate, inconsequential, except in her role as wife and mother. But these observations made her feel that maybe she had failed in that arena as well.

She tried shrugging the comments off, but the words struck a nerve. They became tender, raw spots and began to fester and grow. She revisited an old feeling that she'd tried to put away; it was the feeling that she was unloved because she was unlovable. That's why Peter treated her the way he did. That's why her mother had never really been able to love her. She had always been awkward and strange. She frustrated herself, so how could she help but irritate others? She pondered the idea, and the depression came.

Ada began to move vacuously through the life that her husband created for her. It was Oz, or should have been. She cared for the beautiful house he provided and tried to nourish the children she loved. She was an anomaly. For a while, she was able to continue fitting in. She was well thought of and respected although she couldn't phantom why. And she had friends who loved her, but the reason for that also was difficult for her to comprehend.

And her behavior was becoming more erratic and harder to conceal. She found herself waking up, or coming to, when she hadn't been asleep. She got lost in counting things, counting anything and everything. It made it difficult for her to leave the house. She was obsessed with details, with cleaning and with words and ideas and thoughts. She could spend hours chasing down cars, trying desperately to read the license plates. Sometimes when she was driving, she'd retrace her path in order to read a road sign or a billboard. She felt an unusual, and growing, preoccupation with death and dying. She often had to fight off the urge to point her car in the direction of oncoming traffic or to drive it off the road.

She thought of easy, painless ways that would make her death look accidental, so her kids wouldn't know, so they wouldn't suffer the shame of a mother who took her own life. She realized that she'd become afraid of certain words, afraid that saying them out loud would cause harm to her children, or to others she loved. The counting became more frantic. She was always counting something: her fingers; her words; cars on the road; streetlights. She was careful to count way past the ages of her kids; past the ages of anyone she loved. She was afraid that if she stopped counting too close to their age, she would cause him or her to die. She berated herself for her superstition. She knew she was being foolish but she couldn't help it. Her mind played tricks on her, and at times, it refused to cooperate. She'd forget how to add and subtract. Sometimes she couldn't count. She couldn't manage her bankbook or make change. She'd stare dumbly at the calendar, not knowing what it meant.

Language would often leave her and not return for hours on end. There were times she couldn't read. Letters became chaotic things that strung themselves together forming odd words, or they didn't form words at all. She'd lose the ability to speak and resort to writing notes to express herself.

She cried all the time. She cried with Lucy when Ricky yelled at
her, or when dirt got tracked on the clean kitchen floor. She'd look
at her babies, and tears would fill her eyes. She'd watch a Hallmark
commercial and cry. Often she'd cry for no reason at all. She was sad.
She told herself she didn't know why, but parts of her did and the
voices were speaking again and becoming more vocal. And now some
of them were really mad.

Tears, Tantrums and Mood Swings

A da had been crying for months. Even Peter's intimidation couldn't curb the flow of tears. In fact, his disposition lately had little or no effect on her. She was so down that even her fear was numbed. She was a sad, listless soul who roamed the house in a rag-tag assortment of old, black dresses that hung mournfully on her thin body; a woman always in black, out of place in a world full of colors. She no longer saw a reason to decorate her exterior when she felt so cold and ugly inside.

Once she'd completed even the smallest task, she rewarded herself by crawling into bed. The funny thing was, the house was always clean and meals were prepared; the kids were fed and bathed, and on weekdays, they were shuttled off to school. Ada knew that she had somehow done the work, but she couldn't remember performing the tasks, or explain where the energy had come from.

Sleep was a prize that eluded her, so her dull eyes were deeply rimmed with circles and when she spoke, her voice was as lifeless and flat as her emotions. She avoided friends and isolated herself when it was possible. When it was not possible, and she had to leave the house, her appearance usually wasn't much improved. She began wearing her faded black housedresses out in public now, which irritated Erin to no end.

On the rare occasion when Ada did emerge looking like Ada, people were relieved, hoping the improvement would be permanent. The transformation, however, would be fleeting. Soon, a deflated Ada would appear again. But she continued deluding herself. The depression was obvious to those who knew her, but Ada labored under the notion that she had everyone fooled. When she encountered her children, she smiled at them through her tears. If anyone asked what the problem was, she answered: "Nothing." She couldn't be pressured to comment more. She hoped that her apparent distress would be taken for a mild case of the blues. It wasn't. Everyone knew there was a problem, but nobody knew how to help. And then one day, when Erin was 13, a radical change took place in the house. Erin assumed the position that Ada had treasured for so many years before. She became full-time mother to her two younger siblings, and she mothered her mother, as well. Peter watched Ada quizzically. He didn't know what to make of the resident evil that possessed his wife. For the first time in his life, he was faced with a problem he felt powerless to fix. Ada started exploding in fits of anger. The kids called them her hissy fits. They came from nowhere, and when she calmed down, Ada seemed as surprised as anyone that they had occurred. The first time it had happened, Ada aimed a glass at Peter's head and threw it. He'd just entered the room and spoken to her. The next thing he knew, shattered glass was at his feet, and Ada stood there with a defiant look on her face and venom in her eyes.

Moments later, he couldn't believe his ears when she cursed at him like a seasoned sailor. "What the heck?" The question was rhetorical. He was too stunned to expect an answer. They had been married for more than 13 years, and he'd never heard her curse. Neither of them smoked. Neither of them drank much. And neither of them cursed. In fact, they didn't allow foul language in their house. But this day Ada swore at him, without provocation. Then she turned on her heel and stomped out of the room. She was angry; something she seldom was. And Peter was dumbfounded, which *he* seldom was. Several times when he had made her mad, he heard her mutter under her breath. When he asked her what she'd said, she repeated herself in a strange, unfamiliar tone, and he wondered if she had lost her mind.

She developed the annoying habit of speaking French when he irritated her. She would spit strange-sounding words at him, and though he couldn't decipher their meaning, he knew she hadn't wished him well. He didn't think it was funny, but the kids were amused, and Ada was, too. It was bad enough when this happened at home, but in public, it wasn't tolerable. A couple of times, Ada had laughed at him and called him nitwit in front of their friends. Peter knew she had snapped.

It was important to Peter for his house and his wife to be in order. He was used to Ada's moodiness and her tears, but he usually knew what caused them. Most times, he admitted to himself, he had. But lately, more often than not, when there were tears, they had nothing to do with him. And the temper confounded him. Where had that come from? He never knew she had one. She'd never shown it…not as long as she'd been with him. Her mother always said she'd been a hooligan as a child. That was hard to believe. He had always assumed Ella exaggerated. But now, it was obvious she was tapping into some hidden reserve of belligerence she'd stashed away. He didn't like it. Where was the timid mouse he had married?

She was listening to some people who used to be his friends. Several women he worked with criticized the way he treated her. She was listening to them; becoming unpredictable. That would have to stop. The public tears and the outbursts; both made him look bad, as if he had done something wrong; like he couldn't control his woman. He had a nagging suspicion that he was losing control, that he wasn't running things. It was getting under his skin. Peter had no idea, but one day, these days of tears and tantrums and mood swings would be looked back upon as the good old days. Things were going to get much worse.

Intervention

Carol Stone was a good friend of Ada's. She and her husband Matthew had met Ada and Peter shortly after they moved next door to them in Fox Run Green, their subdivision in West Bloomfield. They were one of the very few white families who welcomed them. They shared a back yard and a fence, and a love of children.

Although the Stones didn't have children they were the proud parents of two dogs, a spunky miniature poodle named Billy, and a chocolate chow named Holliday. Both of the Stones were especially fond of Ada and the kids. Carol took an instant liking to Erin, although she had a fair amount of mischief in her. Lydia was quieter and more withdrawn, and more sensitive than her older sister. But she, too, was just as cute as a button with the largest, most beautiful brown eyes anyone has ever seen. Lydia had an amazing smile and extraordinarily deep-set dimples, like Erin.

Little Pete had more sensitivity than both of the girls and Matthew immediately sensed that he was troubled. He craved the attention that his father denied him and which Matthew was more than happy to give. But from the start, they had reservations about Peter. And with time, the misgivings grew. Carol saw Ada as an easygoing young woman with a good heart and a sensitive nature that she had managed to bestow upon her children. She also was able to discern, early on, that there were definite issues surrounding Ada; issues that she may or may not be aware of. Carol was concerned. She studied the strange mood swings and the abnormalities of her personality, and she made a decision. She needed to talk to Ada, and to encourage *her* to talk with someone who could help.

Carol was waiting for the right time, not wanting to rush into things, when the opportunity presented itself. Ada had been out with Carol for the better part of the morning, and she had been inconsolable. She had been crying all day. Her body was racked with violent, pitiful tears. Seeing her friend in such distress was almost more than she could stand. Fear and apprehension for Ada forced her to broach the subject that had occupied her mind for several months. "What's wrong, Ada? You can tell me what's hurting you." There was no way Ada could answer. There were many things hurting her, but she couldn't put names or faces to any of them. She'd been hurting for a very long time. Tears were her only release. She'd cry until she fell asleep, or into oblivion, whichever condition came first. The tears could be counted on. Eventually they'd fatigue her or numb her so that all she wanted to do was sleep. If she could sleep, she knew she'd be OK for a while; but only for a while.

Ada somehow managed to articulate that thought, although it actually hurt her to speak. "I'll be OK, Carol," she said. "I just need to get some sleep. I'm… I'm just tired, that's all. But I'll feel better if I can get some sleep."

Carol had picked Ada up that morning. When they were out together, Carol usually did the driving. Ada often didn't trust herself enough to drive. She knew from experience how quickly she could disorientate. It was too easy for her to get lost. She might be only a few short miles from home, when she'd suddenly become foggy and sometimes she'd black out altogether. It didn't matter how many times she stopped to ask people for directions, it didn't help. The directions seldom made any sense to her at all.

No matter how simple, the words would be gibberish to her. Or the voices inside her head would try to drown out the voices that directed her from the outside. Or she'd 'come to' and find herself on the road again without a clue as to how she got there, or where she was going. She was afraid she might end up in Chicago or Timbuktu, or some other uncharted parts of the planet. So she drove very little.

They were still in Carol's car. When Ada's tears had gotten excessive and brutal, Carol pulled into the parking lot of a restaurant. She parked where they had some privacy. "Ada, sleep probably will help you," Carol started. She was carefully measuring her words. "But I think you need more than sleep. Something serious is going on with you, and you need to face it head on. I can promise you, you can feel better, Ada, but not without help. Without help, the pain and confusion you're feeling won't just go away."

Ada couldn't stop crying long enough to form an answer. She buried her face in her hands, to hide her shame. She was making a spectacle of herself; she did that so often lately, and there was nothing she could do about it. She was embarrassed. She wanted so much to be strong and in control. When Carol asked the next question, it was official. Ada just wanted to die.

"Ada, have you ever talked to anyone about why you're so depressed? I mean someone who is trained to listen and who can help? I mean a doctor, Ada." Ada was horrified. She had a hard time *seeing* herself as depressed, although deep inside she knew she was. She had to be. There were terrible things going on in her mind, and thoughts she was finding hard to control were taking over. Her mind was communicating with her in strange ways, revealing to her foreign things. And she found herself listening to weird messages that made no sense to her at all.

Some of the messages weren't directed at her. There were voices in her head talking to other voices in her head, and she knew she was going insane, but she wasn't quite ready to admit it yet. She refused to say it out loud. As long as a thought was merely a thought—and hadn't been put into words—then it wasn't really so. That was the way her mind worked. Bad thoughts *remained* only thoughts or ideas, as long as they were unspoken.

So Ada countered: "I think I just need to get more sleep, Carol. I'll be OK. I think you'd better take me home." Carol was adamant. She knew she needed to be.

"OK, Ada, I'll take you home, but you have to promise me that you'll see someone—and soon. You have to talk to someone, Ada; either a psychiatrist or a psychologist or a therapist; someone who can help you." And then Carol told Ada something that floored her.

"Ada" she said, "I've been in therapy before. I needed it because of things that happened to me when I was a kid. And the funny thing is, I thought I was fine. I thought I was coping with my past, but when I hit my thirties, I had a complete meltdown. I hit rock bottom. It got to the point that I couldn't handle anything. So believe me when I tell you…I know how scary this all can be. I know how hopeless and how alone you can feel. And I know how terrifying it can be to feel like you might be losing your mind. I've had all of those feelings before. Ada, I used to be where you are now. Therapy helped me, and I know you'll feel better if you get some help with whatever it is that's bothering you."

Carol paused to gauge the effect of her words on her friend. Then she continued, "Ada, not many people know this, but my mother suffered from a mental illness. She was diagnosed with schizophrenia when I was a little girl." Carol stated the fact simply, like it had caused her no pain at all. Like always, Carol's voice was calm and soothing. "My mother was very ill, and eventually she had to be institutionalized. By then, though, the damage had been done. My mom abused my brothers, and me, I think without meaning to, probably without even being aware of it. Finally, we ended up in foster care. Those were some dark days; those were not good times at all. I thought I'd put it all behind me. But when I was a young woman, the pain caught up with me and I fell apart. I *had* to get help, Ada. And there is no shame in it. I learned, in therapy, that whenever pain goes unresolved, it almost always simmers beneath the surface but it doesn't go away. It *has to be dealt with*, and there's no shame in getting help if you need it."

Ada was flabbergasted. Carol always seemed happy and composed. She couldn't imagine her ever feeling out of control. She just assumed Carol had always had a perfect life. "Carol, I don't know what to say. I never would have guessed any of this," Ada told her friend.

"I was in treatment for several years. It wasn't easy for me to admit I needed it. There's still such a stigma attached to mental illness. But look at it this way: if you broke your leg, you'd see a doctor. If you had an ulcer, you'd do whatever you needed to do to fix it, right? You'd go looking for help. Well, when you have problems with your mind, it's the same. You have to find someone who's trained to help you. Ada, you have to promise me you'll talk to someone. I'll help you find someone, and I'll even go with you if you want me to, but you have to promise me this. I love you, Ada, and I'm very worried for you. You owe it to yourself and you owe it to your kids. You are going to have to promise me."

Ada did promise, but the idea of therapy scared her to death. To her knowledge, no one in her family had ever seen a psychologist. She was nervous. More than that, she felt like a failure. She felt like a loser. And Peter would have a fit, because he'd have to pay for it. How would she find the nerve to tell him? She had to find the nerve somehow. If something didn't give, and soon, she knew she would completely fall apart and would never be able to pull herself together again.

"You have to think of the kids, Ada. They need you, and *you* need to be well enough to take care of them. You have to listen to me," Carol told her. Ada was listening and she was thinking of the kids. She did know they needed her. And she also listened to other voices, more familiar now, as well. "Yes," someone called Liz had replied, from somewhere deep inside her head. "The kids need us." And Ada had heard. And *The Boys* joined in, "And don't worry about Peter," they assured her. "We'll take care of him." Ada heard them, too, and she smiled to herself. *Allies*, she thought. She rested a little easier that night. She was glad for the help.

Decisions

Several days later, Ada told Peter she'd been talking to Carol Stone. She was in bad shape, she told him, and she needed to talk to someone. "I don't know what's going on with me, but something is wrong. I'm depressed and it's getting worse instead of better." Peter didn't throw a party, but he didn't throw a fit, either. Ada was proud of herself, because it was *she* who had informed him of the decision; not one of the unnamed parts of her who always seemed ready to give an opinion these days. She knew *that*, because the conversation was firm in her mind. It hadn't been dreamlike or surreal.

They were preparing for bed. The kids were tucked in and fast asleep when she approached Peter with her concerns. She didn't break down, cry or go into hysterics. She stayed focused and alert. She was direct and matter-of-fact. Simply, she laid out her case. "I need help to get back on track. If I'm ever gonna be able to cope again, I'm gonna need professional help. I'm not functioning at all right now. And I know it's gonna get worse if I don't get a handle on things."

Peter looked pensive. His head was tilted slightly and his nose was in the air, like it usually was. He looked down on her through the slits of his eyes, and his look was careful and guarded. Ada said to herself, *he's mastered that look.* She couldn't read his eyes, but that didn't matter. She had made up her mind. She'd committed to the idea; now she was anxious to get on with it. If it would help her to unload, then she'd unload. She trusted Carol and valued her advice. And she'd stumbled onto a truckload of resolve, and tapped into it. She was prepared for a fight. "How much will this cost?" was all Peter asked. "I don't know. I don't have a clue, Peter, but I'm sure our insurance will cover most of it." That's what she said, but what she thought was, *you're the reason I'm about to lose it, Peter.* No matter what it cost, she wanted to find out what was wrong with her. So she dug her heels in, ready for his attack;

the fight wasn't out of her yet.But the onslaught never came. "I'll check with our insurance," was all he said, and once more, Ada was amazed.

She didn't know Peter had almost squashed the idea, but he stopped himself. Ada had been weird for a while now, even more weird than usual. And he had been wondering, too, what was wrong with her. She was getting stranger by the day, more out of control. It was harder to manage her. He was tired of the moods and the tears. And if she threw one more fit, or muttered once more under her breath, he knew he'd lose it for sure.

He was trying to deal with her rationally. She *was* important to him. He had groomed her. She looked good at company functions. The image of the secure, well-adjusted, intact family was an important one to maintain. It was a mirage, but a vital one.

A few days before, Ada had refused to move when he told her to nuke his dinner. "Are your legs broken?"she had asked with sarcasm, and he couldn't believe his ears. *She's nuts.* He wanted to hit her. He almost did. Out of reflex, his fist had curled, but the kids were in the room. They looked at him accusingly, and Erin came to stand by her mother's side.

He thought about all he had done for this family. They were living like kings, he thought to himself. Then he corrected himself. They lived better than kings. She had never worked a day in her life. Yet here she was turning his kids against him.

He fought off the urge to hit something. It was really hard. Ada's face came easily to mind, but Erin still stood close to her mom, and she continued to scowl. That made him mad, but he reined in his rage, and shoved past the two of them on the way to the kitchen, to nuke his own food. As he pushed past them, needlessly close, he tossed his own menacing scowl, but it didn't tame the looks on their faces. Their expressions were still an indictment.

So now he was thinking, *maybe a shrink can straighten her out, before I have to kill her.*

Ada couldn't read any of these thoughts, but it wouldn't have mattered. She didn't care what he thought. She'd come to a wall of derision with Peter's name all over it. She had already decided; she made the decision even before she spoke with Peter. *I'll call Carol tomorrow,* she thought, *and tell her to find a therapist for me.*

She called the next morning, the moment the kids left for school. Carol called back an hour later with good news. She'd found someone Ada might like. It was a woman, recommended by an acquaintance. "She's supposed to be a virtual genius, a female Freud in designer clothes. She's been in private practice for more than 15 years. Before that, she worked at a mental health facility for four years. And she taught at Michigan State for several years before that. She's supposed to be really easy to talk to, Ada," Carol said. "And I think you're gonna like her."

Ada thanked her friend and hung up the phone, but she was nervous. *Well. It's done,* Ada thought, and then she said aloud, "Relax, it'll be fine," but to no one in particular. Then she climbed back into bed. She pulled up the blankets, covering her eyes and blocking the sun, and she drifted quickly into a very much-needed, uncommonly peaceful sleep.

The Shrink

Dee Schreiber's West Bloomfield office was in a large medical complex that oozed affluence. The cars that decorated the parking lot exuded opulence, too. The elevator ride to the third floor office took just long enough for Ada to ponder the merits of her decision. Like she'd promised, though, Carol was at her side. She looped her arm through Ada's, as if to steady her. Carol could sense her young friend's fear and apprehension, and she noted the small tremors that shook Ada's hands.

When the elevator reached the third floor, Carol accompanied Ada to the front desk where she filled out papers. They made small talk until the stiletto-heeled shoes of one very attractive Dee Schreiber made her ascent toward them, down the long hallway. Ada's first thought was *let's call the whole thing off*. Earlier, when Carol had asked her requirements, Ada only specified that the doctor should be female. She knew she couldn't unload on a male doctor under any circumstances.

With the moment of truth so close at hand, she also determined that in addition to being a woman, the doctor should be mature, grandmotherly, and laid back, almost to the point of reclining. At first sight, this woman definitely did not fit the bill. On second glance, she did.

Dee looked from Carol to Ada with a slight puzzle in her eyes. She seemed to be asking, 'So which one of you is the *nut job*?' (That was Ada's word for *client*). Dee's questioning look gave Ada a moment of pause. She had always assumed that there was a capital *N* for *NUT* scrawled across her forehead, but evidently, Dee couldn't see it. "Umm," Ada thought, "Well, that's good."

Carol introduced both of them, solving the mystery. Ada thought. *OK, this is it. Let the games begin.* "Please, call me Dee," the woman said. That took care of one mystery. The therapist, who extended her meticulously manicured hand, claimed to be in her mid-fifties, but she looked years younger than that. Later, Dee joked she was pushing sixty with a stick. Ada didn't believe it, but she laughed. She liked the woman's sense of humor. She sounded more like an old black woman than a middle-aged Jewish one.

Dee actually extended both hands, and when she had grasped one of Ada's sweaty palms between them, she held it warmly between her own, alternately squeezing and patting and grasping it until Ada abashedly pulled her hand away. Ada wiped her palms against her white linen pants and hoped that she hadn't made a stain. Her palms were wet, and she worried that they would give away the depth of her nervousness. She was sure that Dee Schreiber didn't have one sweat gland in her entire body.

This woman was so polished, and so sophisticated, that Ada immediately rethought her newfound stance on psychology. But, she had nothing to lose. She had promised to give it a try, and she would. Dee was short for Dee Andhra. And her voice was smooth as silk and as warm and soothing as a steaming mug of hot chocolate on a very cold day. Her shoulder-length hair was a beautiful bronze color, and had a tendency to sway in front of her eyes with the tiniest movement of her head. She was constantly tossing her head to clear her vision, the way white girls do. It was obvious, though, that it was out of necessity, and not vanity. Her dark eyes were as kind as her voice and Ada basked in the warmth that lived there.

Individually, her features weren't perfect. Her nose was rather large, her mouth was overly generous, and her smoky dark eyes were deep set. But all together, they made for a surprisingly intelligent and interesting face that on closer observation was surprising in its handsomeness. The more you looked at her, the prettier she became.

Ada sized her up in a matter of seconds. She was put together well enough to be snooty, but there was something in her air and mannerisms that made haughtiness impossible for her. It had taken Ada one hot second to decide she didn't like her and then just one hot second more to determine that she did. Still, she was nervous as heck, and she wasn't so sure that this 'talking things out' was one of her better ideas. She gave her friend one long forlorn look before she followed her therapist down the long corridor to her office. She felt like a kindergartener who was torn from her mom too soon on the first day of school. Or better yet, like the first-time felon who hears the cell door clang shut, and knows he's on the wrong side of it.

Ada checked out the room. She studied Dee's diplomas, her credentials. They were displayed in nice wooden frames on one wall. So, she was licensed. Ada wanted to ask what the credentials meant. She'd been given permission to call the doctor by her first name, but she didn't feel comfortable. This was all very new. Was she a doctor? She wanted to know, but she didn't want to be rude. She didn't ask. The two women sat in silence for a moment, feeling each other out. Five minutes later, Ada was crying. She hadn't meant to be so weak, but the tears had a mind of their own. It hadn't taken much. A couple of well-placed questions, elementary ones, and the floodgates opened.

The first question was simple enough. "Why have you sought treatment, Ada?" Ada answered with an unprovoked barrage of tears that came uninvited, out of nowhere. *Why are you crying, you idiot?* She was upset with herself. She wanted to wipe her eyes, but she didn't. She ignored the tears and sniffed hard to snort snot back up into her nose. *OK, this is great! That's just nasty,* she thought. Dee screwed her face into a mask of genuine concern. She got up quickly, grabbed a box of Kleenex from the mahogany table between them and held the box out to Ada. Ada obediently took several tissues from the decorative container and scrunched them between her hands. But she didn't dab at her tears. Wiping at them would bring attention to them. If she ignored them, they didn't exist. Dee asked the next question. It was an equally simple one. This one completely unraveled her. "Ada, why are you ashamed for me to see you cry? Crying is a way of showing emotion. It's not wrong to show emotion. Especially, in here. I *need* to know what you're feeling."

Ada sniffed, but when she didn't look up, and she didn't answer, Dee continued, "When we hurt, when we are in great pain, tears are a natural response. It's a natural release for us to cry." Still, Ada gave no response. She wanted to go home, right now. She was still thinking, *this was a bad idea.* "Ada," Dee tried again, "everybody cries. It's OK to cry."

OK, Ada thought, *that does it,* and she broke down completely. She lost control, and practically emptied the box. She blew her nose until it was red and sore. She wiped at her eyes until the tissues were sopping bits of pulp. But her actions didn't stop the tears; she just made room for more.

Ada heard what Dee had said; almost all of it. But her words didn't matter. Ada was still embarrassed. She tried to hide her face. Dee's discourse had come too late. A more lasting lesson had already been taught. Ada learned that lesson early on. It was an ancient one; one diligently taught to her in childhood. It had to do with tears. They were useless, even dangerous.

Ella had beaten it into her children; a severe lesson taught with the aid of spindly branches they were forced to fetch from trees that grew in the back yard or more often the thin, whip-like cords or belts they found around the house. They'd see the switch or the belt and cry out in fear or dread, before even the first lick came. Sometimes, Ella would tell them how many strikes to anticipate. Sometimes, the number was unknown. In any case, she'd warn them, in no uncertain terms: if they cried, they were making matters worse. But inevitably, the cries came, and so did Ella's rage.

"Stop that crying!" she'd scream in a shrill, out-of-control voice. "You better stop that noise. So, you wanna cry? Well, I'll give you something to cry about." She'd warn of dire consequences if the *noise* continued. She'd tell them, "I'm gonna beat your behind until it 'rokes' like okra!" They'd seen their mother cook okra. She boiled it until it was a slimy mess. They didn't know for sure, but they supposed that's what she meant. She was going to beat their butts until they were a slimy mess. The analogy wasn't lost on them.

No matter how they tried, it was next to impossible to stifle the tears. Even before the harsh sting of the switch or the belt found the bare skin of their arms, butts or legs, they cried out. And true to her word, the display would cause Ella to discharge a greater, more volcanic blast of anger.

So tears were almost always an enemy. Ada had learned that lesson from Ella, and later, Peter reinforced it. On their first night together, their wedding night, in the 'honeymoon suite,' Ada had cried real tears; they were tears of desperation. She would have been frightened under normal circumstances. But being there, in that disgusting place with a man she was forced to spend her life with…well, it was too much. She was horrified. Peter was annoyed, and the tears provoked him. To Ada, he seemed like a man possessed. It was the first time she'd ever seen this much anger in him, or at least, directed entirely at her. Now, not only was she afraid of the situation, she also was afraid of the fury that pervaded the room. She just couldn't understand. Where was the rage coming from?

The simple fact that 'his woman' didn't want to be there, to be with him, that's what had made Peter furious. Priscilla, the retarded one in the room next door, was crying like a ninny. That irked him. But Peter couldn't believe Ada had the unmitigated gall to be throwing a fit. "Shut up, Ada. People can hear you." He had spewed it through gritted teeth.

And then, "Women cry to be with me, Ada, not to get away from me. I have women lined up who'd be happy for this chance. Stop that noise. You sound like an idiot." He was ranting.

"I want to go home, Peter. Please take me home. I don't want to be here. Please, take me back home, Peter." Ada couldn't help herself. She wanted to be calm; she tried to, but the dilemma got the best of her, and she was hysterical. Peter slapped her. He didn't hit her hard but his movement was unexpected, and very fast, like a cougar. Ada was caught completely off guard. Then he pushed her.

"Get your skinny butt in the bed. And shut up that noise. I'm through playing with you, Ada."

His voice didn't need to be loud to transport his rage. And the lesson he taught was the same one her mother had tried beating into her. 'You must try not to cry. Things get worse if you cry. Don't cry.'

Now Dee's voice was calling softly to her. She had leaned further forward in her chair. "Ada." Dee called her name again.

She sensed that Ada was somewhere else…somewhere far away. She was right.

"It's alright to cry, Ada." She repeated herself. She was almost convincing.

"I really hate it when I cry." Ada apologized. "It makes me feel stupid and weak. But I seem to be crying all the time now. And I promised myself I wouldn't do it in here." That was an emotional mouthful, and when it ended, Ada rewarded herself with a fresh flow of tears. "Well, it's OK for you to cry here, Ada. You're safe here. No one will judge you, and no one is going to look down on you. You don't have to hide your tears. If you feel like crying, go ahead and cry. It's perfectly alright, Ada. I promise."

To prove she meant it, Dee moved the tissue box even closer to Ada. Then she waited a moment before continuing. Ada peeked at Dee's face to see what she was up to. The woman looked tragic, like she'd just watched *Beaches* and *Terms of Endearment* back to back, all on the same day.

Then strategically, Dee took a different tact. She stopped discussing the merit of tears. "So, why don't you tell me about yourself, Ada? What can you tell me about your family?"

Remarkably and very abruptly, the tears ebbed. Ada was silent several long moments.

Dee was about to restate the question when Ada closed her eyes and tilted her head slightly to one side. Dee watched with curiosity. When she opened her eyes again, she surveyed the room like she was seeing it for the first time. Then she focused on Dee and looked boldly into her eyes.

So, where'd this bravado come from? Dee wondered, but she said nothing.

"My father is dead."

That was all Ada said when she found her voice, and the voice she found was frozen, numbed and devoid of emotion. Dee made note of the change. She scribbled onto her little pad.

"Oh, I'm sorry, Ada. And when did he die?"

"When I was 21, my father died. I had just started getting to know him again. My parents were divorced when I was three or four, and we didn't see much of him after that." Ada stopped to breathe.

"My mother hated my father. She wanted us to hate him, too. But I didn't. I loved my dad. I loved him very much. I'd liked to have seen more of him before he died." It was a recitation, presented as merely a matter of fact.

"So, do you have siblings, Ada?"

"I have only one sister, Angela. She's two years older than me. I have two younger brothers. Anthony is two years behind me, and Roman Scott is the baby. We call him Scotty. I think Scotty is 10 years younger than me. Yes, 10 years." She finished in a tiny sigh.

"That's a big gap. He really is your baby brother, huh?"

"Yeah." It was a whisper; just under her breath.

Dee didn't comment. She gave Ada an encouraging smile that said 'Go on.' So Ada did.

"I had another brother, an older one. He was the oldest of all of us kids. But he died. His name was August. He died when he was 14 years old and I was 10. I don't think I ever got over it."

Still, there was no emotion.

"So, how did August die, Ada?"

"He got hit by a car."

"That's very tragic. Death is always a traumatic thing to go through, Ada. And you were just 10 when this happened?"

"I was 10," she said, and then she closed her eyes and rubbed her head, like a blood vessel had just burst there.

Dee changed the subject. "How is your relationship with your other siblings, Ada?"

Ada opened her eyes and struggled to focus. "I love them all very much. I'm proud of them. They've all worked hard to make something of themselves. They're smart and ambitious. You might even say driven. All of them have hearts of gold. I don't have any problems with my brothers or my sister, except maybe that they're too far away, and I don't see them often enough. And I miss them."

Ada looked up to catch Dee's smile. Then she continued. "I'm sort of the black sheep of the family."

She smiled when she said it. The smile touched her lips, but not her eyes. In fact, her large eyes were very sad, and Dee thought probably they had been for a very long time.

"Why do you say that, Ada?"

"Well, I'm the only one who hasn't done anything of importance with my life. I didn't go to college like the rest of them did...I got pregnant when I was 16, and I had to get married. I didn't finish high school until a year after the baby was born, and that was that."

Dee scribbled a moment, and then looked up again. "Why did you think you had to get married, Ada?"

"I just had to."

"You didn't want to?"

"No."Ada looked down. She smiled the world's saddest smile when she said it. There was another moment of frozen silence. When she looked up, she saw that Dee was writing again in the little notebook.

"Ada, how did your mother feel about you getting married so young?"

"She made me."

"Oh," Dee said quietly, as if trying not to upset her. But she looked at Ada intently, urging her to go on.

"My sister, Angela, she got married too,"Ada offered. "She got pregnant at the same time I did. She was 18, a freshman in college, and she got pregnant, too. Our babies were born one month apart, to the day. She had a boy, Gary, and I had my little Erin. But she didn't drop out of school. She went on to get her bachelor's and then her master's, and then her doctorate in education. I've always envied her."

Now Ada's eyes were dripping slow, sorrowful tears. She sat up straighter in her chair and squared her shoulders. But her composure was gone. Her head really ached and her body was tense with emotion. *I'm tired, I'm through,* she thought. She wanted to go home.

"So, it was you, your sister and your two brothers. What about your mom? How did you and your mother get along?"

Bombshell!

Ada visibly tensed and grabbed both arms of her chair.

She didn't answer. Instead, for a second, she sought out an invisible spot on the wall just past Dee's right shoulder. Then she adjusted her eyes, and found the case full of books against the wall and focused there.

Dee watched Ada's eyes. They were frenzied in their movement. She realized the young woman was counting books like her life depended on it. To Ada, it felt like it did.

"Ada?" Dee called her name. Ada tore her eyes away the wall.

"Uh, sorry, I forgot the question."

"I asked how you and your mother got along."

"OK, I guess."

"So she divorced your dad when you were three or four, I believe you said. She must have still been a young woman. Did she ever marry again? Ada was finding it hard to breathe, and her voice got thin.

OK, drop it, she thought. But she said, "She married several times." She looked at the floor and then again at an empty place on the wall. She recounted the volumes on the bookshelf against the wall. Finally, her eyes rested on the hands in her lap and she started counting her fingers. Dee noticed it, too, that Ada had been counting for some time. Scribble. Scribble. Scribble. Her pencil scrawled in the little notebook.

"Did you like your step-fathers, Ada?"

"I only lived with one." She avoided the question. "The others came after I left home." Ada's eyes remained glued to her fingers. She counted them frantically. She couldn't count them fast enough. *You're going to hyperventilate*, she warned herself. She knew the name for this tightness in her chest that blocked the passageway from her throat. Ada leaned forward in her chair. She clawed at her throat and clutched at her chest. There was air in her lungs, but she had no way of catching it. She fought to calm herself, and chased after the illusive air.

Yeah, panic attack. I know what this is! Dee leaned forward in her chair. Her voice was calm but commanding. Ada tried to listen. "Ada, breathe with me. Slow your breathing. Take slow, deep breaths. Ada, breathe with me. Take slow, deep breaths with me."

Dee demonstrated and Ada followed her lead. She measured her breathing. She slowed it down; controlled it until her heart calmed itself inside her chest. "That's good, Ada. You're fine now. That was an anxiety attack. But you're fine now. You're going to be alright." Dee assured her as Ada relaxed into her chair.

Dee decided not to push, although she had found the appropriate buttons. She took a different approach. "Your friend who brought you here today, I assume you are very close." The older woman still sat forward in her seat, and Ada wondered whether she was comfortable.

"Yeah, we're very close. I consider her one of my best friends." Ada thought, *I know what you're doing. You've got me calm; and you're making sure I stay that way.*

She stole a peek at the big numbered clock on the wall. She tried to be covert; she didn't want to be seen. She was afraid Dee would think she was bored, or anxious to leave. That would be rude. She fixated on the clock. It wasn't there just for function.

It looked expensive. It was pretty. *Hmmm, designer,* she thought. *Well, that's not surprising.*

"Your friend is Carol? How did you meet?"

"Oh, good." Ada said, aloud. "We're back on solid ground again. This is safe enough."

Ada looked at Dee thankfully and smiled when she said it, and Dee smiled back.

*So, she has a sense of humor in spite of the pain,*Dee told herself. And she sensed there was lots of pain.

"Carol and I are neighbors. We moved in next door to her and her husband. We hit it off immediately. Peter was friends with her husband, Matthew, at first, but their friendship has kinda cooled off, I think."

This is easy, Ada thought. Then she proceeded to explain how Carol and Matthew had come to their defense when other whites in the area had petitioned to block their moving into their Bloomfield subdivision.

Carol wrinkled her face in disbelief and looked absolutely repulsed. She commented on how terrible a thing it was to find prejudice in this day and age.

"Your husband, so his name is Peter, and you have three children, two girls, Erin and Lydia, and your boy, who is the youngest, is named Peter, too?"

Dee was reading from papers contained in the pages of a manila folder. "Umm…tell me about your family, Ada. What's Peter like?"

Oh, shoot, Ada thought. *This is most definitely a wrong line of questioning. And here I thought I was home free.* She took a stab at it, anyway. "Well, I love my children with all my heart. They really are precious. They're smart and sensitive. They're just good kids, and I know they love me. I guess I feel guilty, because I know they've had a hard time. I haven't been the best mother I could be to them, but they love me anyway. I'd do anything for them, anything in the world. I think they're the best part of my life, but I feel sad for them because I don't really think they're happy…." Ada's voice trailed away. She hadn't meant to say that. Where had that come from? She willed her mind to doze off, but instinctively, still, she dug into the box of Kleenex again. Her eyes had begun to seep. Dee avoided commenting on Ada's statement that her husband was no longer friends with their neighbors. And she didn't comment that Ada failed to answer the question, "So what is Peter like?" She noticed, but she was focused more *on what wasn't said.*

Ada had spoken glowingly about her children. Obviously, she loved them, although she felt guilt in connection to them. She regretted the way they'd been raised. That needed to be explored. She had no obvious problem with her siblings, either. She clearly loved them. But Dee noted that questions about her mother and her stepfather hit tender nerves. She didn't comment on any of this. But she noticed, and she scribbled, and then she tucked the observations away for another time. Their hour was nearly up. She wanted to give Ada a few moments to compose herself. "It upsets you a great deal to talk about your family, Ada." It wasn't a question. It was a summation. But Ada nodded anyway, in the affirmative. She was relieved when Dee looked at her watch and announced that it was time to end their session. "We'll talk more next week, Ada."

"Alright."

Dee stood up, and then Ada did. Again, Ada smiled, and again, her eyes were dead…and her voice reflected that. She extended her hand, but she wiped it first, one last time, on her linen pants. The expensive slacks felt damp and were wrinkled from an hour of sitting, and the moisture she sweated didn't help. *I hate linen*, she thought, and made a mental note never to buy it again; especially not white linen. She felt unkempt. She wiped her hand again, compulsively. She wished there was something other than her pants leg to wipe it on. Dee took Ada's hand and squeezed it. Ada hoped it wasn't too clammy. If it was, Dee didn't seem to notice, or she didn't appear to mind.

Dee assured her, "I know how sad you are feeling, and frightened, but we'll get to the bottom of things, and you'll feel better, Ada. Therapy is hard work. It's like an emotional roller coaster. It can be a difficult ride. I believe you have some serious issues here, and they need to be dealt with. I can promise you, if you're willing to work hard, you'll start to feel better. I'm glad you came to see me. I know it was hard for you, but it was a very brave thing to do."

Ada nodded. She was right; it was a hard thing to do. However, she'd gotten that first hour under her belt, and she didn't die from it. And it made her feel good that Dee called her brave. She didn't feel brave, but she decided she'd try to be. Yes, she'd try it again.

"This same day and time next week; will that be convenient for you, Ada?"

Ada nodded and smiled. She's got a nice smile, Dee observed.

"Yes. I'll be here." She answered with a tentative touch of pride, and Dee noticed that, too.

"OK, then, I'll put you down for this time next week," Dee told her. Then she added a commendation. "And, Ada, you should feel proud of yourself. You're taking steps to help yourself."

Dee smiled at her like a proud mother at graduation. Ada basked in the praise.

"And Ada, if you need to talk to me at any time before then, I want you to feel free to call me. If it's after hours, there's a hotline on the back of this card. You can call that number 24 hours a day, Ada. OK, so, I look forward to seeing you next week. It's nice to have met you, Ada."

As she spoke, Dee handed her the card with her information and guided her toward the door. Ada carefully placed the card into her bag, and then checked several times in the space of a few moments, to make sure it was still there. The card was like a lifeline, and suddenly she didn't want to let it go. "It's nice to know you, too," Ada mumbled. She still felt embarrassed about all of the tears during the session. *That wasn't called for,* she told herself. She also knew she had grown foggy and had lost a little time. She hoped Dee hadn't noticed. Back in the office, when Ada first came to her feet she was standing on rubbery legs. She felt better now, although still slightly sedated and weak. But she managed to control her limbs enough that they carried her back to the lobby.

Dee was at her side. She handed her over to Carol, who immediately had come to her feet. Her expressive face was one big question mark. Dee smiled at both women. "It was nice meeting both of you," Dee said as she shook Carol's hand.

"And I'll see you next week, Ada."

As she turned to meet her next client, her very high heels clicked on the polished tile floor. Ada wondered how she didn't fall. *No, not everyone is clumsy like me,* she chided herself. As they walked away, Ada watched Dee's back, and the back of her newest victim. The matronly woman accompanying her down the hall was wiping her hands on the sides of her expensive, crisply tailored slacks, just the way Ada had done. *Been there, done that,* Ada thought. *I hope Dee has an extra supply of Kleenex stashed away somewhere, because I just cleaned her out.*

Carol's voice broke through her thoughts. "So, how did it go, kiddo?" She had asked it a little too cheerfully. While they walked, Carol fished the keys from the bottom of her large Coach bag. When they reached the car, she unlocked both doors. Then she climbed into the driver's seat and maneuvered the car expertly into the heavy rush hour traffic.

"It was OK. It went well," Ada answered. But she was glad she wasn't driving the car.

Chumps and Dykes

Peter came home in full interrogation mode. All that was missing was a brightly burning overhead bulb and one good cop to round out the good cop/bad cop scenario. Earlier that day she'd had her session with dee schreiber. She came home pensive and moody and was still that way. Peter wasn't happy. He hadn't been from the start. He had expected more immediate results, but they weren't forthcoming. What's more, she wouldn't share with him the particulars of the sessions. After the first visit, she told him they had talked about her childhood. That satisfied him. Ella definitely had screwed her up, and it pleased him to know the therapy was going in the right direction. Ada told him they talked mostly about her upbringing, her mother, and her real dad. They talked about the kids and their problems. Then before she knew it, dee said the hour was up.

"The time flew,"she said. "It didn't seem like an hour."

Ada didn't mention how difficult it had been, or how emotional she had become. She didn't tell him about the panic attack. She was afraid he'd find a way to use it against her. She wasn't about to share any real emotion with him. She had said that she thought therapy would help her, but after that first week, Ada clammed up. Either she begged off, saying she didn't feel like talking, or she came up with some generic answer that didn't really tell him anything. Now he asked her, "So, you had your session today? What did you guys talk about?" The question was innocent enough, but his eyes studied her. They were intense, and his voice had that quiet, before the storm, quality about it. He was restraining himself, and she knew it. "What is this woman like?" Those words were a clue. There was no doubt that he was upset. *Oh, this is great,* she thought. *He's on a faultfinding mission, and Dee Schreiber is the target.* He was referring to her as *this woman.* He knew her name. 'This woman' was *Peter-Code* for a female who'd lost status in his world. That could be for any number of reasons. Usually it was that he saw her as a threat. Maybe she was too much the feminist, and didn't know her place. Or it might simply be that for some reason or reasons unknown, he decided he didn't like her. And a man who was a danger to him became *a chump*. Peter knew lots of chumps.

Many of his friends from work, and from their social circle, had lost status. They'd been relegated to the rank of *dyke* and *chump*. They became 'those women' or 'those people.' Peter Collins wasn't hard to figure out. He was devious and cagey, and crazy like a fox. Daily, he purchased friendships …the way school kids bought lunch. He'd give the shirt off his back to anyone who was on his good side. When it suited him, he was generous to a fault, and not just with his money. If he liked you, he'd walk a mile in the rain to ensure your allegiance. But if ever someone crossed the invisible line, by challenging him or irritating him, that person was no longer Peter's friend. Suddenly he was a nameless punk. His presence and memory were barred from Peter's house. And his banishment involved Ada and the kids, as well. Peter's family could never mention, defend or in any way side, with the exiled one.

Dennis Mallory was a good example of someone who somehow broke The Code. Ada asked, and finally she was told how. Dennis was a good friend of Peter's, a young guy Peter knew from work. He had been beside himself, cramming for the second try at his electrician's license. He had choked on his first exam. He was terrified of taking it again.

Where this test was concerned, it was 'two strikes you're out,' and Dennis knew he was coming up for his second strike. If he failed again, he'd have to wait six months before he could take it again, which seemed like an eternity. Peter took him under his wing. He assured Dennis that with his help he'd ace it. Peter set about tutoring him.

They worked together, all day and late into the night, for weeks on end. When Dennis passed the exam with flying colors, he gave Peter his props. He told anyone who'd listen that he couldn't have done it without Peter's help. From that day forward, to Dennis, Peter was a demigod. No one could say anything derogative about Peter to him. For years, they were close friends, thick as thieves. Dennis was the young protégé who knelt at the feet of the master. One day, though, all of that changed. Peter accused Dennis of making a play for Ada. It was ridiculous and it wasn't true. Both Ada and Dennis pleaded their case, but in the end, Dennis was barred from the house…for life.

Without evidence or proof, Peter rendered his judgment. He based it on his suspicions. Ada thought she got off easy. Peter gave her a vicious verbal lashing, and he pushed her around a little, but he didn't hit her. After that, no one in the house was allowed to talk to Dennis ever again, or even to mention his name. "Dennis is dead," Peter told them. And the matter was not open for discussion.

Peter's gut told him that Dennis was guilty, and Ada was too. He'd listened to it many times in the past. More than once, Ada found her behind on the floor because of it. Some of the guys from work, knowing Peter's reputation, started calling him Petermeini, after the Ayatollah, Khomeini. Peter liked it. The name suited him, he thought, and it stuck. He found a perverse kind of humor in it. It proved that he was seen as a formidable foe, someone who was not to be crossed. He was autonomous, self-governing, and perfectly capable of standing alone. Ada thought differently, although it would be many years before she could say so. *He's a tyrant*, Ada thought, *without the good sense to know that isn't a good thing.*

Peter often had problems with women. With one leg knee-deep in the nineteenth century, women, he thought, should always be silent, barefoot and pregnant. He summed up the problem of loud-mouthed women who challenged him, like this: they were dykes. They didn't like men, and they didn't like women who liked men. Or else, they were jealous. They wanted what Ada had, a good man who provided well for her. She couldn't see it. She was stupid enough to think these people were her friends. They really wanted to break up their marriage, to come between them. So they attacked him, and put silly ideas in her head. In Peter's book, the nosy woman next door was definitely a dyke. She meddled too much. And her husband was a punk who needed to control her.

She was the one who'd put the idea of therapy in Ada's head. It was an expensive luxury and it wasn't working anyway. Ada was as nutty as she ever was. "Ada, what do you talk about in these sessions?" Ada was about to answer his question when he popped out another one.

This one was more to the point. "Have you been talking about me, Ada?"

"Not really. I…I mean, I guess…maybe…maybe sometimes." Ada stammered it as she studied the floor. But a defiant voice in her head whispered, "We hate you, Peter."

"You're a bully, and we're not afraid of you," another voice said.

"OK, so Ada, what have you been telling her? What do you say about me?" The question accused her.

"Ada, go on. Don't be afraid. Tell him!" This voice was familiar. She had heard it before. It was steady and strong but still somehow always tinged with benevolence. "I don't know, Peter. I think maybe Dee thinks you're…domineering." She was careful with her words. She was afraid, but she continued. "She thinks you sometimes intimidate me. She says that's a form of abuse. We talk about my mother more. She says Mom is overbearing, too, but she thinks you have the same effect on me."

Peter didn't speak. He stared at her through his squinty eyes.

"She thinks I have a lot of stress, and I'm having trouble dealing with it. So…she wants to start seeing me twice a week for a while, so we can resolve some issues." The words poured out of her mouth. She hadn't planned them. It sounded like her voice, but it was propelled by a force deep within. Her first reaction: she was shocked at herself. Her second: she was frightened that she'd spoken the words, but third: she was glad that she did.

Peter had two reactions. For a moment, he was dumbstruck. Then the words sank in, and he blew a serious gasket. This was exactly what he'd been afraid of. This woman was causing trouble, stirring up some mess, putting ideas in Ada's head.

OK, so he'd hit Ada, pushed her or shoved her a few times, but only when she deserved it. And yes, he lost his temper. She had a knack for driving him to it. But he never *abused* anybody. And here she was, using his hard-earned money to tell this quack that he did. Any issues Ada had, she had gotten from Ella. She was unhinged when he met her. He wondered if she'd told this woman that. Did she really think he was going to agree to pay twice a week for these male-bashing sessions? Not gonna happen! "Ada, are you lying to this woman about me? I asked you what you've been saying about me." His eyes became murderous.

"I told you, Peter, we really don't talk about you. I mainly tell her how I feel. I mean…you do have a tendency to be domineering, Peter, and you do make me anxious and nervous sometimes. But that's about as far as we've gotten in therapy. She does say she needs to see me twice a week, but we mainly talk about me. We haven't gotten very far at all into my therapy." That part was true. Dee said therapy was a slow, arduous process that would take time and patience. She believed Ada had memories bottled up inside and that they needed to escape, but they needed to surface slowly, she said, like steam escaping a pressure cooker. She really hadn't spoken much about Peter at all. Dee didn't know that Peter had choked her, thrown her down a flight of stairs, or through the big picture glass window in their living room on Station Street. She hadn't told her about the time he socked her so hard that she fell backwards, and landed in a crumpled heap on the hard concrete at the bottom of the basement stairs. She didn't even tell her how he routinely humiliated her in front of their friends; telling them that she was frigid. Right in front of her, he would throw out the question for general discussion. "What do you do when your woman is frigid?" he'd ask.

"If your woman is afraid of sex or doesn't like sex, what is a man supposed to do?" Peter inquired with innocence in a sincere tone while he stood near her, smiling sweetly with his arm around her. And Ada would just want to die. Ada would be mortified, but she'd keep silent. She wouldn't know what to say or how to defend herself. Their friends would look mournfully at her and she wondered if Peter really knew the depth of her humiliation, or if it would matter to him if he did.

When Ada tried to express herself, Peter's eyes glazed over with ennui, and she quickly learned neither she nor her opinions were important to him. Ada figured it out, all of it. Peter was sadistic; she knew that now. And he was Machiavellian, but she kept these findings to herself.

She had never told Dee, or anyone else, any of these things. And there were other things she hadn't disclosed. She wanted to. She'd come close a couple of times. But what would it say about her—the fact that she was still with him, and had been for so many years? And she'd exposed her children to him. No, there were things she would never tell. Some things were just too embarrassing to talk about. For instance, Ada never said the word abuse when she talked about the way Peter treated her. Abuse was Dee's word, and it made her feel nervous and uncomfortable. Ada had a hard time admitting, even to herself, that it applied. She thought, *If Dee calls it abuse when Peter threatens me or raises his voice at me, what would she think if she learned of him hitting me?* It was too shameful. She could never tell.

They did talk about how overpowering his presence was. He was overpowering in the same way Ella was. And Ada was intimidated by both of them. "I'll ask you once more, Ada…" Again, Peter's question intruded on her thoughts. "If you never told her I hit you or abused you, why would she think I have?"

"I don't know Peter; I've never told her that you hit me. She asks me questions about how I feel…and I answer. That's all." It was the truth. "Well, she got the idea from somewhere, Ada. And now she thinks I've messed you up so much that she needs to see you twice a week. What does that say about me? Ada, aren't you smart enough see through the game she's playing with you? These people are trained to keep you coming back as long as you're willing to pay them. That's their business; to drum up problems where there are none. We were only going to try this for a few weeks to see if it worked. Well, it's not working. You're as spaced out as ever, maybe more. You're still stressed out and moody, Ada. And I don't see how you listening to some strange woman bash your husband is gonna help you or our marriage."

"Seeing her will eventually make me feel better, Peter. It's only been a few weeks. It's gonna take time. I need to keep seeing her. And if she thinks twice a week is necessary, then maybe I need to commit to that."

"Well, here's what I'm thinking, Ada. I'm thinking you need to commit to me and our kids." He raised his voice an octave in a crude imitation of her voice. "I knew this was a bad idea to begin with. But, it was something you wanted to do, so I gave in. I should not have. I always shoot myself in the foot when I go against my better judgment."

Ada's eyes swelled like a flash flood and very quickly overflowed. Peter was unmoved by the theatrics. He continued. "Now this doctor decided that you should see her twice a week instead of once. Even with the insurance coverage, the co-pay is adding up. You must have found the most expensive shrink in the book, Ada. We simply can't afford this."

"Peter, we can afford it. We waste a lot of money eating out and going out. We waste money all the time on unnecessary things. We can cut corners in other ways, but I don't want to give up my therapy, Peter. It's something that I really need. I know it's going to make me better."

"Ada, I'm the head of this family. I pay all the bills. I know our finances. You don't. You never have. I make the decisions for this family. I knew from the beginning this was a bad idea. I knew I couldn't afford to have you running off to a shrink every week. And twice a week is out of the question. If she told you she needed to see you three times a week, you'd believe that, too. Well, we can't afford it! But more importantly, this is not a good thing for our family. You're getting strange ideas in your head. You need to concentrate on home, Ada. And besides, you're supposed to be such a big Christian. Why isn't your faith enough now?" His voice was sardonic.

"I just know that I need to keep talking to Dee, Peter." She was tired; she was losing her resolve.

"I said no," Peter repeated. "We can't afford it. Now, save yourself some grief, and drop it!" His tone was icy. It added a period to the conversation.

Final Session

Dee Schreiber met Ada in the lobby before she'd had a chance to sign in. Ada was a few minutes late. It was difficult to come in at all. What was the use? This was her final session. They hadn't had enough time to resolve anything, and ada really wanted more time. She felt like a rug had been snatched out from under her, or like she'd been tripped, and there was no way to break her fall. But she managed to hold onto her tears until she heard the familiar click of dee's high heels on the buffed lobby floor. Then she gave them to dee, like she'd been saving them just for her, special delivery.

As soon as they got into the office, which by now for her was warm and comfortable, Ada blurted out her sad news. "I can't see you anymore. Peter says it's a waste of money and we can't afford it. This is going to be my last session."

"Oh, Ada, I hate to hear that. Do *you* want this to be your last session? Dee asked. "Do you think it's a waste of time?"

"No, but it's not up to me."

"Why isn't it up to you, Ada? We're talking about your mental health. It's your life."

"I know."

"Did you tell Peter you wanted to continue?"

Ada felt like a child in the principal's office. "I tried to, but he doesn't care."

"Well, Ada, if you're worried about the money, we can work that out. Your insurance pays quite a bit. Sometimes, when it's necessary, I see patients at a reduced rate. I think it's crucial for you to continue with your therapy. I think we're just at the brink of some important breakthroughs, and this would be a very bad time to stop."

"Well, Dee, the truth is, Peter doesn't want me to talk to you anymore. I think the money is just an excuse. He's been asking what we talk about. I think he's afraid I'm saying bad things about him, and he doesn't want me to talk to you anymore."

"Don't you find it suspect that he's more concerned with possible negative comments about himself than he is with you being able to function and feel better? You're an adult, Ada. Your husband doesn't have the right to keep you from nurturing yourself. I believe you're very depressed. We haven't met often enough to get to the root of it, but I believe you have some real issues surrounding your childhood as well as your marriage. I think it would be dangerous to end these sessions so abruptly. Your depression and confusion are only gonna get worse. I think we're making progress; it's slow, but its steady progress and I'm convinced that you'll continue to improve with time. It's going to take time, Ada."

"I know. But he's gonna cut off the money."

"We can work around the money, Ada. If you want to continue, I'm willing to see you at a reduced rate." She was speaking to her as someone would to a young child. "And if he has a problem with twice-a-week sessions, we can keep it at once a week for a while. I'm willing to do whatever I can to help you. Do you think it might make a difference if I spoke to Peter? We could invite him to sit in on our next session, or I could agree to meet with him alone, if that would be more comfortable for you."

"I don't know." Ada was chewing her bottom lip, and she had been counting up a storm from the time she sat down. She had completely lost her resolve, and all she wanted to do was go home to sleep.

Dee was right about one thing. She was depressed and confused, and her brain hurt when she tried to think. Peter's mind was set, and she didn't think anyone could change it. "You can talk to him," Ada said. "But it won't do any good. He's stubborn, and I don't think he's gonna budge." Ada felt guilty, like she was letting Dee down. And Carol was disappointed in her. She knew she was being a wimp, but what more could she do?

"I'll call him one evening this week, Ada. But promise me you'll stick to your guns. You have to let him know that you really want to continue the sessions. Let him see how important it is to you. You never know. Maybe he just really doesn't see how strongly you feel about it."

"OK." Ada said it without conviction. And that's the way they left it.

That Thursday afternoon was the last time Ada was in Dee Schreiber's office. When she saw Dee again, it was a little more than a week later. She was strapped to a bed in the emergency room of Henry Ford Hospital, highly sedated, barely conscious and in a great deal of pain. And her truest regret in life was that she was still alive.

Suicide

Dee stood by Ada's bed. Her voice, full of concern, came from some distant place and penetrated the thick haze of pain and confusion that engulfed her. Ada would not look at Dee, who was softly rubbing her arm and speaking quiet words of consolation to her. The words made her sad. Ada heard the pity and compassion in Dee's voice, and knew they were undeserved. *You've failed miserably. You can't do anything right. You never do anything right.* She accused herself from within, or somebody else did. Repeatedly, the message was filtered through her brain. She knew she couldn't speak, even if she had been willing to.

Her throat was on fire, scraped raw, more sore than it had ever been, and her larynx was useless, like it had been crushed. It was incapable of producing sound. She kept her face turned toward the wall, away from Dee; away from the sad questioning faces of passersby who wondered at her plight. *I want to die,* she moaned to herself from inside her head. And she meant it. More than anything else, she did want to die. She was desperate for it. The very idea that she was still living and breathing and that nothing had changed was more than she could bear. But no, she reminded herself, actually, there was a change, and not a good one. Her situation now was worse than before.

Now you're in trouble, she thought. *You've really made a mess of things and you're in real trouble.* And other voices chimed in. "Now they know. Now they know. Now they know."

The words were relentless. They were hurtful, palpable things that percolated in her brain while silent tears flooded her eyes. They completely drowned out the soft words of comfort that Dee spoke into her ear. She felt hot and cold and frantic and fatigued. But the verbiage inside was merciless, and that message assaulted her brain. "Now they know. Now they know. Now they know." *Who knows?* Ada wondered. *And what did they know?* Her head hurt. She was so nauseous. She wanted to vomit some more, but her belly was empty. They had pumped her stomach, and all she could do was heave.

"Well, you made yourself sick. You deserve to be sick." This voice was, at the same time, sad and sullen. "No, she deserves to be dead!" Another voice piped up— the truculent voice of an angry young man.

Yeah, I know. She acknowledged both indictments. Ada was consumed with raw guilt and shame. Yet she couldn't quite label her thoughts. She wanted to feel sorry for herself, yet she knew she had no right.

She was ashamed, angry, weak, and scared. Most of all, she hated herself. She'd done this to herself, and now matters were worse than before. She did deserve the pain. She told herself, *just lay here and endure it.* It was hard to do. A blazing tube, an implement of torment, had been shoved down her throat. They were trying to save her life. They tortured her in the process. The tube was gone now. But in its wake, her throat was on fire; it was burning like an open and oozing red wound.

She could never really describe the pain except to say it was beyond terrible; it was excruciating. But she welcomed it, embraced it. She deserved it. She wished she could die from it. She knew she needed to die, because now, in addition to her other shortcomings and sins, she had tried to take her own life.

The Phone Call

Two days before, it was Friday, the start of the weekend. It was a bright, sunshiny day, just like in the song. That night, in the early evening, Ada was having a Tupperware party. She expected a houseful, and she had started baking the night before. Ada still loved entertaining. It gave her a chance to show off her culinary skills, one of the few things she could be proud of. The ladies would be working off calories for weeks to come.

Carol contributed cookies, which of course were homemade. And she was bringing her large-capacity coffee maker.

People came to Ada's parties as much for the food as anything else. Besides, everyone loved Ada. She had a lot of friends, and when she asked them, it was hard to say no.

The kids were as excited as she was. They had cleaned their rooms without squabbling and they'd completed the rest of their chores on time. Each of them was allowed to have one friend come over to play.

Ada's big plan was to occupy them upstairs in their rooms while the grown-ups had their party in the large living room. Ada looked forward to the evening. She'd been in bad humor all week, but her mood changed the night before. She'd been cheerful and energetic— giddy, almost, all day. Everything was ready ahead of time, and when Carol showed up, they had time to sit and chat a while before the other guests arrived. She hadn't spoken to Carol for a few days. She had dreaded telling her she was stopping therapy. She predicted Carol's reaction. She felt wishy-washy. But she told herself there was no way she could ever have swayed Peter. She tried. His final word on the subject was, "Its dead, Ada. Drop it!" She did.

Somehow, she was able to snap out of it, and by the end of the following week, she was all sunshine and smiles. She was that way still, sunshine and smiles, when Carol stepped through her door on Friday night. Carol wasn't convinced. And though Ada was always glad to see her friend, Carol's presence that evening unsettled her. She felt like she'd let her down, and she knew she'd disappointed Dee.

Carol had started right in with her diatribe. She wanted Ada to force the issue with Peter, but Carol didn't understand. Ada was reluctant to wake a sleeping monster. Peter had made his position clear. Even Dee hadn't been able to sway him.

Dee called earlier in the week, and when Ada answered the phone, she felt a surge of hope. Dee was convincing. She had this calm but forceful manner about her, and Ada hoped she'd be able to break through Peter's resolve. *If anyone could*, she thought, *Dee could.*

After they'd chatted a moment, Ada called Peter to the phone. She resisted the urge to listen in on the extension. Instead, she pretended to be busy in the kitchen, within earshot. Peter seated himself at the long marble dining room table. He leaned forward in one of the off-white, upholstered high-backed chairs, and propped the phone to his ear. Ada strained to hear his end of the conversation. There was annoyance in his voice and his brow was deeply creased in a frown. Ada felt a sensation of doom wash over her. The conversation was short. There were a few long moments of heavy silence while Dee was speaking. Peter listened impatiently. Several times, emphatically he muttered 'no'. Once, he took the phone from his ear and looked at it, like it was some peculiar object that had somehow attached itself to his hand. When he placed the receiver up to his ear again, he spoke firmly and finally. "I am sorry you don't agree, but this is my family, Dr. Schreiber, and I make the rules in my family. The answer is still 'no.'"

Peter didn't call Ada back to the phone. He hung up, and without a word to her, he headed for the garage. A moment later, the ignition fired, the garage door opener hummed its mechanical song and Peter was gone. The big house was asleep. The kids were outside, playing with neighbor kids somewhere, and Ada was alone. She sat down at her beautiful dining room table and squished her bare feet into the caramel-colored carpet. It was new carpet, and Ada loved it. There was a large, expensively framed picture of a happy young family on the wall in front of her.

Then there came the familiar babble of voices inside her head. "Leave me alone," she said and she realized that not only was she was talking to herself, but she was answering, too.

OK, she thought. *I'm definitely not in the mood.* She blinked several times, and sniffed, and then she gave up. She placed her wet face against the cold, smooth marble top of her table, and she cried.

The Note

Three days later, when Friday night came, Ada was in rare form. She flitted here and there like a busy little bee, organizing games, passing out door prizes and overseeing the serving of refreshments. She had energy to burn. "Sit down, Ada,"the Tupperware lady insisted. "You're making me nervous." But she couldn't know that it was not nervousness, but something more, that kept Ada in motion.

Ada's brain was a menagerie. If it was still for even a moment, dark thoughts began creeping around, and the irksome clatter of disparate voices intruded again, making her fear she was crazy. So while everyone oohed and ahhhed over the coffee and cake and the ice cream punch, Ada busied herself with myriad mundane tasks, all designed to preserve her sanity. She sold lotsof Tupperware and when they saw the prizes Ada earned by throwing her party, several of the girls scheduled parties of their own.

The evening was a success. Carol and some other friends stayed to help clean up, so the house was as immaculate when they left as it had been when the first guests arrived. Ada, though she was glad for the help, found she was wishing her friends would just leave. She'd played the role of happy hostess all night.

The academy award goes to me! she mused. But the pretense had taken its toll. She was drained, and tired of the charade. Ada's old friend, grief, was knocking at the door. It was scratching, like the family pet, left too long in the cold, begging to be let in. Finally, when the house was quiet and still, Ada let loose an extended sigh of relief. She sat for a moment on the comfortable sectional sofa and stared out the sliding glass door.

She could barely make out the outline of wooden patio chairs, and the matching gliding sofa on the big porch at the rear of the house. The moon was high, but it had cloaked its light. She turned her view from the window. There were still untapped reserves of nervous energy to burn.

Her eyes roamed from ceiling to wall, and back again. She studied her nails and the crease in her pants. When she could sit still no longer, she wandered throughout the house. She got a feather duster and went looking for cobwebs. There were none. So she blazed a trail through the house re-mopping already spotless floors, and polishing dust-free furniture. When she passed through the kitchen again, she poured herself a big mug of coffee. Then she went to the den and switched on the TV set. *The Twilight Zone* was on. *This is just great*, she thought. *The cosmic universe is having a laugh at my expense.*

She got up to cut herself a hunk of her prize-winning cake. She wolfed it down without tasting it. *This might as well be cardboard*, she thought. *Wasted calories!* But the coffee was good. She got up and poured herself another cup. It was decaffeinated, yet she knew it didn't really matter. She felt like she'd never be able to sleep again. However, her eyelids did grow heavy. She stumbled like a drugged woman toward the stairs. She needed to check in on the kids. She slipped into each of their rooms. They were all sprawled on their beds, fast asleep, without a care in the world. Their friends had gone home hours ago. Ada gauged how good a time they'd had by the amount of disorder they'd caused to their rooms.

She smiled at their sleeping faces. Looking at them made her sad. "I love you so much," she whispered. "Why do you make me feel sad?" She didn't know. Peter was gone. He was making himself scarce, he said, "because the hens were taking over the house"; but Ada knew that wasn't the reason. He often was scarce these days, and Ada had her suspicions as to why. She was happy he wasn't there. He haunted her like a ghost even when he was gone, but the flesh and blood sight of him upset her more. Her plan was to be in bed when he came home, pretending to be asleep. And she hoped he wouldn't disgust her with his sickening attempts at lovemaking. Ada got undressed, and then she checked on the kids one last time. She smothered each of their sleeping faces again with kisses; half-hoping they would wake up. They did not. She tucked them again into their blankets and shuffled barefoot to her room. She closed the door behind her.

She climbed into bed and lay there, both drowsy and restless, for more than an hour. Wide awake, she stared impatiently at the walls, and it agitated her.

Once it was clear she could not fall asleep, Ada climbed out of the bed and made her way to the master bathroom at the far end of the room. She opened the door that separated the bathroom from her dressing nook, and turned on the light. She peered into the medicine cabinet. It was well stocked. (Ada was a certified, card-carrying hypochondriac). When she spotted the pills she took almost nightly in order to fall asleep, she eyed them like they were solid gold. She pulled a tiny cup from the wall dispenser and filled it with water from the tap, and then she filled another one.

Then she snatched the sleeping pills, and for good measure, she grabbed one of several economy-sized bottles of aspirin. She turned off the light and padded back to her bed with the precious drugs in one hand and both sloshing cups of water in the other. She climbed back under the covers, turned on the TV and opened both medicine bottles. She poured two sleeping pills into her hand, then she stared at the small, oblong pills and reevaluating the severity of the problem, she took out one more. She popped the pills into her mouth and swallowed them with a big gulp of water that almost gagged her. Then she popped three aspirins into her mouth, gulped them down, too, and fell back against the fat pillows on her bed…and waited for sleep. Even drugged, it took a while. It was nearly two in the morning when she switched the TV off and fell into a fitful sleep. Peter still had not come home.

When the sun came through the sheer curtains in Ada's bedroom window, she opened her eyes. The house was still quiet. It was Saturday morning, and the kids were sleeping in. She had an urge to go look at them, but Peter was snoring loudly in bed next to her. She turned her head to look at him instead. She was careful not to wake him.

She'd been asleep when he came home and didn't hear him come in. She was glad. She was always thankful for small miracles. She scooted away from him, closer to her edge of the bed, still careful not to wake him. He was facing her. His face was peaceful, like he'd been having a pleasant dream. She hated his face. She couldn't remember why it had once seemed so attractive to her. She studied him while he slept. *It's funny*, she thought. *He doesn't look like a demon when he sleeps.*

She re-adjusted the covers. She tucked them between them like a barrier, so that no part of his body touched hers. It made her flesh crawl when he touched her, even though her bedclothes.

Peter stirred. "So, how was your party?" he asked. His voice was sticky with sleep.

Drat! Ada cursed inwardly. "It was good, I guess." She answered, but it taxed her to speak to him.

"Kids still asleep?"

"Yep, I guess so."

"Well, I've got an early morning meeting with a client. It's a business breakfast. So I gotta get out of here," he said. He rolled off of his side of the bed and started to throw one of his spindly legs onto the floor. Then he got a better thought.

Ada blanched and braced for the onslaught she knew would come. It came swiftly, was ineffectual, and it left her angry… frustrated and as usual, not even remotely satisfied. When he finished, he collapsed heavily on top of her. She struggled to breathe. And within half an hour he was dressed and on his way out. He stood in the frame of the bedroom door.

"I guess I'll see ya around noon." His voice sounded strange when he said it. His gaze settled on her. His eyes were those of a wounded hound.

Good! she thought. She hoped he had sensed her aversion.

She watched his back as he left the room, and then exiled him from her mind. When she was certain he was gone, she got up to clean his filth from her. Then she climbed back into bed and covered her head with the blankets. She snuggled there, entombed in her covers, in the diffused light, and tried to reclaim sleep that refused to come.

She felt suddenly overwhelmed by the most potent strain of sadness. It was familiar, recognizable, but much deeper… and infinitely more painful than it ever had been before. She was drowning in it. She was smothering in a cavernous, woe-filled pit of it. Tears formed in her eyes. She brushed them away, but they soaked her pillow until it was cold and wet.

Both bottles of pills still sat on the table beside her bed, where she'd left them the night before. The impulse was strong and undeniable. It attached itself to the strange message that resonated from somewhere deep in her brain. She strained to listen, to decipher. She wasn't quite sure that words were formed, but the meaning was all at once painfully clear. "You ought to be dead. You need to kill yourself. You need to be dead!"

Ada sat straight up in bed.

There was a chorus of them, these troubled and troubling voices. Some were angry, some frightened, and some sad.

They all sang the same song. It was harmonious. They agreed. "You ought to be dead."

Of their own accord, Ada's eyes moved to the pills on the table beside her bed. The bottles were both practically full. There was almost a full glass of water there, but the cup was small, and she wondered if it was enough. She dragged her tired body from bed and willed her feet to cover the distance to bathroom. She ran the water in the tap until it was cold, then she filled two more cups with water and drifted back to bed. She sat up there, tucked beneath the covers, with her back against the thick, king-sized pillows. She had plumped them until she felt comfortable. Then her mind nodded off, and went to sleep.

When she opened the bottles, it was without conscious thought, like a sleepwalker out for a nightly stroll. She poured the contents of both of bottles into her lap, hoping there were enough to do the job. "It's enough." A very sad voice spoke softly inside her. One fistful at a time, she swallowed the pills until only a few remained. She looked at the leftover pills, and then she swallowed them, too. *I haven't written a note. Maybe I should write a note,* she thought. She tried to compose one in her head. She reached for paper and pen from the drawer beside her bed. *This is impossible,* she thought. But she managed to write:

To my children:

I'm sorry. I'm so sorry. Please know that I love you. This is not your fault. I love you all so much. Please forgive me. I just don't know what else to do.

She didn't sign the note. *They'll know who it's from.* There was nothing else to say. She lay back against the soft pillows and waited to die.

Still Alive

Ada couldn't gauge how much time had passed. She had drifted into a fluid semi-consciousness, but her mind wouldn't turn off. She thought about her kids, and felt pangs of conscience, and guilt. She shut them off. *They'll be hurt for a while*, she thought, *but they'll be better off without me. I haven't been any good to them for a very long time.* She wondered how long it would take her to die. She thought of her friends, of how sad her sister and brothers would be, and she thought of Ella. She would like to have seen them one last time.

She thought of her children again and the fact that Peter would have to raise them. This was a new thought, and it was jarring. It jolted her brain. A fresh batch of warm, salty tears sloshed out of her eyes.

She wanted to call her kids to her bed, the way she often did in the mornings or late at night. She wanted to snuggle with them, to feel them near until she was gone. She missed them already. But if she called them to her, she would start to cry and then they would know; they'd know what she had done.

No, it's better this way, she told herself, *and if the kids find me, there won't be any blood. I'll look like I'm asleep. They'll just think I'm asleep.* She closed her eyes and drifted off.

Sometime later (she couldn't say how much later) she came to with a start. She was surprised and confused at the excited din of anguished words that pushed through the murky sieve that was her brain.

I'm alive, she thought, and the realization stupefied her.

There was chaos and commotion. An authoritative voice asserted itself. It was an angry one, and it belonged to Peter. She realized he was holding her. He was carrying her in his arms, like she was a precious child. But she was not precious to him. She never had been precious to him.

They were standing in the hallway, at the top of the stairs. Other voices joined in. They were frightened ones. Between terrified sobs, her children were calling her. She had no way to answer. She tried, but her throat was uncooperative. Her lips were rebellious. Her eyes were asleep.

"Momma," they cried. "Daddy, what's wrong with Momma?" And then, "Momma's dead," they wailed. "Momma's dead." Ada drifted back to a time a very long time ago. She and her sister, and her two brothers had yelled those very words as their own father carried the lifeless body of their mother back into the house after wringing the breath from her lungs. They had known that she was dead. Killed by the father they all adored. The vision was imprecise; it was weirdly warped. But she reconnected with the fear she had felt then, and her heart, treacherous and still beating, pounded more wildly in her chest.

Peter's demon voice cut through her thoughts. It reeked of antipathy. "Look what you've done." He tossed the words out and they fractured the air. "You've killed your mother. I hope you're all happy. You're bad kids; you're selfish and spoiled. Are you happy now?"

Peter's voice grew even more ruthless, maniacal and harsh. The children responded with heartbreaking, pathetic wails of despair. Their pain hurt her ears. She thought she might choke on it. "You drove your mother to kill herself," he yelled.

"Get to your rooms, all of you. You get in your rooms and you stay there until you hear from me. And don't you dare call anybody. This is family business, and it stays in this house. Do you understand? What happens in this house stays in this house! Now get to your rooms!"

The dark haze thickened; it was closing in on her.

Ada tried once again to open her eyes. They still were fused shut. She could only manage an incompetent flutter. She wanted to speak, but only the tiniest moan escaped her lips, like the meow of a kitten begging to come in from the cold, damp rain. She couldn't help her children. She couldn't comfort them. She couldn't help herself. "Please God," she begged, "I'm supposed to be dead."

Maybe I'm dying now. Is this how it feels when you die? she wondered.

She was certain her prayer had been answered when she slid further inside of the eerie, dense fog and tumbled into a coffin of sleep.

Woodhaven

Ada awakened sometime later. She opened her eyes and squinted to focus. The room was as cold and as dark as her mood was. With difficulty, she maneuvered her head, and surveyed her surroundings. Then she remembered: *I'm in the hospital.* She said the words inside her brain, to no one in particular. The scenery had changed. Before, she had been in the emergency room, she guessed. She wasn't quite sure. Now she was lying on a clinical cot in an actual hospital room. The sheets on the bed were stiff, and the artic chill enveloped her and mocked the paper-thin blanket that covered her. She looked to her right, and saw another bed, an empty one. *Good!* she thought. *No roommate. I don't need to see anyone, not now. Not ever again.*

Then she recalled: *Dee! Where is Dee?* Dee had been there when she first came to. She'd been with her, stroking her gently, speaking warm words to puncture the fog that clouded her brain. It wasn't so much the words that had registered; the caring did. She hadn't known it at the time, but she needed that warmth, the softness of that touch. And now Dee was gone.

I have to get out of here, she told herself. Panic set in.

Ada cried again. The tears came into her world like they owned it. And time was a thief that kept running away. She opened her eyes once more. She looked at the clock but couldn't make sense of it.

What time is it? What day is this? The confusion grew more extreme. She closed her eyes again and evoked sleep. The lights went out. On Monday afternoon, when the lights came on, Ada understood the enormity of her troubles.

She was no longer in Henry Ford Hospital. This was another place. She knew it was Monday only because she was told it was. And she knew that her troubles had multiplied because of the conversation she was having right now. Or rather, the conversation she couldn't have.

Ada was in the office of a well-dressed, middle-aged, Middle Eastern-looking woman who sat at a big desk to one side of her. She was very dark, and pretty. Ada covertly studied her face. It fascinated her. *Brains and beauty,* she thought. *She might have been a beauty queen. But instead, she was…what? A doctor or maybe a psychologist?* Her intelligent face, like her voice, was kind. Her brown eyes were keen and full of concern. There was a chart on the table in front of her that she pulled from a pale yellow folder. Ada knew that it was hers. Her faults and misdeeds had been spelled out in black and white. Ada studied her feet; she averted her eyes in shame.

"My name is Riesa," the woman said. "Riesa Bashour, Ada. And I want to help you. I'm a social worker here at the hospital. We want to get you better so you can get out of here. This is a top-rate facility, but I'm sure you'd rather be home with your family."

Ah, Ada quantified the information…*so she's a social worker.* Ms. Bashour's voice was cultured, refined. There was no trace of the accent Ada expected to hear. Ada's natural curiosity was awakened. She wanted to ask where she was from, but being well mannered, she didn't dare. "You could help me by answering just a few questions. Ada, all of us here, the staff, would really like to help you. And I believe that we can." She said it sweetly. Her voice was so calm and still. The words almost brought comfort. Ada focused on the voice, but her mind wandered. She wondered if Ms. Bashour had learned that tone in school. Dee had much the same soft timbre to her voice. *The two could have been classmates,* Ada mused. *Psychiatry 101, Lesson 1: How to speak soothingly to a distraught patient.*

"Ada?"

The sound of her name on Riesa's lips ended Ada's rumination. She focused again and remembered the problem at hand. For a moment, with her quiet eyes, Riesa studied the chart in front of her. Then she looked up, smiled at Ada, and gently dispatched her questions. She cloaked them in compassion, and they came to her at a snail's pace. Still, the questions were hard. They made Ada's head hurt. She didn't want to talk. She didn't want to think. How could she explain herself to someone she didn't know and who didn't know her? No one understood the turmoil inside her skin. Ada didn't understand it herself and she could never put it into words.

"Ada, do you know where you are?" It was the mythical Siren's voice. Ada felt compelled to answer. It would be rude not to. *Well, I guess I can give her that much,* Ada told herself. She opened her mouth to utter a word. She'd give her just one short syllable for the sake of politeness. She tried to say 'yes,' but she couldn't.

"This is Woodhaven, Ada." Riesa answered for her. "I know that," Ada wanted to say. "I know where I am." But there was no sound. Nothing! *Drat!* Ada said to herself. She tried again. Her lips moved to form the words, but they stuck at the top of her chest like a too-big gulp of water swallowed too quickly. She choked on the words. The matter was out of her hands. Like bright light flooding a darkened room, it dawned on her, and tears came to her eyes.

This thing had happened to her before, this sudden inability to speak. Even without diagnosis, she'd known: this was emotional laryngitis. It was just one more of the many unspeakable things that caused Ada to think of herself as her strange. It sometimes happened when Peter interrogated her or unnerved her in some way. It sometimes happened with Ella, and it's what was happening now. The sad thing was…now she actually wanted to speak. She hated appearing stupid, or rude, or both.

I need to get out of here. This woman can help. Ada turned her face to hide her tears, and wondered how long the condition would last.

Mental

Three weeks passed and Ada still had no voice. To communicate, she had to resort to paper and pen. The predicament mortified her. At her doctor's suggestion, she began keeping a journal. To her surprise, she soon found that she was prolific, fertile, but not so coherent. Mostly, what went into her notepad was gibberish. She'd line up her thoughts and sort them all out in her mind, but when they gained freedom they'd run amok. It would take a team of linguists, she decided, to decipher them. For a while, her own thoughts, or rather her lack of rational thought frightened her to the point that she stuck her notebook beneath the thin mattress of her bed and disregarded it.

Riesa Bashour had given her the grand tour on the day she arrived. That had terrified Ada, too. She had observed the people who would be her 'cell mates' (Ada's name for them). There were both men and women, people with dead, or wild, or haunted, eyes, who *looked* disturbed…dramatically and outwardly so. There was something about them that announced their illnesses.

Do I look like them? Ada wondered.

She felt a major twinge of guilt for the way she labeled them. It was prejudice, she knew, but she couldn't help it. She didn't *want* to be like them. She'd struggled her whole life not to be. Oh, Ada knew she was strange. She'd been strange for as long as she could remember. But nobody knew *how* strange. She always felt she hid the depth of her weirdness.

Being here, in this place with these people made it official. She was a mental patient, certifiable and certified. It was all written down in a chart. From one member of the staff to the next, it circulated. She'd been stamped and labeled; there was no way she could forget.

And no amount of wishing, praying, or pretending could wash the stamp away.

The stigma brought with it a new brand of anguish. The unnamed thing she fought so hard to disguise was now fully exposed and open to public scrutiny. And it was given a name that people would know: mental illness.

Mute

Ada's odyssey had started three weeks before. But the weeks had passed and now strangely, the place felt like home. She was acclimated to it, in an unnerving kind of way. She attended the various therapies required of her, and even looked forward to most of them. She couldn't draw, but she loved art therapy, and she tried to express herself with her captioned pictures that really looked like kindergarten scrawl. She made decoupage artwork, for the kids' rooms and won praise for herself, and was really proud of her efforts. This was a skill she already had, something she could feel good about.

She congregated in the break room with other patients and got to know them as people. They were friendly and accepting. She liked them, and it saddened her to hear the problems that had brought them to this place. But still she was silent, and communicated largely through gestures, nods and smiles, and by using her eyes. But also, she had picked up her notepad again, and kept it close at hand, for those times when gestures weren't enough. She began to see the other patients as normal people who simply had problems they couldn't surmount.

Some were addicted to alcohol or drugs. And to her surprise, when they told their stories, Ada learned that it was easy for her to put her prejudices aside and muster sympathy for them.

She learned, and accepted, that alcohol and drugs were symptoms of deeper underlying problems that hadn't been resolved. Some of the patients, both men and women, had bad marriages or bad childhoods, or both. Some were schizophrenic, and Ada listened with interest to learn what that diagnosis entailed. She learned about other mental illnesses, as well. She was surprised at the various postures these illnesses assumed.

Some of these people had struggled a lifetime, like she had. And like her, many had masked their problems for years. Some were new to treatment, and as unsure of themselves as she was. Some had been in and out of institutions their whole lives. These places for them were like swinging doors. That was information she could have lived without. But she shared an affinity with all of them. It was a kinship based on understanding, and it bordered on friendship. She liked these people, and her candid interest flattered them.

Ada still dreaded the private sessions with the doctor and with the hospital's therapist. She participated because she had to. Her mind was full of words. They scurried around in her head like little mice searching for bits of food. They formed maddening, tangled webs of thought, like the jumbled ones that fled from her pen. They were ill mannered, like mischievous children, and she wanted to spank their little behinds. She wanted to straighten them out and make them behave. But she couldn't.

Little by little, with the passage of time, a curious mix of some new-fangled drugs (in healthy doses), and assiduous hours of therapy, the words unraveled themselves, and started to trickle forth.

Calling Home

Two months passed and Ada had not seen her children. She had regained her voice, but she hadn't phoned them. She wanted to, but the thought terrified her. She knew they must be terrified as well, and always, that knowledge cooked up a fresh batch of remorse and despair. What must they be thinking? Would they ever be able to outrun this trauma? Finally, after a lot of coaxing, she got up the nerve to call the kids and talk to them on the phone. The conversations were bittersweet—at the same time happy and heartbreaking. Ada gathered interesting bits of information from Erin, who was relieved to hear her mother's voice.

The kids thought she was in Indiana, at Ella's house. That's what they'd been told. It had been almost a week before their father let them know that she was even alive. When he finally did give them the news, he said she needed a break from them, to rest, so he'd sent her to her mother's house. This news came after five long days of torment, when he'd left them alone in the big house believing their mother had taken her life.

He came home to see them weekly, bringing Erin money for their expenses and groceries, but gave them few details about their mom. They stopped asking questions; they learned to subsist on the meager bits of information their dad tossed at them. His parting instruction to them was always the same. "Don't tell anyone what's going on in this house. Do not call your grandmother. Do not bother your mother. She's in no condition to talk. We'll have her call you when she's able."

He left them with a phone number where he could be reached, and his office number. Erin was in charge. And she was only to call in case of emergency. Sometime later, when Ella called asking to speak to their mom, Peter could have been Mohammed Ali; he danced so fast on his feet. They'd been in the family room when the call came.

"We thought Momma was with you!" Erin wailed at her grandmother, shrieking into the phone before Peter could snatch it from her. But he didn't miss a beat. He rushed from the room, ran to the master bedroom, picked up the extension, and yelled for Erin to hang up the phone on her end. She had raced up the stairs behind him, still screaming her dismay. He shot her a long withering look before slamming the bedroom door in her face. What he said to Ella didn't take long. Soon enough he was demanding the children's presence, calling them into his room, the one he had shared with their mother.

"I've been trying not to have to have this conversation with you. I'm going to tell you kids the truth now," he began. His voice was calm, level, but his eyes and his tone still said, *this is your fault.*

"You know your mom tried to kill herself. She had a nervous breakdown and she tried to kill herself. I've been trying to spare you guys all the gory details. Your mom is here. She's not with Ella. She's here, in Michigan. She's in a mental hospital, and she's been committed. That means they signed her in and they won't let her out until she's better. She'll be OK, but it's going to take a lot of time. So she'll be there for a while."

He made certain, once again, that they knew it was their fault, and that they weren't allowed to see their mother or to try to call her. And absolutely no one was to know where she was. He complained the affair was costing him money; a recurring theme with him. "This is an expense we could do without," he told them. "We're throwing away money we could be spending on other things. We won't be taking a vacation this year."

"If it gets out, it'll hurt my business and my reputation. Something like this could destroy everything I've worked hard for." For good measure, he threw in, "They're restricting her visitors. You can't see her or talk to her right now. If she saw you now, she'd relapse for sure. She'd have a setback. Then there's no telling when she'd get out. As it is, they're talking about keeping her for good. So, if you want to see your mother again, you've got to do exactly what I tell you. Try not to do anything to make things worse!"

Then he left them to digest the bitter words; he retired to his basement studio to calm his nerves by writing and playing his music. Erin was 14 years old, she was in charge, and she didn't know what to do. She watched helplessly as Lydia turned to her with dead eyes and then wordlessly walked to her room. Little Pete clung to her like his life depended on it. Later that night, like a mother hen with her chicks, she called her younger brother and sister to her. With one weary child on either side of her, Erin cradled them both equally. The three of them huddled in her full-sized, grown-up bed she had always been so proud of.

Erin watched her baby brother and sister as they fell into fitful, dream-filled pockets of sleep. Finally, in the wee hours, she turned on her side and stared at the shadow men on the walls until somnolence called her to sleep, as well.

M.I.A.

Nearly every day, Peter took breaks from tormenting the kids, and came to torment Ada. Her resentment of him made her feverish. She hated him more and more. Why didn't he just stay home? He managed to look wounded, sad, and concerned when he talked with her doctors, or other members of staff. But once they were alone, he stared at her with sly, accusatory eyes that set her adrift in a sea of despair. With no words, or with well-chosen ones, he'd launch his quiet attacks, leaving her devastated and stripped naked before him.

Her illusions about him were finally shattered. They could never be pieced together again. The long hours of therapy had shown her finally what he really was, and the hateful image that she now carried in her head was indestructible. This knowledge was both a blessing and a curse. Once again, she was being warned, taught about his motives, and this time she knew the lesson would stick. But at the same time, it heightened in her a sense of misery and powerlessness.

After each of his visits, she returned to her room to find that a new tomb of depression, engraved with her name, had been reserved for her. Each one was a bottomless pit. In time, the staff restricted his visits. She didn't miss him. But she was lonely for her kids, her family and her friends. She couldn't call Carol, who was the only one who had known about the therapy sessions. She could never admit it had come to this. Carol warned her, but she ignored the advice. So she could never tell Carol where she was. She was too ashamed.

Dee visited a couple of times, but she didn't want to interfere with the treatment. She'd arranged to see her when she was released. Meanwhile, there was no one else to call. It was funny, but Ada made friends. And in time, Woodhaven almost became a pleasant retreat. It was a good hospital, Ada thought. First class, as far as *nut houses* go.

It was clean and well staffed and not at all like she'd imagined when she'd first come there.

The food was actually good, once she regained the ability to eat, and she enjoyed the games, and TV in the break room and lively conversations (when she could speak again). On the wings of a bird, time flew, and Ada was surprised when the conversation turned to release dates and follow-up treatment. She was diagnosed: clinical depression, and anxiety disorder with obsessive tendencies. She talked with staff about what those analyses meant and how to identify and control the symptoms.

She remembered and identified long-buried traumas that had scratched and clawed their way to the surface of her brain. She could speak of them only in general terms, but she recognized them just the same, and they survived the long trip. She learned to *say* words that she never mastered before, words like 'hit' and 'beat,' and 'abuse.' She still had a hard time directly linking the words to herself, and she mentioned them with detachment. That coated her psyche with a protective covering.

Ada wanted desperately to see her kids but 'did they still love her?' Could they, after what she had done? She didn't know. How could she explain to them what she didn't understand herself? And what had their father said to them? What lies had he told, or worse yet, what truths?

She remembered some of it, but the memories were vague, like they'd been filtered through rose-colored glasses. She didn't know if she'd ever see that dreadful night clearly, or if she wanted to. And what could she say to her friends? She had abandoned them, or had very nearly done so, by attempting suicide. She wondered where her faith had been, and why it hadn't been enough, and why it still didn't quite feel like enough to make her strong. She decided that her friends could never know. But would she be able to conceal it?

She'd been M.I.A. for nearly three months, gone without a trace. There was no way to explain that. She admitted she did feel better. She felt rested and composed. She was in touch with her feelings. But she was still fearful of so many things. Most of all, right now, she was afraid of going home. Ada fit in here; she felt at ease, comfortable. Woodhaven was home. Here, people knew her. She didn't need to pretend. Out there, she knew, the charade would begin again.

Dr. Spinner told her this fear was natural, that many patients experienced it. Woodhaven had been home for three months, and now her real home (and he emphasized that) and her family were uncertainties to her. But he assured her she was ready to go. He told her she'd be fine.

Ms. Bashour did, too. "You're armed with the tools you need to survive, Ada," she said. "You're self-aware. You're going to be fine. I have confidence in you."

Her friends in the joint (that's what they called it) all said they would miss her, but they thought she was ready, too.

"You can't stay here forever," one of the girls informed her. "Nobody does."

People had regularly come and gone in the time she'd been there. She'd watched the new arrivals with empathy and whenever anyone left, she was sad. When it came to be her turn to leave, Ada had strong misgivings. But she took her doctor at his word.

There was a lot of work still ahead, but that could be accomplished on the outside, as an outpatient, he assured her. "You have worked really hard, you've accomplished a lot, and you're going to be alright," Dr. Spinner told her.

She literally breathed those words in like a soothing balm, until she could feel them warming her chest. She left Woodhaven with a small overnight case that Peter gave her. The suitcase was new, it was pretty, and Ada liked it, but she didn't say so.

She didn't say much as she cleaned out her room, said her goodbyes and counted the steps to freedom. Then she signed the papers that freed her, and she fell into step beside her husband. They walked through the front door and out into the lot where Peter had parked the car. *Emancipation*, she thought. But she wasn't the only one leaving that day; she wasn't leaving alone. Another large cat had jumped out of the bag and it followed her. This wasn't a Kathy; it was a beast, wild and ferocious, and searching for blood.

Like the terrible beasts of Revelation, it was a force to be reckoned with. It hissed its muted intent through bared teeth, so Ada didn't hear. This was a rapacious four-headed, many-fanged beast. One of the heads bore Ella's face. One of the faces was Jacob's and another one mimicked Peter. But the fiercest, most sinister face of all was an amalgam. It was the other three faces fused into one. It was predatory, and like a predator, it stalked Ada patiently, followed her home, and awaited its chance to pounce.

Homecoming

They couldn't curtail their excitement. The kids flew out the front door the moment Peter pulled into the driveway. They had to quickly retrace their steps, though. Peter didn't park in the driveway. They raced to beat their mom into the house. Instead, he pressed the remote for the garage opener and easily maneuvered the car into one side of the three-car garage.

Ada gave credit where credit was due. Peter was a good driver. It didn't hurt, she guessed, that he owned several sports cars, and that he raced in the semi-pro circuit.

Ada saw her babies run into the front yard and a burst of adrenaline flooded her veins. Like a puppy in a pet store, when she saw her kids, she pressed her face against the window. Her tears awakened and started to flow. She had told herself not to do that. The kids needed to see her calm and serene. They should see that she was well and happy to see them. Her homecoming had to be as normal as possible.

She was glad Peter didn't park in the driveway. His driving into the garage gave her a few extra moments to pull it all together. She wiped her eyes with the sleeve of her shirt, and then reached for the mirror of her compact to survey the damage. She closed the compact and prepared to face her kids. She didn't look at her husband.

When the door to the house flew open, the kids fell over themselves in their haste to get to her. And for her part, Ada couldn't reach them fast enough. It seemed like years rather than months since she'd seen them. Often, she'd feared she might have died from the longing, and she pictured, replayed, and imagined the homecoming in her head almost every day. She was surprised now at how quickly her nervousness vanished. It was replaced with a simple excitement she couldn't contain. It rushed over the rim of her emotions and spilled into the room. The children felt it, and returned it to her, and she knew they'd be all right. Her latest vocation, her new life's work, would be making sure of it. She'd make it up to them; undo the anxiety she caused. She'd give them stability, security, a sense of worth. They would know that they were loved.

Ada didn't know what Peter had said to them but she knew him. These past three months away from him had caused her to know him better than she ever had before. She imagined he tried to poison their minds against her. She had worried that he might succeed, but now she knew that they still loved her. Their happiness was genuine. He hadn't been able to pilfer their love. They had folded it neatly. They put it away like a treasured thing and saved it for her, then presented it as a welcome home gift when she returned.

They greeted her with generous tears, snotty noses, and great slobbery kisses that mirrored her own. She couldn't get enough and she couldn't have been happier. This was what she'd dreamed of and prayed for: a second chance. She didn't deserve it, she knew, but she'd always be grateful. And for the first time in months, she talked to God and she told him so.

When Erin found out her mother was coming home she baked a cake. And when Lydia informed Ada proudly, "And I helped," she sounded like the TV commercial. The cake came out of a box. It was a little rough around the edges, but to Ada, it was the best-looking cake she'd ever seen; the most delicious one she'd ever eaten. They had it for dessert, after they feasted on a KFC dinner with all the trimmings.

It was the middle of August and the kids were out of school for summer vacation. This was a happy time of year for them even under normal circumstances, but having Ada home was an extra cause for celebration. She planned something special every day: a trip to DQ or to the dollar movie show, or new video games, or soft drinks and hot buttered popcorn on the family room floor while they watched made-for-TV movies. They laughed at Little Pete's antics when his favorite TV show, the *Dukes of Hazard*, came on. He'd jump up and sing the 'Duke Boys' song and he'd do his 'Good Old Boys' dance, and life was back to normal.

Ada started driving again and was functioning nicely. She would load the kids in her shiny Dodge Caravan and take off on uncharted adventures. She'd heighten their excitement by refusing to tell them where they were headed, and they loved the game.

At night, Peter joined in the family fun but his presence always weirded them out. For the most part, he hung back, watching her and the kids with a puzzled look on his face. He provided them with everything they needed to make their adventures fun, but he looked like he didn't belong.

It was remarkable: he didn't complain about money. He handed it out like he grew it out back on a tree.

But to Ada, it seemed he studied them like lab mice in their little cages or butterflies under a scope. He unnerved her, but she tried to ignore him, remembering the things she learned at Woodhaven. She breathed deeply, slowly to ward off panic attacks, and she'd take herself to a pleasant place in her mind to settle her nerves. For the most part, those techniques worked.

And there were other things she learned during her hospital stay. She now knew Peter's role in her illness. She saw Ella's part, too. And she finally remembered Jacob's role, and acknowledged it.

Jacob Daddy. He was where her problems began. Like layers of swaddling slowly peeled away, the gradual truth was exposed; in time, she did recall. She recalled, but she couldn't afford to dwell on it.

The Plan

Before leaving the hospital, Ada was given the name of an agency that specialized in depression and anxiety disorders. Contacting this clinic would constitute a change. It was a new idea to get used to. She was torn. She wanted to go back to Dee. She trusted her old therapist, and she missed her. But for some reason, Dee seemed to think this agency would be a better fit for her.

"I think this agency will make the transition home easier for you, Ada. They have an in-house pharmacy, and have access to the medications that they've started you on. They specialize in psychoanalysis. The doctor there can directly prescribe and monitor your meds. I know this agency, and I know Dr. McKinsey. These are good people, Ada. They're very qualified."

When Ada didn't answer, Dee continued as if reading her thoughts. "Of course, I would love to continue seeing you, Ada. And if you don't think you'll feel comfortable seeing them, then of course I'll keep seeing you. But I think you should try this agency. They provide more comprehensive services. They have a really good program for outpatient care. You'll like them, Ada, I know." Ada didn't know. She felt rejected. She wondered if this was Dee's payback for wimping out and ending her therapy. But she didn't think she had much choice. She would do as she was told.

Within a week, Ada's life was normal again. But normal for Ada was not a good thing. When the leaves changed in the autumn, and Ada surveyed the beauty of the colorful new season, she felt familiar spasms of sadness. She really couldn't say why, but her moods came and went like the seasons. And like the seasons, this moodiness became a way of life. Ada fell easily back into this unnatural routine of things and soon found herself eerily planted in the netherworld that separated the living from the dead.

The mental health facility she'd been referred to was called 'Mercy Network,' and the agency was wonderful. But as far as she knew, they weren't miracle workers. And Ada felt it would take a miracle to rescue her from this existence of living death.

She had promised herself and her doctors and more importantly, her God that she'd never attempt suicide again. It was a shame she'd never live down, and she battled with guilt from it every day. Yet there were still powerful urges to end it all. This struggle would last for almost seven years, and it led to nearly as many hospitalizations.

Simply staying alive became her new life's work. It was a full-time job. She eventually reached the point where dying was an obsession with her. She saw it as the ultimate peace, a very long and restful sleep. But the process of getting there, the method, that was the problem.

In the subsequent years, Ada would give in to urges to slit her wrists. She drank a mixture of ammonia and rubbing alcohol. She downed handfuls of sleeping pills, which she chased with large quantities of scotch. But there were more urges that she resisted. She battled the urge to jump off bridges, and from the tops of high buildings. She stopped herself from swallowing rat poison and routinely resisted the impulse to step off curbs and into the flow of fast-moving traffic.

She toyed with the idea of using gas. It seemed like a nice, peaceful way to go. And she would have, except she couldn't quite figure out how. On more than one occasion, she defied the urge to swerve her car into oncoming traffic. The thought of injuring innocent people enabled her to defy that temptation. As her therapy progressed, she found herself able to talk about these urges. She tried to describe to the doctor and to Michelle, her new therapist, what they felt like, how powerful and consuming they were, and how nearly impossible they were to resist.

These urges came out of nowhere. They actually spoke to her in watertight voices that gave no room for reprieve. While inside the fog, she was taught by them. She learned that she needed always to have a workable plan of escape. And she never left home without it. Her purse became an arsenal, an armory. She'd been caught unprepared before and was forced to resort to painful and messy ways of killing herself. It was better to have a plan that included means as well as opportunity.

The extreme, blinding fear she had was that she'd be out in public when an urge would hit her. She'd be unable control it or act on it properly. She might then be forced into some rash, irrational action. She had learned from experience that slicing her wrists, when she was under duress, was messy, but surprisingly painless. That became her first choice for *getting out* in an emergency (for Ada, getting out was euphemized suicide).

After the initial fear of the first attempt had worn off, swallowing pills became choice number two. So she carried a razor blade, a very small and very sharp knife, and a large assortment of prescription pills with her at all times. She kept these items in her purse, in her coat pocket, and in her car. She never told a soul about her emergency stash—that was how she thought of it. When all else failed, and there was no other way out, dying became the logical solution to all of the problems of her life. Her problems were many. In addition to severe and immobilizing depression, there were the voices. They were back, and they were louder and more troubling than ever. The turmoil of the troubled world around her could never compare with the warfare going on inside of her head. And the compulsions were a major problem. The obsessions were totally out of control.

There were so many of them, and they made no sense at all.

Being an intelligent person, Ada constantly warred with herself and with her fractured mind, but her mind always seemed to win. She was reduced to counting and re-counting. Ada counted everything in sight. She counted cars on the freeway, and street signs, and stoplights and billboards.

She counted her steps, she counted the words that people spoke, and she counted her own words. And the growing list of phobias was suffocating; they both baffled and stifled her. Ada had always been afraid of *things*. She was afraid of the dark, and of monsters, and of being murdered in her bed. She was afraid of thunder and lightning and of taking a shower, and of getting her face wet. She never rode escalators, and had to psych herself to get into an elevator. She was afraid of tall trees that grew too close to the house; they could be uprooted during a storm. And she was afraid of fire and of boiling water.

Ada especially feared cemeteries and dead people and funerals. She even feared *words* that had to do with death and dying. There were some words she couldn't say out loud. Certain words released negative energy, and she was terrified of those words. Uneven numbers always had frightened her, but her obsession with them grew worse. She still had to count in her head, higher than the ages of everyone she knew and loved, as high as she could go, up into the thousands, to make sure that all of her loved ones would have long, uninterrupted lives.

She refused to breathe in, to inhale, when something frightening was on TV. She was scared that inhaling when a troubling scene was being played out on TV or when menacing words were being said would bring the trauma into her body, or that it would somehow cause harm to her kids.

She was afraid of germs, and of hospitals and sickness. She was especially afraid of cancer. Several of her very good friends had died that way. She'd watched them deteriorate until they were no more than skin stretched taught across fragile bones. Ada saw death as merely an end to life, so the prospect of dying didn't faze her. But dying from cancer wouldn't be a good death. There would be too much pain involved, for herself and for her loved ones. Her Big Mama had cancer, and at least one of her aunts and two of her favorite uncles had died from it. So she could only see cancer as the 'C' word. She avoided saying the word at all costs.

Most troubling of all, Ada was losing more and more time. She would wake up…or come to…and have to rack her mind for clues as to where she was and how she got there. She was routinely losing days and weeks, rather than hours. The children had begun to notice. She'd disappear for a time and return like nothing had happened. The kids would look at her with confusion, and she had no answers to the questions in their eyes.

The truth of it was, the missing time, and her strange behaviors, were becoming impossible to explain, even to herself. The strain was taking a toll. And even stranger than the blackouts was that Ada was causing trouble and acting out, like she did when she was a kid. She became a vandal. She would poke holes in tomatoes and squish fruit in a grocery store. She broke eggs, crushed bags of potato chips, and tore the wrappers from canned goods. She tore the tags from clothes in department stores. A couple of times she awakened to find she had ripped the seams of garments with the razor or the knife she had in her purse.

She only learned of these offenses when she was told about them, or when she discovered the mutilated evidence of her crime. Once Ada became aware she was missing time, she dreaded entering any public place, not knowing for sure whether she could be trusted not do something illogical or illegal. On one occasion, she had been asked to leave a store for malicious destruction of property. She was banned from ever coming back.

The mortification she suffered could not be described. That was another reason she felt always on the brink of suicide. She had become an unwitting liar and thief. She had to lie to conceal her condition. She couldn't control herself and she didn't know why. Ada no longer thought of herself as merely eccentric. She reached an inescapable conclusion—she was psychiatrically disordered. She was incurably insane; she had to be. Her situation was hopeless. Already she was too sick to live, and she was getting sicker by the day.

To make bad matters worse, it had become obvious to Ada that Peter had gone back to cheating. Ada didn't love him. She didn't even like him. She had to pray real hard every day not to hate him. She wasn't jealous; she really didn't care, except that he rubbed her face in it, and expected her to like it. The humiliation…that's what he relished.

He chose women who looked and acted like common street whores. He hired them as secretaries for his firm, although they were nearly illiterate and as back-up singers for his band, when they could barely hold a tune. Her friends and family looked on with undisguised pity and sorrow for her plight. Ada appeared oblivious, but she was not. She stewed and steamed, and thought of thousands of ways that he should die. His unfaithfulness was blatant and bold, like a slap to the face. Yet she was not allowed to comment on it or to show the least bit of consternation.

His temper had returned and it restrained her. It was accompanied by new and even more vicious verbal onslaughts, which Ada was never prepared to withstand. If she asked a question, cloaked in false innocence, he lied to her. He ridiculed her. He accused her of being crazy; of being out of her mind, off her meds, said she was imagining things. If she made the mistake of questioning him further, his fists finished the conversation.

Peter had cheated on her when they were young. Ada feigned ignorance then, too. Even then, it had been too humiliating to acknowledge, and the consequences of a showdown were severe. The staff at Mercy Network took special interest in her case. Ada moved from one medication to another. She moved from one program to the next. In addition to her office visits twice a week, she received visits in her home several days a week. They tried to monitor her meds and tried various therapies.

Her therapist, Michelle Braden, became a trusted confidante and friend. Ada remembered things, opened up and she started to talk. She remembered the episodes in the basement of Ella's house, the school days when she'd come home for Campbell's soup and then be raped by Jacob Daddy before returning to school for afternoon classes.

She remembered Ella's temper, Ella's beatings and the longing to tell, that was eventually crushed out of her. And she remembered the day she met Peter as a record low point in her life. He was the torpedo that sank her crippled ship. He had been cheating on her from day one. A long parade of her friends had lined up over the years to tell her so, but she had refused, or been unable, to listen. But she did start saving money in Columbus.

In the beginning, she had only allowed sneaking suspicions of Peter's other women. But in time, she had undeniable proof. She learned the extent of his unfaithfulness; and was flabbergasted.

The first time Ada knew Peter had been unfaithful he had gone to L.A. on business. When he came back, he confessed to sleeping with some girl he met at a club out there. He seemed remorseful. He told her he'd been unable to live with the deception. He begged her forgiveness and promised to spend the rest of his days making it up to her. Ada bought it. After all, she reminded herself, he didn't have to confess. If he'd kept the secret, she would never have known. He said he loved her, and he couldn't live without her and the kids. They were his life, he said, and this girl was just a mistake. It was what she needed to hear. Ada forgave him.

The second time she learned he cheated; it was from a letter she found. He'd written to a woman he worked with, and although it was obviously a love letter, he managed to explain it away. Ada forgave him again, but this time she didn't forget. Her sense of security was gone. And she learned once again what she had forgotten—that neither his words nor his tears could be trusted. And so with renewed fervor, Ada began to save. Money became her security. It was a constant, in a way that Peter had never been. He vacillated in his treatment of her, between adoration and abhorrence, which kept her ungrounded and off-centered. One minute he was telling her how smart she was. The next, she was a fool. One day she was his beautiful wife, and the next, she was shapeless, skinny and buck-toothed.

Ada thought of one close friend, a young woman named Jordyn, who lived in Columbus when she did. Not only had Jordyn and Ada been friends, but their families had become close, as well. Jordyn's husband, Jim, looked up to Peter, and Jordyn was like a younger sister to Ada. One day, very suddenly, Peter turned against Jordyn, and he began a campaign to end their friendship. Peter could never give Ada a good explanation, except to say that Jordyn was a bad influence on her. Suddenly she wasn't welcome in his house. They had to take their friendship underground.

Ada found out later, after many years had passed, that Peter tried to rape Jordyn. He came close to it, but she fought him off. When she threatened to tell, Peter threatened to hurt her husband. He said he'd accuse her of coming on to him. He assured Jordyn that Ada would believe it, and that her husband would, too. Jordyn knew Peter well enough to believe him. He had an eerie kind of persuasion over Jim, and she didn't doubt that he could turn her husband against her. For years, Jordyn had been too terrified to tell, too afraid to talk, but now, Ada saw Peter unclothed and unmasked.

Long-buried secrets and fretful revelations were excavated; they stood on their feet and started to talk. Every session with Michelle brought a new exposure. This period for Ada was as Dickens had described: It was the best of times and the worst of times. She was stronger and weaker, more resolute and more fearful. She was gaining ground and losing her way. But she remained determined to work her way through the tears and pain; to examine the truth of her history once and for all. That, she'd been assured, was the only way she'd heal.

If she didn't continue her therapy, didn't follow through on what she was being asked to do, she would be lost, and her kids would be, too. Her children would never know their mother. She loved them, but she had never been there for them. They really had never known her. They didn't have a father, Ada decided. He'd merely supplied the sperm that brought them into this hellish existence. He was Chameleon-like, the worst kind of a monster; the kind you couldn't see.

And she had exposed them to him. She *had* to continue her treatment. She *had* to get better. She owed it to them. Her sanity, her life and theirs depended on it.

Moving On

All the apples were out of the cart now. Ada knew everything… and she had survived. She'd been in therapy for many years. She'd had numerous hospitalizations. But she knew now that she was better, stronger than she'd ever been. She'd come to terms with Peter and she coped with him. She accepted the fact that he would never change. More than that, she realized that *she didn't care*. She didn't love him anymore.

Her marriage was over; she knew that. And though she still lacked the strength to leave him, she knew it was only a matter of time. But still, thinking about her father, about Jacob Daddy, almost always demolished her. She simply could not understand why that was so. She told herself that, and she told Michelle, too, in the middle of one particularly rough session. "I really need to get over it. I mean…that was all in the past. And I know I need to *leave it* there. I remember things now; nearly everything, I think. We've addressed it all and I should be able to move on. So why can't I? I can't understand why it's still such a big deal to me. I mean, after all, the man is dead, for Pete's sake!"

Jacob Daddy *was* dead. He had been for many years. But Ada neglected to tell her therapist that it was her husband who had killed him.

The Prediction

When he was in his seventies, Jacob Daddy was indicted for molesting three little girls who lived near her mom. The news didn't make headlines, but Peter heard about it. He was livid, but his anger was misplaced. He was angry with her. It had been during one of his visits to Woodhaven, when Ada was being treated there, that he'd brought Ada the devastating news. It was her father's crime, but Peter managed to implicate her in it.

He turned *on her*, as he had done years before when she'd told him how Jacob molested her. She had confessed *that* horrible secret on the advice of one of her therapists. It was against her better judgment, and it was a hard thing for her to do. The therapist didn't know Peter, certainly not the way Ada did. But the woman had reasoned, "If he knows your past, Ada, it may help him to understand better what you're going through; what you're dealing with." Ada didn't agree, but she complied, hoping the woman knew best. After all, she was degreed in psychology, which affirmed her ability to read people.

He had accused her of having an affair with her father. That's what he called it. "You said you were a virgin when we met," he charged. There was simultaneous fire and ice in his voice, and Ada couldn't answer. He continued, "So, you lied. When you said you'd never been with anyone but me, you lied." The words stung, and even knowing how vicious Peter could be, Ada had a hard time believing the words he directed at her. When he demanded details, she couldn't relate them. She remained speechless.

When he demanded she tell him what *other affairs* she'd had before they got married, it was all too much. Ada had answered back then with a barrage of tears. That angered him further.

When Peter learned that her dad was under indictment, he hurried to bring her the news. His eyeballs bulged and his temples throbbed with the weight of it. He threw it at her, and with the merciless swiftness of a fastball, it hit its mark. And before she could recover from the absolute shock of it—from the incredible idea that this man who had ruined her life—had *continued to molest* for a period of more than thirty years, Peter floored her with a prediction.

"He'll never stand trial," he foretold. "He's got one week to live." Peter said this simply.

His face and his voice had calmed, and he might have been speaking of luncheon plans, or of which shirt he would wear on the following day. But Ada believed the threat. She knew Peter's violence, and she begged him not to do anything.

"No, Ada," Peter repeated, he'll never stand trial. I can promise you. You can look at it this way; I'm saving the taxpayers money. And this will never touch me. I can promise you that, too."

Ada dissolved. About a week later when Peter told her that Jacob Daddy was dead, she was numb, but she wasn't surprised. "I told you," was all he said. Ada didn't ask questions and they never discussed it again. What few details she gleaned about his death came from her mother and other family members. They talked about how strange it was that he was found dead in his house, sitting upright in his chair, with a half-empty can of beer near his body.

Her mother and Jacob had divorced by then, though they still had contact. Jacob lived alone. He'd been dead for several days before he was found. Ada recalled there was talk that his fair-complexioned skin had turned an abnormal black or purplish-blue. And his death was ascribed to unknown causes. She couldn't be sure of all she'd heard. Much of that period was still a blur. But it didn't matter. Jacob was dead within a week, just as Peter had promised. And she knew that Peter had done it.

She shook outwardly now at the memory, and then was surprised to find herself crying. Tears always came unbidden when old emotions waltzed in on her, all sassy and rude, yet still fresh and new. It angered her when she cried like this. *I've never cried so much in my life*, Ada thought, *as I have these past few years.* And again, Jacob was at the root of the tears. When Ada mentioned him, mentioned the fact he was dead, it opened the door, and so Michelle asked about him again.

It was never an easy subject. It was one that Ada avoided with the skill of an Olympic gymnast. She *had* spoken of him before but when she did, she was careful. She only reported the facts.

She related the details of a horrible existence, but the facts she revealed were missing sentiment. That day's conversation with Michelle started out the same way, too. She was precise; matter-of-fact. But for Ada, the past was still a tangible thing, so the emotion that accompanied it breezed blithely into the room and sidled up next to her. At some point, strong feelings rose in her throat like bile and they stuck there.

Then a hard, heavy, and unyielding pressure constricted her chest. She felt like air was being sucked from her lungs. This sensation had happened before, and Ada knew what came next— but there was no way to stop it. She heard Michelle's voice. It came from a distant place, from somewhere far away, and reached out to her. It almost touched her, almost comforted her, but not quite. She strained desperately, trying to cling to it, to grab hold, but her consciousness, even her body, was being pulled in another direction.

Other voices, inside ones, were calling to her, too, imploring her to sleep, like they had done when she was a frightened child. These voices also were caring and kind and Ada didn't *want* to resist. The chaos was *outside*. She wanted to be away from it. She moved away from it. She drifted into a safe corner of her mind, and disappeared there. She semi-slept for a while; she had no idea how long. And then the vague and calming allure of Michelle's voice was reaching for her again. She stirred…opened her eyes…and awakened. She noted the time; she had lost more than half an hour of it. She noted the concern on Michelle's face. "Ada, do you remember anything about the past thirty minutes or so?"

"No. Not really. I know I lost time again." Ada was sheepish.

"Yes, Ada, you did." Michelle's eyes never left Ada's face.

Ada was mute. "Ada, do you remember anything at all?" Michelle pressed again, but there was still no response.

"Well, this time, Ada, while you were 'gone,' for lack of a better word, something unusual happened. Someone else came out to talk to me. In fact, two people came out, and they told me a little about what's been going on with you."

Ada didn't answer. There was nothing she could think of to say.

"One of the people I met, the first one, was just a child, Ada. She is a very young and very frightened child. I know her name. Her name is Adie-baby; that's what she calls herself. But actually, she's a part of you. She's a part of you who carries horrible memories of abuse you suffered. She remembers details of your abuse at your stepfather's hand. She's frightened because in her mind, the abuse is still going on. She doesn't feel safe. She has to be assured that she's safe, and that Jacob is dead. But she's hard to convince, because she's so young, and she's frightened. She's been very traumatized."

Michelle paused. Her silence, and the look in her eyes, said she was waiting for acknowledgment, for some sign of understanding. Ada didn't answer. "Do you understand what I'm telling you, Ada?"

"Yeah, I think so," Ada finally said, but saying the words made her feel weak.

"We had diagnosed you before with borderline personality disorder, Ada. And we have talked about what that means. But Ada, I've had suspicions that perhaps the lost time, the blackouts and the memory losses were indications of *dissociative states*, which are just a step beyond borderline personality disorder. People with your symptoms were at one time said to suffer from multiple personality disorder. The name has been changed. I think we need to test you for Dissociative Identity Disorder, or DID. I think we need to talk about scheduling an appointment with a doctor who specializes in DID. There are tests that can be performed. Ada, would you be willing to submit to some testing?"

"So, are you saying you think I have multiple personalities?" Ada asked, ignoring the therapist's question. It sounded incredible when she heard herself say it aloud.

"Well, Ada, today I've spoken briefly to a petrified little girl who could only cry and stammer out basic words. She was so frightened; that's all she was able to do. And I spoke at length with another person, a person who sees herself as a teenaged girl named Liz. She seems to hold a lot of the anger and hostility that you've always been unable to show. She gave me information about the little girl; she called her 'one of the babies.' And she indicated there are others. I think we definitely need to pursue this as an avenue of thought."

Ada was crying again, now for different reasons. She knew exactly what Michelle was saying, but she wasn't sure how she felt about it. The uncertainty unnerved her. If it turned out to be true, if she had multiple personalities, would that be a good thing or a bad thing? If it were true, it would explain a lot. But, Ada had to wonder, would it mean she was even crazier than she always feared she was? Michelle read her mind.

"Ada, if the diagnosis were to be made, it wouldn't mean that you're crazy, or strange or weird. If this truly is Dissociative Identity Disorder, it's no more an indication of insanity than is obsessive-compulsive disorder. You were able to accept that you have OCD, and we've been able to treat you for it. And with treatment, see how much better you've gotten? Well, Dissociative Identity Disorder, like OCD, is simply a coping mechanism. It was a tool you needed in childhood. It served as a protection for you then. It helped you to survive. You had to be pretty brilliant to devise these ways to protect yourself; to preserve your sanity. And actually, Ada, that's exactly what you did. You had lots of reasons to want to escape. There were terrible things in your childhood that threatened your survival. You should feel proud that you're a survivor. Ada, you survived a lifetime of abuse. You survived *multiple* kinds of childhood trauma. Your childhood was physically, psychologically and emotionally traumatic. You were sexually abused as a very young child. Your stepfather raped you until you were a young teenager. And then Ada, you were forced to marry a boy you didn't love when you were still virtually a child. Then, Ada, you survived the cruelty of an abusive and manipulative husband, a man who has terrorized you for years."

Ada was silent. She studied her hands, her feet, and various spaces on Michelle's wall. She couldn't force her gaze to meet Michelle's. She couldn't answer. She didn't know how. Michelle continued, "As I told you earlier, Ada, this personality, Liz, told me a little bit about you. She indicated that there are *more* parts of you split off inside. I think, in light of this, we do need to talk with Dr. McIntyre. And I'd really like to send you to see a specialist. There are tests that need to be run, but I do think you may have a dissociative disorder, Ada. It would explain a lot. And we can help you."

Still, no answer. "Ada?" Michelle prodded. Ada felt Michelle's concern. She looked up, nodded and struggled to smile through her tears. She hadn't said much, but she had been listening; thinking. She noted Michelle's calm, like this was the sort of news that she presented to clients every day. Michelle's composure helped to calm Ada.

Ada also pondered another fact: that her voices, those who only had spoken to her, these people who whispered inside *her* head…her people…could speak to others, too.

Joker Charlie

It was late in the evening when Charlie Foster came. Peter had been away for several weeks. He was away on business in Atlanta, he claimed. He called the night before his return, to say he'd be home the following night, so Ada and the kids were expecting him. But he hadn't mentioned Charlie. Charlie was a surprise, and it turned out, she was not a welcome one.

Even for Peter, who was inclined to be scandalous, the Charlie episode was incredible, an all-time low. She was the straw that broke the camel's back. And although it was a long time coming, Charlie marked the beginning of the end of the Peter and Ada show.

On first impression, it appeared that Charlie Foster had nothing going for her but youth. She looked rough, like hard times in the 'hood. She actually stupid, like there wasn't a brain in her head. And when she spoke, she appeared to confirm it. But that was her ruse. Charlie wasn't dumb. She was street smart. She showed up all sugar and spice, bashful and appreciative and full of homespun innocence.

She orchestrated her power play with a ruthlessness that uncovered her worldliness and belied her years. And years later, it still taxed her brain when Ada thought of her own naiveté; when she thought about Charlie and the relative ease with which she maneuvered herself into Ada's home. When Charlie came, she came to stay.

She disguised herself as an aspiring singer, looking to make her mark in Detroit's record business. Peter was going to manage her, he said, and he asked Ada to help. "She can sing background vocals for you," Peter told Ada. "We can write songs for her, teach her the ropes. She has raw talent. You can help her with her vocals. Help her develop a style and help her with her stage presence."

Ada wanted to become a songwriter. She was prolific, and she loved the writing process as much as she enjoyed performing. She never had developed an ego. In the beginning, she didn't want to be out front, to be on stage. But that's where Peter pushed her, and finally she started to the limelight. She learned to crave the praise she got when people heard her sing. She expressed herself through the words she wrote and sang, and through the words of other singers who influenced her.

Still, she wanted to be a songwriter. She dreamed of hearing someone famous singing songs she wrote. She appreciated talent from whatever source so she was anxious to hear Charlie sing. And Charlie had her story intact. She was only recently married, a newlywed, and her husband was fighting in the Gulf War. She was alone, a young Army bride, with nothing but a dream and a voice, and with time on her hands, she said, until her husband came home from the war.

She missed her young husband and seemed frantic with worry for him. Ada's heart went out. Always the hopeless romantic, Ada pictured the young couple, so sad, and separated by oceans and continents and war. Charlie spoke bravely of her husband. She showed Ada some of the letters she received from him. It seemed she treasured them deeply. There were tears in her eyes when she spoke of how much she missed him, how worried she was, how much she loved him, and how she was pursuing her dreams as much for him as for herself. He believed in her and had always supported her, she said, and she wanted to make him proud.

She left her home in Georgia, she claimed, just like in the song, to follow her dream. Her dream was Motown…Detroit, the city of bright lights and opportunity. Miraculously, Charlie claimed, she met Peter on a plane to Detroit from Atlanta. Atlanta was a big city, too, but she hadn't known anyone there. She had lived in Atlanta for less than a year. That was where she met her husband, and she had married him there.

It was her husband's home. Charlie didn't have family, she said. And she didn't fit in with his. They thought she was too and too ghetto. They made her feel uneducated and dumb. Ada felt sorry for the young woman.

Her original home was a small town a couple hours south of Atlanta. Tuscaloosa or someplace like that; someplace that Ada had never heard of. "Nobody has," Charlie told her. She had no reason to go back there, and no reason to stay in Atlanta, either, she said. So with 500 dollars in her purse, all the money she had, she boarded the plane to Detroit, a place she had never been before and had only read about. All her worldly belongings filled two suitcases, and a carry-on bag. But she had prayed to God, and she knew that somehow things would work out for her.

When she sat next to Peter on the plane and he said he could help with her music career, Charlie claimed it was providence, and she jumped at the chance. So she ended up on Ada's doorstep, not knowing anyone and with nowhere else to go. Peter didn't ask; he announced that Charlie would be their protégée; she'd be living with them for a while, until she found a place of her own.

It seemed plausible, even innocent at first.

By now, Ada and Peter did have connections. They were making a name for themselves in Detroit. Peter's skill and knowledge of engineering and electronics paid off. He invested in expensive sound equipment, and was soon running the 24-track soundboard in their well-equipped basement studio. He was a talented musician, producer and composer. People lined up to practice and to record in their studio, which he called S.O.U.L. Detroit). Peter was in his element. He was doing all the things he did best, and loving it. He was making music and making money.

Ada had come into her own, as well. She wrote catchy dance tunes and haunting ballads, and the lyrics that accompanied them. When she fronted their band 'Merging Traffic,' and they performed the songs she'd written, Peter arranged and the result was magic. They developed a huge following and performed regularly in exclusive Detroit-area hotels, clubs and restaurants, sometimes five or six nights a week. People started to recognize Ada when she was out in public.

A couple of their songs even had modest success on the R&B charts. They heard themselves on the radio. They were written about in the papers and appeared on local radio and TV shows. They gained a reputation in Detroit's music industry. So when Peter disclosed his plan to promote Charlie, to help with her career, Ada gave him the benefit of the doubt. Or rather, since by now she knew Peter's reputation, she decided to trust Charlie.

Ada's good nature got the best of her. She took Charlie under her wing. She tried to clean her up, to teach her how to dress and how to conduct herself. She took Charlie into her own closet; she schooled her. She tried to impart to her some of her own fashion sense. It was a task. Charlie had no style. Ada was petite, and had acquired, from somewhere deep within, her own sense of style. She always looked polished. Although she wasn't tall in stature, the way she carried herself made her appear much taller. People were amazed when they stood next to her, to see how diminutive she really was.

She tried to help her new friend with her hair and makeup, and with her speech and her demeanor. She coached Charlie on her vocals and Charlie watched Ada like a hawk, studying her, copying her manner on stage, and mimicking her showmanship. People who saw them together joked, calling Charlie 'Ada Two.' Ada was the mold that Charlie poured herself into. She treated Charlie like a younger sister. Ada decided to trust her. It was a mistake; her trust was misplaced. The signs of betrayal were almost immediate, and so apparent Ray Charles could have seen them. And in fact, Ada did see them…she just pretended not to.

Those signs first became evident in practice sessions at home, where Charlie sat at Ada's table and ate Ada's food, wore her clothes, used her perfumes and usurped her position in Peter's life. Later the signs were even more apparent on stage during live shows, when Peter started giving Charlie numbers to sing that had been Ada's signature songs. When Ada asked Peter to learn songs she liked and wanted to sing, Peter would not, but he always had time for new material for Charlie. He learned any song she presented to him. He was constantly writing original music for her to sing, and badgering Ada to do so, too. When gradually Charlie was moved from the background to take over the lead vocals, band members and club owners, and even fans started to comment and to complain.

Charlie didn't have Ada's voice, her look, or her style…she didn't have class. And for all her imitation, she didn't have Ada's presence on stage. She lacked the natural and easy rapport with an audience. Everyone noticed, and Ada heard the comments.

"We came to hear you, Ada." Or, they'd say, "Charlie can't even sing. Why are singing background for ? I don't get it." They'd look at

Charlie and Peter with calculative eyes that brimmed with disgust. They looked at Ada with commiseration.

Their pitying, knowing expressions were easy to read. Ada felt the sting of humiliation.

She now surveyed the 'hully gully belly and hully gully butt' on the younger woman with revulsion. Her weaved hair was matted and the dime-store makeup she applied with a too-heavy hand made her look garish. Her mouth was always crimson, and very large, and it spread too easily into an empty grin that completely spanned the distance between her ears.

And this was the new and somewhat improved Charlie. Ada had done her best, but she had failed. This was as good as it got. Charlie was grotesque, inside and out, and when Ada looked at her now, it was only with contempt. The kids, who were obsessed with all things Batman, had early on taken to calling Charlie 'The Joker.' It really was funny, and Ada finally confessed that the comparison fit.

It amazed her that her husband could find anything at all in this slimy, ill-shaped woman that was appealing to him. But obviously, he did, and the something that he liked definitely was not her voice. Ada knew it had to be .

When Peter hired Charlie to work as his executive secretary and he sat her in the big office next to his, Ada thought she'd choke on the ridiculousness of it. It was so absurd that she could almost laugh. The girl had no intellect. She couldn't spell executive. She couldn't type; couldn't turn on a computer without detailed instruction. Her phone skills were a joke and it was shameful how she mistreated the English language.

The office gossips quickly ascertained what her real title, her job description, was. Charlie's husband, who she claimed to love so much, all but vanished, never to resurface again. Charlie got her own place; she bought a new SUV and leased and furnished a nice condo in Southfield. Ada knew the money had come from Peter. She didn't care. Charlie wasn't in Ada's house anymore. That was a relief.

Ada had to speak to Charlie in order to reach her husband at his office during the day. It irked her, so she only called him in cases of emergency. And she learned to work through emergencies, so her calls to the office were few and far between. She stopped visiting the office altogether.

She didn't correct the kids anymore when they called her 'The Joker.' When she thought of Charlie, or was forced to see her, the word 'slut' immediately sprang to mind. And once, when she realized she'd actually uttered the word under her breath, (but still loud enough to hear), in front of both of them, she was glad. She hoped they had heard her.

Empty Nest

Years flew by, and one by one the children left home. Ada marveled at how time had passed. Her kids had grown so quickly and soon they drifted off into their own nightmares.

By the time she hit her mid-forties, Ada was alone in the big house on Kingsfield Drive. It wasn't really a bad thing. She loved her kids and she missed them, but living alone had advantages. She knew the children had suffered because of her. They lived with her illnesses much more than her husband had. They'd seen her mute with desolation. And they'd seen her manic, in the throes of illegitimate glee. They'd visited her in psychiatric hospitals, and they had known that the corpse-like woman who stared sadly at them with dark and gloomy eyes was not their mother.

They were brave little soldiers because they had to be. And they had been there for her, especially as they grew older. But they'd been damaged as a result, and Ada blamed herself as well as Peter. She shielded them and protected them as much as she could, but it had not been nearly enough. The illnesses that tormented her were very strong. There were so many symptoms. It required tremendous effort to control them. And when they were full-blown, control was impossible.

Being alone in the house meant Ada was free to be herself. With the children gone, there was no need to pretend, no one to fool. She felt she'd come through the roughest part of the storm, but still sometimes there were dark and unsteady days when she didn't feel stable enough to face anyone. There were still days when she couldn't get out of bed; times when the fogginess descended so abruptly that she had no time to plan or prepare. There was no escape. She remembered reading about the old film star Marlena Dietrich. In her later years, she'd become eccentric. People joked about her. But Ada thought she understood how the old actress must have felt. "I vant to be alone,"she said.

The long years of therapy were paying off. Ada understood herself better. She felt stronger and more in control. The change was starting to show. It caused Peter to have spastic fits, but gradually Ada and the kids rebelled. At first, in subtle ways, they began refusing to play the games he'd dictated for so long. Soon though, their rebellions became flagrant.

The first coup came while the kids were still at home. All of them stopped lying for him, stopped covering for him. The rule had always been: no one was to know that theirs was not a happy home. To Peter, this was imperative. "What happens in this house stays in this house," he always said. So it was a well-guarded secret that Peter had other women, and another life that Ada and the kids were no part of.

No one knew his life was lived elsewhere. When people called for him, they weren't allowed to say, "He doesn't live here." So, for years, Peter's family was merely his messenger service, relaying his messages when he got around to collecting them.

It was absurd, pretending that Peter lived in a place that he merely visited a couple times a month, and Ada found it increasingly impossible to live with the lie. It was anybody's guess where Peter actually lived. Erin, always the avenger, encouraged Ada to try to find out. Erin spied on her dad. She relished delving into his personal life and into his finances. She used the computer he bought her to do so. All of the kids inherited Peter's aptitude for electronics.

Though Peter lived elsewhere, he insisted that the kids, as young teenagers, pull tours of duty, working for him. He had several offices, and he interned his kids at all of them. He seldom saw them personally, but by proxy, he taught them many things, always saying that one day his kids would run his business. He underestimated them, and the level of their disdain. In time, the kids began to use their skills against him, and they offered to do the same, to help their mother.

Although Ada was sometimes curious, she really didn't care where Peter spent his time or his money. When he was away, he couldn't harass her. She didn't miss him, and as long as the bills were paid, she saw no need to stir the pot.

When Peter showed up, it was always unexpected, and it always
boggled her brain. Sometimes Peter would come around dinnertime
and sit at the table like nothing out of the ordinary was taking place.
Ada and the kids would look at each other in disbelief, but none of
them dared to challenge him. They could have gone months without
seeing him. They might have been leaving messages on his office or
cell phone, trying to contact him about some urgent matter, but to no
avail. Peter returned calls only when it was convenient for him.

It usually was important to him only when business matters or money
were involved.

Sometimes, in the middle of the night, Ada would awaken to find
Peter crawling into bed beside her. He'd snuggle up next to her like it
was something he did every night of his life.

On those occasions, they would not speak. Peter never explained
himself, and Ada would quickly scoot to the far corner of the bed,
always careful to punch the covers between them so his body would
have no chance of touching hers. She still was not yet outwardly
defiant, but for a woman who had lived in morbid fear of this man
for the better part of their married life, this moving away was a
monumental statement. And even more telling was the fact that Peter
never responded.

911

Near the end of the '80s, Peter made a startling revelation. He learned that his children despised him. For the life of him, he didn't know why. He was a good provider. His family had a roof over their heads; they had food to eat. And Ada parked the late-model car he bought her on one side of a three-car garage in the big, colonial-styled house. He had planted them smack-dab in the middle of West Bloomfield, Michigan, in Suburbia, USA. In his mind, that made him a doggone good father. There was only one explanation. The only thing that made sense was that Ada had turned the kids against him.

Really, that didn't make sense, either. Peter had given his wife everything she could dream of. She never worked, never lifted a finger unless she wanted to and all he asked in return was that she respect him. He demanded that. For the most part, Ada was in charge of the house. He expected her to care for and rear his kids. Somewhere along the line, she turned on him. He was pretty sure that all the therapy he'd paid for was behind that.

It especially annoyed Peter to know that Erin despised him. She had been his 'Little Grasshopper.' She was his first-born, the daughter he adored so much. He had molded her to be able to walk in his footsteps. He had plans for her. She would help him run his business, and she'd be the one to take over when he retired.

Erin was smart—a quick study, with a quick wit. She had sprung from the womb that way, imbued with common sense. Peter was proud and saw it as his mark in her.

Now Erin used her wit like a razor against him. She was pugilistic with her barbs and jabs. Her eyes blazed when she cut him with her pointed words. Peter was puzzled, even hurt, by the hatred his kids tossed at him.

Peter couldn't see it, but the truth was they had stopped looking for their father. They learned not to expect anything from him. He had taught them not to trust. Too many promises had been broken. He was make-believe, like the fairy tales they'd outgrown.

They had seen too much. Their short lives had been filled with disappointment, and were rife with bizarre, erratic behaviors. It was true, their mother's behavior was often strange, but they knew it wasn't deliberate. On the other hand, their dad seemed intent on hurting them. But they were resilient. They tapped into vast reserves of will power that Peter didn't know they had.

They experienced more than children should have to, but they coped. As they got older, their expectations lowered and their anger increased. Being the youngest child and the only boy, Little Pete especially needed his dad. For a long while, he craved Peter's attention, but in time, this craving turned to apathy, and then naturally, into hate. Ada was surprised at the intensity of anger her children developed toward their father. He brought it on himself, but still she felt a little sad for him.

If someone asked about their dad, Little Pete said he didn't have one. Both of the girls routinely answered that their father was dead. To Peter, Erin was the ringleader. She was the head of the beast. She led the rebellion against him. It was Erin who gave him the hateful nicknames that the other children adopted. She called their father 'the sperm donor' and said the term perfectly defined his relationship to them. She called him *crackpot* and *crack head*, to characterize the volatile nature of his personality. The nicknames stuck like crazy glue. Once, when he made her mad, with the feigned innocence of a child, she had asked him, "So, Dad, do you remember the precise moment you went out of your mind?' It was blatant disrespect. At first, he was mystified by the insolence of his family, but eventually, his puzzlement turned to rage. In frustration, Peter fell back on time-tested defenses he knew so well. He revisited his violent nature. Like a sleeping volcano, the violence that lay dormant in him awakened and erupted full-force. When he came to his house now, he was cautious, like a soldier entering a war zone. The battle lines had been drawn *by his family who waged war on him.*

Peter came home late one night, tired and wanting to climb into bed. He missed his house, which was always neat and clean, and the way the place smelled when Ada was cooking. He missed his wife and wanted to snuggle with her for a while. Peter tried his key in the lock, found that it no longer fit, and was baffled. He jiggled the doorknob and rang the bell. The television was blaring, and he could hear his family inside, but there was no response.

Ada had changed the locks on the doors, and had not given him new keys. He yelled Ada's name first, and then the kids'. Still there was no response. Half-blinded with rage Peter kicked the door down and burst into the house.

Ada shouted to Erin, "Erin! Dial 911."

Erin wasn't fast enough. Peter was on her in a moment's time. He snatched the phone from his daughter's hand. He yanked the cord from its socket and then threw the phone against the wall, knocking a large picture from its place. It was a picture Ada loved, of a happy family walking down a country road. The mother and father were holding hands, and all of them were in their Sunday clothes. As he grabbed the phone, Peter shoved Erin hard, and she fell.

Ada sprang to her daughter's defense. She flew into him. All at once, it seemed, her fists were flying, her feet were kicking, and her nails dug into his flesh. She managed to land a blow to his nose. Peter was shocked. Ada had never fought him before. None of the kids had either. Quickly, Erin rebounded. This time she jumped on his back. She scratched and clawed at her father's face, drawing blood.

Peter retaliated. He tossed Ada against a wall. And then, in one fluid motion, as he flung his daughter free he sucker-punched her so hard that she saw stars. The basement door was open. As she stumbled and fell backwards, Erin grasped frantically at the walls on either side of the basement door. She couldn't catch hold. Ada watched in horror as her daughter tumbled down the hard basement stairs, landing in a crumpled heap on the concrete floor at the bottom.

Once again, Ada sprang to action. And again, Peter was caught off guard. She flew at her husband with the adrenalin-fueled fury of a tigress protecting her young. She scratched at his eyes, and pummeled his chest with her fists. When he yelped in pain, she realized that a large portion of his arm was clenched tightly between her teeth. She had drawn blood there, too.

Erin, who lay dazed at the bottom of the stairs, roused herself after a few moments. She hadn't been knocked unconscious, so it only took a moment for her to re-gather her wits.

She heard her mother's screams, and her little sister and brother were crying pitifully. Her father was roaring in a voice designed to incite terror. Normally, it did, but not tonight. Erin noted that her mom's cries sounded angry rather than scared. She raced up the steps again, ready for round two, and found that her mother was engaged in battle. This was something she'd never seen before. But her father was massacring her mother. He was just too big for her.

Erin was even smaller than her mom, but she was so angry she felt sure she could take him. In the end, though, Ada and her daughter both were battered and bruised. To themselves, they admitted defeat, but not to him. For the first time, Peter had bruises of his own. Seeing his injuries made their wounds hurt less.

The next-door neighbor called the police. There was a loud knock at the door, and the fray was over. Ada wanted Peter in jail. She told the cops he didn't live there. They were separated, she told them, and it was not his home. But Peter had friends in both high and low places. Some of them were on the police force. They'd been to that house several times before, and although there was often evidence of her abuse at his hands, nothing had ever been done.

"We had a complaint of a disturbance," one of the cops said. "Is there a problem, Mr. Collins?"

'Is there a problem, *Mr.* Collins?' Ada could have spit nails, she was so mad. "Yes, there definitely is a problem." Ada answered for Peter.

And Erin chimed in, "The problem is he just beat the crap out of my mother and me. He doesn't live here. He's never here, and we want him out of here!" She looked her father full in the face when she spoke, and she forced the words through gritted teeth.

Peter cocked an eyebrow at her. He wondered when his older daughter had become this angry young woman. She had always had fire, he reflected. He could almost respect that in her. Almost.

"Erin," he told her, "your mother is upset. She's not on her medications. She's not thinking straight. But I'm your father, Erin. You know I'd never hurt you guys. Your mom is on the verge of another one of her breakdowns, Erin, and you're not helping."

"No, Peter," she told him, "*you're* not helping. And you're not my father. My father is dead."

She pierced him with her gaze, as she purposely called him by name. Peter knew at that point that Erin could give as good as she got. Their eyes met, but there were questions in his. Ada sent the younger two children to their rooms. Then she moved to stand next to her daughter. "He doesn't live here," Ada said, supporting Erin's accusation.

"We are not together. He has a girlfriend somewhere in Southfield, and he lives with her. I want him out of here!" The cops glanced her way, as if to survey the situation. Ada thought the situation was clear. The two younger kids had been cowering on the floor, in a corner of the living room, when the cops came in. Erin and Ada were hysterical, almost in shock. Ada's nose was bleeding, one eye was nearly swollen shut, and her two front teeth felt loose.

Erin hadn't fared much better. There was a goose egg on her forehead *the size of a goose egg*. And she had bruises all over her body from her fall down the stairs.

"He kicked my door in. He just beat the crap out of us. He broke in here, and he needs to go to jail. He threw my daughter down the stairs. I want him out of here! He needs to go to jail!" Ada was fighting for composure.

One cop shot her a dubious look; the other one avoided her eyes, as they pulled Peter aside. Out of earshot, they spoke to him in confidential tones. She strained to hear, but couldn't. Their attitude annoyed her. When they returned to her, they spoke with condescending voices, as if she were a child, or an imbecile, which goaded her further still. She was so aggravated she wanted to spit. "Mrs. Collins, are you on any medications," they asked.

"Why?" Ada's voice dripped ice.

"Well ma'am, your husband says you're on medications but you haven't been taking them. We're trying to get to the root of the problem. We can see you're upset, and we want to help. We want you to be safe."

"You want me to be safe?" Ada asked. "Then make him leave. He assaulted us! Why are you still talking to me? You need to be taking him to jail."

"We have told your husband that it would be better if he leaves for now, to give both of you time to cool off. But he's concerned about you and the kids. Will you be all right here alone with the kids? Should we call anyone for you?"

"He's not my husband," Ada repeated lamely, "we're separated, and he doesn't live here."

But she knew the statement wouldn't hold water. His mail and his driver's license and his clothes in her closet all said that he did live there. His long-standing plan was obvious now. And Peter had resorted to one of his favorite tactics. He was once again the loving, long-suffering husband with the crazy wife. He *told* them she was crazy, delusional. That she was in and out of mental hospitals, and he had the paperwork to prove it.

He had only been trying to restrain her, he said, just to keep her from hurting herself. *She* flew into a rage and his bruises confirmed his story. The children were naturally frightened and confused. He didn't blame them, and he didn't really blame Ada, either. It really wasn't her fault. They just didn't understand.

Ada had to concede: he was good! She didn't know whether they actually believed him or not, but it was clear that Peter wasn't spending the night in anybody's jail. *Well, that's all right,* she consoled herself. *For now, it's good enough that he's leaving.*

That night, Ada made two vows. The first one: starting then, when Peter threw his weight around, he wouldn't be the only one throwing punches. And second: in spite of his money, and regardless of his threats, even if it killed her, she'd be divorced from Peter Collins before the year was out.

The Loan

Years passed, and Ada was still married to Peter Collins. There were a lot of reasons for that, and not one of them had anything to do with love.

Every day she remembered her promise to leave Peter, and reproached herself for not keeping the vow. But the truth was, despite her immediate bravado on the night of their last fight, was she was still afraid of him. In fact, she and the kids were more afraid than ever.

For nearly a month after the incident involving the basement stairs, Ada hadn't seen Peter. But she knew it was part of his strategy. He was biding his time. Their standing up to him on that night was the same as rebellion. His ego wouldn't allow that. His absence and silence unnerved her. She wasn't idle, though. She started planning her escape. She knew she'd need money. She'd have to have help. She'd have to find a place to live. And she'd need physical help when she actually got ready to move.

Ada had never been independent. She couldn't read a map and had never paid bills. She'd never worked, earned a paycheck or paid taxes. Peter always had taken care of the finances. Any money she had, he had given to her. And she no longer had a nest egg.

When they were moving to Bloomfield, looking for houses, she'd made the stupid mistake of telling Peter about the money she'd been saving over the years. Actually, he had asked her point-blank if she had money saved. She wanted to say 'no,' but she had the feeling that somehow he knew. She was afraid to lie. And before long, Peter had managed to get her money away from her. He made good money, but he always seemed to have money problems. It was always feast or famine for them. It was that way when they moved to Bloomfield, too. But as usual, he had plenty of excuses.

Peter had a large expense account, and he was being completely reimbursed by the company for the move. "The reimbursement from my expense account is always running behind," he told her. "We've got some cash flow problems." When he started complaining that he was short on the down payment he needed for the house, Ada knew what was coming next.

"I'm waiting on a big check. I just landed a major contract with the city of Detroit, and I'll be getting a big bonus in a couple of weeks. But right now, I'm a little short. We need twenty thousand to put down on the house. I want to keep the payments low, down where I can afford to make them. I have ten thousand, and we could close with that. But it would be tight. I don't want to stretch myself too thin," he told her.

Ada didn't answer. She was thinking of the house in Southfield. She had loved that house so much. She loved the older, more rustic feel of it. It was less expensive than the Bloomfield house. They could easily have afforded it. But back then, Peter and Erin had conspired. They'd out-voted her. He had listened to his daughter, who was still a preteen at the time, rather than to her. She couldn't help but think that if they had moved into the Southfield house back then, today, he wouldn't need her money. Her money would be safe.

When she took too long to answer, Peter's irritation surfaced. You'll get your money back," he told her. There was ice in his voice. She didn't believe him.

"Peter, that's all the money I have in the world. It's taken me years to save it. It's in case something happens to you, or to me, so the kids will be alright."

"Ada, we both know that's not the real reason you've been hiding money from me all these years," Peter said. A subtle nuance had attached itself to the word 'hiding' and the implication wasn't lost on Ada.

"In any case," he continued, "that's why we have insurance." You and the kids will always be taken care of. You know that."

She didn't know that, but she didn't respond.

He was losing patience, and the anger that tinged his voice sent shivers up her spine. He actually hadn't hit her in years. She worked hard not to give him a reason to. But the threat was real, and it was always there. When he was away, she told herself she wasn't afraid of him, but it wasn't true. It was true, though, what he'd said about her hiding money from him.

Her brother, anthony, kept her nest egg for her. The account was not in her name, and she knew Anthony hadn't told Peter about it.So how did he know? Ada remembered the early days, when Peter routinely wired their house and their phones, and those of her family and friends. He bragged about it.

Was he spying on her again, she wondered? Had he ever stopped? Once Peter found out about the money, he badgered her until she gave him every penny of it. In the beginning, he promised her that it was a loan. But his word, like always, was worthless, like debris in high wind. She never understood why he bothered giving it since he never kept it. Ada never saw that money again.

After a couple of months, when she found the nerve to broach the subject, Peter scowled. "It wasn't your money, Ada." She managed to glance at him. Both his voice and his eyes were hostile. "It was our money." His tone said it was outlandish for her to imagine otherwise. When she didn't answer, he continued,"You live here Scot-free, Ada. I carry this load all by myself. You don't work. I never asked you to. You don't contribute to this family at all. And now you're gonna hound me for money that you got from me to begin with." His temper stopped her in her tracks. She let the subject rest for a while.

Months later, he got a large bonus and bragged about it. He was in a good mood; she approached him again. "Wow!" Ada exclaimed when he showed her the check. It was more than enough to cover the loan. "So does this mean you can pay me back the money you borrowed now?" She had tried to keep her tone light. She was always careful not to upset him, but the words came out in a nervous rush.

This was the third time she'd asked for her money. As far as Peter was concerned, it was three times too often. He didn't bother to answer. He just looked at her in disgust and walked away. She never asked again. So now, when she needed it, she was broke. It terrified her to think of having to make it on her own. She had no skills to speak of, and she couldn't imagine how she could earn a living.

She could cook, clean, and sew, but she doubted she'd ever be able to make suitable money doing any of those things. She knew she could write, but how could she parlay that skill into money without a degree? And she could sing, but she'd never performed without Peter. Her confidence and self-esteem had been eroded over the years. Peter had convinced her that her talent was marginal, at best. Her success was because *he made her look good*. So she felt clumsy and naive, and unsure of herself. And every chance he got, Peter ridiculed her for it. "You don't have the sense God gave a goat." He told her when she exasperated him. She didn't feel she could argue with it. She knew it was true; she didn't have common sense.

In addition, she couldn't forget her mental state. She knew, better than anyone, how strange she was. To Ada, *strange* still was the word that best described her personality even after long years of therapy. Her memory problems were a constant source of worry and embarrassment. And now she had no real money to speak of. She needed to save again, but it would be much harder now, actually impossible.

Things had changed drastically since that night long ago when the police were called, the night when Ada had fought back. Since then, she was on her own. She was being punished; she knew it, and money was the weapon Peter used against her. He withheld it, or made her beg for it. He wanted her to see what life would be like without him. She did see.

Her life was a paradox. She lived in a huge home, in one of the nation's richest area codes. Yet, there were times when she and the kids had no heat in the winter to warm the house. They slept in layers of clothing, sometimes even coats and scarves, to stay warm. The gas and the electricity were frequently cut off for non-payment. They often used the stove to heat water and to warm themselves. They used candles and flashlights for light.

During those days, they got into the habit of going to bed at dusk, when night began to fall. They accomplished as much as possible in the light of day.

Sometimes there was no money for food. Sometimes they had no phone. Whenever something broke down, some major appliance, it stayed broken. They learned to do without necessities, as well as the luxuries of life.

More than once, they were in danger of losing the house. Trucks even pulled up a couple of times to haul their belongings out. Ada tearfully begged the sheriff to give her enough time to contact her husband. He had taken pity on her and the kids. Peter knew the house was in foreclosure. Even though he was rarely there, she managed to apprise him of the notices.

He said he'd take care it, that they wouldn't lose the house. She sensed that he enjoyed the smell of her fear. Her pride hurt badly as she pawned choice pieces of jewelry, and a couple of furs coats. To raise money, she had garage sales, sold furniture, and expensive designer clothing, for next to nothing. In a last-ditch effort to save the house, she sold her engagement and wedding rings. It wasn't enough. So finally, with the sheriff literally breathing down her neck, Ada swallowed what was left of her pride and called Peter. She did it for the children, who were traumatized. By some miracle, he accepted her call. And as if by design, he bailed them out in the nick of time. But it was a temporary reprieve.

They still hung onto the house by a mere thread. Ada knew that one day soon she and the children would be homeless—out on the street. Just when it seemed that matters couldn't get worse, Ada badly burned her foot when she spilled scalding water on it.

She had been carrying a large roasting pan filled with boiling water to the one of the upstairs bathrooms. The water heater had been broken for some time and Ada had to heat water from the stove for daily chores. She felt like a pioneer woman, like in one of the *Little House on the Prairie* stories she liked to read. She boiled water to wash dishes and mop floors and to add to the cold water she or the kids bathed in.

She never allowed the children to carry the buckets or pans of water. She worried that one of the kids would be burned. Now, *it* was *her* foot that was burned and she thought she'd die from the pain. Ada cursed Peter Collins. And she thought of her mother's seared legs and felt empathy. She knew that Ella still suffered physically from the scalding that had occurred so many years in the past.

Ada herself was in dreadful pain for several weeks. The accident happened about the time Erin graduated from high school. As a result, Ada was on crutches during the graduation. Her right foot was so badly blistered that she couldn't get a shoe on it. She had to use crutches to keep her foot from hitting the floor. On graduation day, Peter showed up with money and a card. He played the proud father, looking and acting like all was right with the world.

He never mentioned her leg, or the fact that she was on crutches. She hated this game he played. It was for the benefit of their relatives and friends, she knew, but she couldn't sense the logic in it, and it galled her. Still, she was civil. But after the ceremony, when he hugged his daughter, shook her hand, and disappeared back into his life, Ada renewed her vow to divorce him.

She was mortified when the grass grew tall and she couldn't afford to have it cut. The maintenance and upkeep of the house was forsaken. She was helpless. She watched as her beautiful home became ravaged by time and neglect. Peter had plenty of money. He raced cars and flew planes. Peter and his women lived in style, but she and her kids were like paupers, in constant worry. And this was even before Ada told Peter she wanted a divorce.

Her tension and anxiety mounted. She was on the brink, always fighting to maintain consciousness. This was no way to live. Her determination deepened. She had to get out.

She looked into the court system to see what protection she could find there. She knew she would need it. In her weekly sessions with Michelle, for the first time, she began to express her desire to file papers against Peter. She articulated both her fears and her determination. Michelle and Dr. McIntyre cautiously approved of her decision. But they both understood her fears. She had reasons to be afraid.

The couple of sessions Peter sat in on had given them very real glimpses into the flawed character of the man who had terrorized his family for years. From their limited contact with him, both professionals were of the opinion that Peter Collins was a sociopath, incapable of genuine feelings of empathy or caring.

Michelle told Ada, "The world revolves around him. Peter can never be wrong. He's not responsible for any bad thing he might do. Nothing is ever his fault. Nothing ever will be."

She explained to Ada all the qualities that made him clinically diagnosable as a narcissist and Ada confirmed each one fit him. It gave Ada further resolve to leave, but she was still afraid. Michelle encouraged her to get out by offering resources to help.

At night, she would lay awake recounting the promises she'd made to divorce her husband and knowing how powerless she felt to act on them. She thought of her children. They had been wounded and scarred. She had to blame herself for that as much her husband. She hadn't protected them.

She needed to combat the guilt. It depressed and crippled her. She felt stymied, caught in a thickening pool of despair. She tried to fight it but she hated herself more each day for not finding the strength to leave long ago. She *wanted* to be divorced, but lacked the motivation to take that first step. And then one day, it just happened.

"Peter, I need to talk to you," she told him over the phone.

The conversation went exactly as Ada expected. The threats were fast and furious. "You're not divorcing me, Ada,"Peter told her. "You are not going to leave me." Had it not entered his brain that *he* had left her years ago? His voice was flat. He was very calm, like he was stating a simple fact. Ada knew this tone, this contrived composure. It annoyed her but she tried reasoning with him.

"Peter, I know you don't love me. I don't think you ever did. And I don't love you anymore. We don't live together as husband and wife. We haven't in years. We're only married on paper. We don't *need* to be married. The children are basically grown. There's no reason for us to pretend anymore."

Peter dismissed her logic as if it were crazy talk. She tried to imagine his face. She was sure one eyebrow was cocked. "We're a family, Ada," he told her. "I don't know who you've been listening to. I don't know what you've been reading. All of a sudden you've decided you want to be independent? Well, I'm not gonna let you ruin our marriage. His voice became intense.

"Someone's been filling your head with crap. Those doctors at Mercy Network have got you all worked up." Peter was the one getting worked up.

"This is bull crap, Ada," he continued. "You can just get it out of your head. It's not gonna happen." Peter started to sputter. "I have never given you any reason for a divorce. You don't have grounds for divorce. It ain't happening. I can't believe how selfish you are. You're just thinking about yourself. Well, I'm not letting you make a stupid mistake that we'll both regret. We got married for better or worse. I put too many years into this marriage to just throw it all away. We aren't getting a divorce. You might as well drop it."

Ada could hardly believe her ears. This man *was* nuts. She tried another tactic. "Peter, if you're worried about how it will make you look, *you* can divorce me."

"Ada, listen to me. He spoke plainly, like he was explaining basic math to a slow child. "There will be no divorce." Ada could picture his face as he repeated, "There will be no divorce."

He was calm again. He could afford to be. He was finished talking. With that, he hung up. Ada removed the phone from her ear. She gawked at it, like it was a snake that just bit her. The two younger children were asleep. Erin was spending the night at a friend's house. Ada sat alone in the darkened family room. She had failed to turn on the lights. For a moment, she stared into the darkness while tumultuous thoughts whirled about in her head. Then, in mental fatigue, she trudged up the stairs and fell into her bed. The next day, early, Ada made an appointment to see an attorney.

The Lawyer

Kathy was a trusted friend, so much so that she had actually met some of Ada's personalities. *They talked to her.* Sometimes, when she was addressing Ada, another personality might be in charge of the body. It was usually a woman, about Ada's age, who called herself Ada Two.

Once, *Liz* corrected Kathy. "You think you're talking to Ada, don't you? Well, Ada's not here." The voice continued, "I'm Liz. Ada is tired, so I'm taking over for a while." That didn't happen often, and it didn't happen with just anybody.

Ada could count on one hand the people who had actually met any of the troops, as they called themselves. But Kathy had, and that was telling. All of the *alters* liked Kathy and they all spoke highly of her.

Sometimes after an encounter with one of Ada's *people*, Kathy would fill Ada in, telling her what she'd learned. When she heard stories one of the multiples' exploits or was made privy to their conversations, Ada always felt like she was eavesdropping, listening in on private discussions. But she liked doing it. She gained more knowledge about them, about herself, that way.

And she never felt embarrassed or intimidated when she and Kathy talked about her illness. They even joked about it. Kathy cracked Ada up when she'd tease, "I don't care what anybody says, Ada. You're my best *friends*."

Ada knew Kathy when depression and eating disorders had reduced her literally to skin and bones.Kathy had also seen her friend through numerous suicide attempts and even more hospital stays. These were times when it was impossible to joke the pain away. Kathy even understood when Ada's bizarre behaviors had caused trouble with the court system, when Ada was arrested for vandalism, shoplifting, and malicious mischief. It mortified Ada to think of some of the things she had done, but Kathy understood, and never judged.

They remained friends through those strange, pitch-black days of mental illness. Ada clung to her friend in the most difficult days of her marriage. It was appropriate then that Kathy was with her when she took the first steps in the process of bringing her marriage to an end.

Kathy drove ada to Rebecca Neilson's office because she was too nervous to drive.Ada left her friend in the lobby when she stepped into the attorney's office and she was relieved to find, upon leaving the office, that lightning hadn't struck her dead. She left in one piece. She'd nearly convinced herself the event would spell immediate doom. But it hadn't. Actually, she'd been *somewhat* reassured; although Ada knew her newly acquired attorney didn't fully grasp the implications of a tangle, legal or otherwise, with Peter Collins. Ada had recounted her history with Peter. She felt a sting of humiliation when she told Rebecca how her husband had beaten her and had raped her for years, and how his threats terrified her even now.

She tried to be candid, because her therapist and her doctor had told her to be, and because she wanted the lawyer to know this could be dangerous. As Rebecca listened quietly, there were alternate flashes of surprise, sadness, and anger that crossed her face.

Then when her client was quiet, Rebecca said, "Peter Collins is just a man, Ada. He's a bully. His control over you is your fear. When you lose the fear, he loses control. That doesn't mean we shouldn't be cautious, but try to remember that bullies are cowards, Ada. They don't like to fight fair." Rebecca stopped for emphasis. She looked hard at Ada and then she continued, "Bullies back down when the odds are no longer in their favor."

Ada listened, and she absorbed the words. But at the same time, she was contending with her own thoughts.

"One thing we have going for us is that Peter is not a fool,"Rebecca said. "It's just that you've never stood up to him before, Ada. Now that you have, you've got the courts behind you. We will get a restraining order, and once we do that, I can promise you he'll back down."

Rebecca was probably 10 years Ada's senior, and she wore confidence comfortably, like a cottony-soft robe on a damp day. Ada knew instinctively that Rebecca was the kind of woman Peter would hate. That fact, standing alone, fortified her.

"I've been a divorce attorney for more than 20 years, Ada, and I've worked with abused women much of that time. And although I know it may seem that your situation is unique, it's not. I've seen this scenario a thousand times. Your husband is controlling and domineering and manipulative. I'm sure of it. And I believe he is capable of great violence. I know he's been violent toward you and the kids and I know and understand that you're afraid of him. But Peter is also a businessman. He's smart. He's known and respected in the community. And he's going to use the legal system, now. He can't afford not to. He may want you to think he is, Ada, but your husband is *not* crazy."

Mercy Network had referred Rebecca Neilson to her. She worked for a reduced fee, and she was plainly passionate about protecting the rights of abused women. Ada liked her. She came highly recommended. Michelle had referred other clients to her, and had always been pleased with the results.

Rebecca was telling her that Peter's threats were all a bluff. Ada lunged at the hope that Rebecca was right but she couldn't hold onto it. She couldn't remain convinced. She knew her husband was smart, but also, she had evidence he *was* crazy. Ada still hadn't told her attorney what she'd only recently disclosed to her therapist; that she was certain when Jacob Daddy died several years ago, it was at her husband's hand.

The Divorce

Ada was in a constant state of agitation once she learned the legal papers had been filed. The papers made it official, and the thought scared her out of her mind. The kids were afraid, too.

The children and she held a family meeting and discussed Ada's decision to divorce Peter. They were in agreement with the idea and they encouraged her. For years they had prodded their mother to file the papers that would legally separate them all from their dad.

None of them wanted anything more to do with him. They thought of this as a *family* divorce. And anyway, they knew their dad well enough to know that in Peter's mind, they would share equal blame. He would hold all of them accountable and his anger would be meted out to each one of them in equal shares.

They fully believed there would be risks, dire ones. They devised strategies to protect themselves and their mother, but they determined that it was time to cut the invisible cord that tied them to the enigmatic man who continued to control them even though, on the face of things, he was no longer in their lives.

It wasn't long before Rebecca Neilson learned that Ada's claims against her husband were not exaggerated. She had underestimated him. Once she met Peter, she decided that Ada deserved a medal. Living with Peter, she decided, would have to have been problematic, even under the best of circumstances. So being on his bad side would have to be a nightmare.

Rebecca concluded Ada was much stronger than she gave herself credit for, and she told her so. She had to admit that she'd never before met anyone like Peter. He wasn't a big man. His height and build were only a little more than average. But his demeanor was large. She immediately noted the presence that Ada often spoke of

when she described her husband. He exuded a cockiness that said,
'I know things you don't know.'

The condescending way he looked at her, like she was just a
meddlesome child, infused in her an evolved form of annoyance
that blossomed into rage. Rebecca considered herself a strong
woman, and an accomplished lawyer. She wasn't easily intimidated,
especially in a courtroom setting, but she could readily see how
her client could be. And she had to admit to herself, Peter was not
someone you'd want to meet in a dark alley.

He *was* a bully, to an extent, she conceded. But he wasn't merely a
bully. It was true; he picked on Ada and the kids because they were
easy game. But Rebecca sensed that Peter enjoyed a fight, fair or
otherwise. The most predictable thing about Peter Collins was that
he was not predictable.

The attorney he hired was his perfect counterpart. Rebecca disliked
both like Peter Collins and his good-old-boy attorney. And as it
turned out, Ada hadn't merely imagined it. Peter did indeed have
friends in high places.

Ada also hadn't imagined his uncanny ability to manipulate the
legal system. Neither Ada nor her lawyer was quite sure how it
happened, but Rebecca had to admit, it was strange the way filed
documents suddenly vanished into thin air. Restraining orders
against him disappeared and witnesses suddenly had nothing to
say.

Ada told Rebecca how police reports had vanished in the past, but
now the attorney witnessed all of it with her own eyes.

As they entered the courtroom Ada made eye contact with her
husband and his attorney. Her fear was palpable. It was when
Rebecca followed her client's gaze that she first laid eyes on Peter
Collins. And from across the room, she felt that aura that Ada
so often referred to. Peter's eyes left Ada's and locked with hers.
With difficulty, she freed herself from his scrutiny and prepared
to attend to the matters at hand. That first court appearance was
routine.

Legally, there were no surprises. But on that first day, Rebecca
Neilson was given definite notice that a battle had ensued. She

had met Peter Collins, but hadn't spoken directly with him. They'd communicated only through his attorney. But during the short proceedings, as she spoke with Ada, she found that her eyes were drawn, impulsively, to her client's husband. He seemed to have lost interest in his wife. His attention was mainly focused on Rebecca.

When the court session was over, Rebecca walked her client into the hallway outside courtroom 'B'. She stood there with Ada a few moments, explaining to her in layman's terms what had just happened. Peter Collins walked up with his attorney. He stood close to them but didn't speak. When Peter walked away, Rebecca noticed her palms were sweating. She let out an elongated sigh, and realized she had forgotten to breathe.

The divorce dragged on for nearly two years, and before long, even the reduced fees that Rebecca was charging became impossible for Ada to pay. And she felt guilty because of the long hours spent, and because of the extraordinary lengths to which Rebecca was forced, in fighting Peter. Several times Ada came close to giving up. Rebecca urged her not to. In the end, the determined lawyer waived her fee. This had become a personal matter for her. Peter was true to his word, too. He made it his mission to plague Ada. He made sure she had no money and few prospects of getting her hands on any.

The house was to be awarded to Ada as a part of the divorce settlement, and Peter had been ordered to keep up the payments. Of course, he did not. Rebecca was optimistic at first. "We'll go after his assets. Don't worry, we'll make him pay." She said it with conviction. After nearly 30 years of marriage, you're entitled to spousal support, Ada. You never worked outside the home. He'll have to support you until you're able to make it on your own." But Peter had other plans. His assets disappeared.

Peter was known to have several businesses, but the ones that could be traced to him appeared not to be profitable. In the end, she was forced to sell her house at a loss, to keep from losing it in foreclosure.

In addition to the financial problems, Peter menaced her with loosely veiled threats of physical harm. He broke into her house on so many occasions that Ada gave up repairing the locks on the windows and doors. He kicked in the front door once with such force that the wood splintered away from the doorjamb.

He sabotaged her efforts at finding work, telling prospective employers that she was unstable and not mentally fit to hold a job. Peter had Ada followed; accusing her of having affairs with any man she was seen talking to. "Ada," he told her, "you've determined your own destiny." The children moved back into Ada's house, formed a line of defense against their father, and devised tactics to arm themselves.

It was Erin's idea to remove all sharp implements from the house. They emptied the kitchen drawers of knives and skewers, anything that could be used as a weapon against them in a surprise attack.

The girls slept in the bed with their mother, with a baseball bat under the mattress and a carving knife beneath the pillow. The bedroom door was blocked each night by heavy pieces of furniture. They knew it wouldn't stop Peter from breaking into the room if he decided to go on a rampage; but it would slow him down enough for them to gather their wits. Weapons would be a last resort.

Little Pete slept in the next room. He had vowed that their father would not hurt their mother again. The women really didn't want to know what measures he had planned to take against Peter. "I can handle Dad,"is all he would say. And knowing Pete the way they did, they felt no need to question him further. This is the way they lived for nearly another year. Then one day Rebecca called. She might just as easily have said Gibraltar has crumbled, but what she did say simply, was…"Ada, your divorce is final."

Ada was divorced, and she was still alive to tell the tale. This amazed her. She moved out of her home, and she lived to revel in that fact, as well. Her first *home away from home* was a three-bedroom apartment that she shared with Erin. Ada loved that arrangement. She was able to pay her share of the rent by snagging singing gigs with a local wedding band led by a gorgeous Greek keyboard player named Lee Pantely. She was proud and happy to be on her own. She was making her own money; doing what she loved to do.

A year later, at about the same time that the lease was up, Erin got an offer for a job in Texas. It was an offer she couldn't refuse, and

Ada didn't want her to. It was a good opportunity for her, and Ada was happy for her daughter, but still, when Erin moved to Dallas, Ada again felt slightly desperate, and abandoned.

She couldn't afford the apartment alone. She didn't renew the lease. She began to feel the familiar downward spiral that had so often led to hospitalization. Mercy Network quickly facilitated her next move. Michelle and Dr. Mac learned of a program for displaced homemakers who struggled with mental or emotional problems. Ada qualified for the assistance. Within a year she was settled in a home with two other women who were also were clients of Mercy Network.

One of the women was a middle-aged widow named Debbie. She suffered from anxiety and depression. Ada could relate to Debbie, and immediately they became good friends. Their other roommate was named Joy. Her name was deceiving. Joy was both paranoid and schizophrenic. She was anything but joyful. And her problems were apparent. Both women came to the home right out of mental institutions. Ada qualified because she had multiple personalities.

Joy told the most fantastic stories, which she believed to be true. Her boyfriend, she said, had flown a plane into one of the Twin Towers on 9/11; she was on the FBI's most wanted list, and there were *hits* out on her life. As she became more and more unstable, living with Joy became an impossible challenge, and eventually…a dangerous one. She pitied the troubled young woman, but when Joy had to be forcibly removed from the home, Ada was relieved.

Of course, it was stressful to live with someone whose life was so emphatically out of control. But more than that, it reminded Ada of her own precarious situation. Once Joy was gone, Ada felt more settled. She and Debbie were just a couple of single women living together to share expenses. They got along well. But Ada knew the truth and the severity of her situation. A team of mental health workers visited the women's house regularly, monitoring their progress. They administered meds and provided in-home therapy sessions. And since, for medical reasons, neither of the women was allowed to drive, they transported them to and from doctor's appointments. Ada knew that the services were necessary, but still, she somewhat resented them. This was a group home, and like soggy bread, the knowledge stuck in Ada's throat. It embarrassed her, and she especially didn't want Peter to know where or with whom she lived.

Soon, Ada began to feel stable and secure again, and she acknowledged that the agency had intervened once more to save her life. She no longer thought of the house she shared with Debbie as a group home. She and her roommate had made their modest three-bedroom house cozy.Once again, Ada felt she was home.

In the summer of 2002, Ada's Aunt Lillian became ill, and Ada returned to Indiana. It was a monumental decision. Staff members at the agency devoted many sessions to dissecting the pros and cons of the move. By now, all of Ada's children were in Indianapolis. Erin and Lydia had children of their own, which meant Ada was a grandmother, affectionately called *Mimi*. She loved it. She loved her grandchildren, she missed them and she relished the idea of being close to them again.

Ada liked the thought of putting hundreds of miles between her and Peter. This was, everyone agreed, a very good thing. But on the flip side, Ada's mom was in Indy, too. Over the years, Ada found that even short visits with her mother could be hazardous to her mental health. The love/hate tug of war that always waged between them had barely improved over the course of time, and even that nominal improvement, Ada knew, was largely due to the great distance between them.

She wanted acknowledgement; an apology for the many years of the sexual abuse Ella had allowed at Jacob's hand. And she blamed her mother for forcing her marriage to Peter.

None of these things were forthcoming, as her therapist warned Ada might be the case. "I can do this," Ada told her therapist, her doctor, and herself. One day in late October, she loaded her car, gassed up, and drove to Indianapolis. Most of her furnishings had been sold. Some things were left at the house in Farmington Hills.

Her kids rented a U-haul and followed her on the trip, transporting the rest of her things for her. Ada had been granted her license the year before, and she saw it as a huge indication of normalcy. The night before she left, Ada wrote a poem in her journal:

With these thoughts so clear in heart and mind

I revisit a world I'd left behind

I return to the scene ofa villainous crime.

A land so painful it left me blind, a villainous place so far away;

Where childhood memories dance and play.

Aunt Lillian

Aunt Lillian's house had once been a hub of activity. Like her aunt, the house seemed vacant, was old and beginning to fall apart. The old woman had been in the hospital for several weeks following surgery to repair a recurring problem with her colon. Ada suspected, and the rumor was, that the surgery had been botched, and her aunt had suffered the needless and prolonged effects.

After she was finally released from the hospital, she was admitted to a convalescent home to recuperate. She stayed there for several months. Lillian's old house, in its perpetual state of disrepair, became Ada's new home. She looked at her new surroundings and felt a sense of sadness for herself and for the aunt whom she loved dearly.

Lillian lost a considerable amount of weight during her illness, yet her continued weight loss had more to do with her weakening state of mind than with physical health. Lillian was depressed, Ada knew, largely because she wanted to go home; to the home she had shared for so many years with her late husband.

Uncle Ernest died relatively young, making Lillian a widow while she was still in her fifties, but he had provided well for her. She never remarried. She supported herself on her salary as a grade school teacher. She earned her master's in education. Lillian taught white children at a time when integration was still a fresh and displeasing novelty in Indiana.

Aunt Lillian had always been an independent, forward-thinking woman, and Ada admired her aunt and looked up to her. But time had taken its toll, and Lillian had fallen victim to Alzheimer's, which seemed to be her family's plague. It was ravaging her mind the way illness had ravaged her body.

"I've got my work cut out for me," Ada acknowledged, although in hindsight, she'd have to concede she hadn't fully grasped the direness of her aunt's situation. Ada moved into the back bedroom of her aunt's house. There were memories in that house, good ones. It was one of the few places that offered her comfort as a child.

Ada attended weddings, reunions, and barbeques there. And a large neighborhood pool right behind the house meant asylum from the hot summer sun. For a short time, when Ada was young, she and Peter lived there, in the basement of her aunt and uncle's house. Peter had been careful, during that time, not to mistreat her. Neither Aunt Lillian nor Uncle Ernest would have stood for it. Ada had actually been happy there.

It was a lovely home then; warm and beautiful, and Ada was determined to make it that way again. She busied herself around her aunt's house. She wanted Aunt Lillian to come home to comfortable new surroundings. She hired painters, installed a garbage disposal, updated the furnishings, and planted a garden. She often lost herself in thought in the beautiful, new garden. She sometimes found herself singing to her flowers, to her cucumbers and her beans. She spoke in loving tones to her peppers and berries.

"I heard you were back." The familiar voice was infused with amusement.

Startled, Ada turned, lifting her head, but shielding her eyes from the blazing sun. "Oh, my goodness! Kevin Coats?" Ada exclaimed. She was astounded. She hadn't seen him in years. The last time was at the house in Bloomfield, when he'd wordlessly gathered his few belongings and high-tailed it out the front door.

Kevin had lived with Peter and Ada for several years, sleeping on the couch in their finished basement. That fact mystified and dumbfounded Ada and anyone else who knew Kevin. Kevin was a tenured professor at Ball State University. He had his master's in music theory and taught in the music department. He was one of the most logical-thinking, intelligent men Ada knew.

She would never know what had gotten into him. It was beyond her, the idea that he would leave his position at the college and move hundreds of miles away from his family and friends to join Peter in his new business venture. Peter was ambitious and smart, and he quit his job at Digital to strike out on his own. Owning his own business was Peter's dream and Ada understood that. But it wasn't Kevin's dream, so she was shocked when he decided to join them in Michigan. Ada chalked it up to Peter's powers of persuasion. His charisma could be hypnotizing.

Ada and Kevin became good friends, but it had been years since they'd spoken. The circumstances surrounding his leaving were sketchy, but she knew that partially at least, it had to do with her. Several months before he left, she had been instructed by her husband to stop talking to him. Peter had accused him of flirting, and her of encouraging it. Ada knew trouble was brewing, but still she was surprised at the swiftness of his departure when it finally occurred.

Now Ada asked him, "How did you know I was here?"

"Let's just say a mutual friend told me."

"We don't have mutual friends,"Ada joked, but with a nervous laugh.

Kevin didn't answer. He just extended his hand and helped her up from the damp soil she'd been working in.

"Ada, I heard about the divorce. Please be careful."Kevin's voice was serious, intense.

"I know you think it's over and that you've won, but you don't know what you're up against."

Ada had no words. She simply stared at Kevin, the man who had once been Peter's dearest, oldest, and only, real friend.

"Let me tell you a little story,"Kevin began. "Years ago, back in Detroit, I went into business with a friend. This man and I went on a sales call, to a potential client. The client turned down our proposal, but that wasn't the problem. The problem was that he was sarcastic in doing it. He insulted my friend. It was a minor infraction, and the details aren't important. The point is, my friend didn't flinch or respond. But when we were leaving the client's office, he turned to me. "I don't care if it takes five days, or ten years," he said. "He will pay for disrespecting me like that. Nobody treats me like that. Nobody gets over on me. I'm a very patient man."

Now Kevin locked eyes with Ada.

"That man was found dead in his office ten years later, almost to the day. Cause of death was never determined,"Kevin said.

Ada's mind raced until it landed squarely on Jacob Daddy and *his* undetermined cause of death.

"My friend has often told me, "I'm a very patient man." And Ada, he's never meant it in a good way. He has his own sense of justice and sentencing,"Kevin said.

"When he feels he's been wronged, and that he's gained an enemy, he'll wait patiently, for years if necessary, to catch the offender off guard."

"So Ada, I hope you're getting my drift. I'm just saying be careful and watch your back. It may seem to be over. But it's not over."

With that, Kevin turned and walked away.

Almost

Peter tracked Ada to Indianapolis in no time and began a quiet harassment of her. But to her surprise, she was more annoyed than afraid. She wondered if he was back in the wire-tapping business, but really, she didn't care.

"I'm getting too old for Peter Collins and his games," she told Erin one night. "He's welcome to any information he gathers," she said.

He showed up one day when Ada was away from home. Aunt Lillian let him in although she was repeatedly warned not to. The sitter, the woman who cared for her when Ada was out, had been warned, too, but Aunt Lillian, who could be surprisingly swift at the most inopportune moments, had beat the woman to the door.

Peter had a nice visit. From what Ada could tell, he gathered small but useful tidbits of information from Aunt Lillian, and was on his way. Many times, Ada spotted him outside Aunt Lillian's house. He just sat there with his lights off surveying them.

Ella was always happy to entertain 'her favorite son-in-law' whenever he came to visit. The two would laugh and talk for hours; eating homemade ice cream and sweet potato pie. Ada could speculate how they traded stories about her, her peculiarities; and congratulate each other on making it through the dark days. Ella would justify her marrying a rumored pedophile. *They were only rumors, after all.* Ella would explain, and Peter would listen to the reasons she allowed Jacob to touch her baby girl all those years. Peter would recount how hard he worked to provide for Ada and those ungrateful children. Ella would emerge from each of their visits feeling understood, fully atoned, and right. Peter left Ella's house feeling refreshed and validated.

He started contacting old friends and acquaintances, and inquiring about Ada and the kids. Well-dressed thugs would deliver messages a wee bit short of threatening to Ada at her gigs right before she went on stage. Peter sent Ada and her kids a barrage of emails, which they blocked and sent directly to junk mail. They refused his phone calls, but he continued to make his presence known and felt. They often had their mail disappear, tires slashed and more often than not, they were followed when they drove.

They jokingly called these his reconnaissance missions but as long as he kept a respectable distance, they decided it was best to ignore him.

Ada hadn't forgotten Kevin's warning. She shared his message with the kids, but they were all determined to move on with their lives. Gradually his power over them weakened, his control dissipated, until eventually, in time, they all felt kind of…free…almost.

Jonathon

Erin had to talk Ada into attending the mid-morning book signing. She was tired and didn't want to go. "There will be lots of good contacts there," Erin said, "people we should meet. People we need to know."

Erin showed up at Ada's house that Saturday morning bearing gifts—bribes, actually; Starbucks coffee, scones, and bagels slathered with cream cheese.

And she told her mother, "There'll be a gourmet brunch, and free-flowing wine, all you can drink. How can you refuse?"

Ada accepted the bribe, but she told her daughter, "You know I don't drink wine. And I'm tired. I refuse to dress up. If I can go dressed like I am, I'll go. But I'm not changing clothes, and I'm not putting on makeup, Erin."

"Whatever!" Erin countered. "Come on, Mom. I'll drive. And you can come dressed like you are, and you can put makeup on in the car. Please try not to be a dud, Mom. We both need to be there."

Indy Bookstore was a 20-minute drive from home. By the time they got there, Ada was in a better frame of mind, and her face was made up. Erin was right. They did need to be there. There were interesting people there, other local authors like Erin and herself. They met editors, publishers and people who simply liked to read. Since Ada was starting to make a name for herself in the Indianapolis music scene. She saw everyone, these days, as a potential groupie. So as she entered the room, she was glad Erin had convinced her to clean up.

Jonathon Bonnay watched the women enter the bookstore from across the room. Ada saw him, too. Her brothers were tall, both well over six feet, but this man, who was impeccably dressed in an expensive, well-cut dark blue suit and tie, was taller than both of them. She figured he must have stood nearly six and a half feet high. Ada wasn't a world traveler, so his chiseled features had a foreign look that she couldn't quite put a name to. She did note, though, in a clinical way, that the dark-skinned man at the far corner of the room was enormously handsome.

During the course of the evening, Erin made her way to the wine table that Jonathon had been guarding all night. He saw his chance, and grabbed it. "So, pretty lady. Red or white?" he asked her. His accent was thick. *Hmmm…French,* she thought.

"Are you the bartender?" Erin smiled her deeply dimpled grin.

"Today, for you, I will be," Jonathon answered.

"Well then, red," Erin said. As he poured her wine, she studied him. He looked familiar to her. *Not bad,* she told herself, *for an older man.* And she instantly thought of her mom.

He filled the glass almost to the top. Erin said, "Boy, you sure know how to pour a glass of wine." Then as Ada approached she added, "And you can pour one for my mother, too."When Erin looked at her mom, there was mischief in her eyes.

"Your mother?" Jonathon exclaimed. "That can't be!" His surprise was genuine. Erin made the introductions, and as she did, she handed Jonathon one of her business cards.

"I'm Erin, and yes, this is my mother, Ada," she said. "I had to drag her here kicking and screaming. She didn't want to come."

"It's nice to meet you both. I'm Jonathon Bonnay. And I'm glad you forced your mother to come." He said it to Erin, but she had the distinct impression he'd forgotten she was there.

Erin noted his interest in her mother and she thought, *OK, Mom, let's give him a chance. He seems nice, he's kinda cute, and he definitely likes you!*

"And Ada, I am glad you came," Jonathon said, as he handed her a glass of red wine. When he said this, he looked at Ada and smiled a fluorescent smile that revealed the straightest, whitest teeth she had ever seen. The man had dimples in both cheeks, which were deep enough to swim in, and he was flirting with her. "Well, I worked late last night," Ada said. She noticed his accent, and she liked it. She didn't like the wine, but she pretended to.

"And this is still pretty early for me. I intended to sleep until noon, today. But I'm having a good time. There are some very interesting people here. Yeah, I am glad I came."

Jonathon looked at the business card Erin had handed him. He read aloud, "Erin Collins Publishing. So, you're a publisher." he stated.

"Yes, I am," Erin smiled.

"And you're a writer, too?" he asked, still reading the card.

"Yeah, you could say that, as well."

"Well, I'm impressed. So, tell me, what do you write?"

"I write poetry, short stories, fiction, and children's books. I'm working on a novel. And what about you, Jonathon? Are you a writer, too? No, let me guess. An editor?"

"Not even close, but I do love to read. It's people like me who keep people like you in business. Actually, I'm a pharmacist," he said with a grin.

"Oh," Erin exclaimed, and her eyes widened. "That's how I know you! I'd been trying to figure out where I've seen you before! You work at the pharmacy near my house."

"Yes, I knew I recognized you. I've filled your prescriptions!"

Jonathon finished his wine and poured himself another glass. "So where are you from, Jonathon? What's your accent?" Erin asked the question Ada wasn't about to ask.

"I'm from Barbados. I lived in France for many years, and then came here to the United States to go to university. I've been here for a while, now. So you think I still have an accent?" he asked.

He amused himself with his little joke. His eyes twinkled and his dimples flashed. Erin liked him, but she watched her mom to gauge her reaction. Her mother was smiling.

Erin surveyed the couple and sized them up. She thought how pretty her mom was, how nice it was to see her smile, especially at a man, and what a nice-looking couple they would make…her mother, and this tall, dark, handsome stranger.

"So, Ada," Jonathon said, and he touched her arm. "Now you know how I make a living. And I know what your daughter does. How do you employ yourself?" Jonathon looked at Ada with undisguised interest.

"Well, I'm also a writer, and I'm a vocalist, a singer. Jazz, mostly, but R&B and Blues, too," Ada said.

"Oh, really, pretty lady? Multi-talented! So, what do you write and where do you sing?" Ada liked the way he'd addressed her: *Pretty lady*. She tried hard not to blush. "Well, I published my first book two years ago, a book of poetry. And I'm also writing a novel. It's nearly finished. And, as for my music career, I sing everywhere, in restaurants and hotels, mostly, and at private parties. I sing all over the city," she informed him.

"Well again, I have to say, I'm impressed. But could you be more specific, maybe? Like, can you give me the *name* of a place I can come to see you, and give me a *date maybe, and a time?* I'd love to check you out."

She told him, "As a matter of fact, I'm singing this coming Saturday night, at the Conrad Hotel, downtown, from 8 p.m. until 12 a.m. I'm with a great little jazz quartet, some very talented musicians. If you can make it, you'll have a great time."

"I'll be there," he assured her, "but although I'm certain your musicians are fantastic, I'll be coming to see you!" Then he asked, "Do you have a card?" And as he handed her his, he added, "I don't want to lose track of you." She gave him her card. It had her name on it in fancy script, with her image above it. He studied the likeness. *It's a very good picture of me,* she thought.

"Hmmm…nice picture," he said, making her smile, "but it doesn't do you justice." And he added, "I'll see you this Saturday night." True to his word, he came to The Conrad on Saturday night.

Loving Ada

Ada saw a lot of Jonathon in the next few months, but only because he came to all of her gigs. He never came empty-handed. He brought flowers, candy, or perfume, and always the perfect gentleman; he treated her like a queen. Still, she refused to let her guard down.

He was determined to win her over. He said and did all the right things. And although he tried to hide it, when he looked at her, his eyes said she was the most precious thing he'd ever seen. Other people noticed it, too, and questioned her. "So, who is this guy?"

"He's just a friend," Ada replied. And she meant it. She refused to let herself like him.

She wouldn't date him. She told him that. Peter Collins was still too fresh in her mind. He had almost destroyed her. It would be nearly impossible, she thought, for her to trust any man ever again. She told Jonathon that, too. She was hoping that he'd lose interest in her, and just go away, but he didn't.

Finally, after months of persistent begging, she did allow him to call her. When they talked on the phone, it surprised her to learn how quickly time would pass. And she read to him from the manuscript she was working on. The script was the story of her life, and her sharing it with him was a major development in their relationship. Not many people, other than family and close friends, were privy to the details of her personal life. She was nearly finished with the book, but she'd confided in him that she was blocked.

"I feel like I've hit a brick wall. I don't know where to go from here,"she said. As she read to him, she relived her life. She saw herself as a troubled little girl, and as a hesitant and confused young woman.

She brought back to mind the disturbing things she'd experienced and she felt—alternately, anger and pain.

Ada was uncomfortable sharing those things with him. She dreaded his reaction. Actually, the idea of disclosing to anyone the details of her life made her feel at risk. But Jonathon seemed intrigued by her story. He hadn't been put off when he learned about her past, about her mental condition; that among other things, she had dissociative identity disorder.

Rather than telling him about it, Ada allowed him to read the details from her manuscript, and then she waited for the other shoe to drop. She expected him to head for the hills. She wouldn't have blamed him. But he didn't go away.

He did ask questions though because, he said, he wanted to understand; but he didn't think she was weird, or strange. "OK," he would joke, "so you're a *little* bit quirky." Ada wasn't offended. She sensed that no insult was intended. "I think you're intelligent, and beautiful, and absolutely fascinating," Jonathon told her. "And I want to know everything there is to know about you." And she felt that he meant it. She started to hope that he did. Jonathon wanted to protect her. He loved being near her. He loved to hear her voice. He looked forward to her phone calls. When she would read to him, continuing her story from where she'd left off, he felt he was watching her life unfold, and he wanted to be a part of that life. Jonathon realized, long before Ada did, that he was falling in love with her.

Unblocked

Ada was having trouble writing. She took a break and pushed her laptop aside. "I'm blocked," she sighed. "I need coffee."

She'd just returned from the kitchen, cup in hand, when the phone rang. Jonathon! She placed the steaming brew on the nightstand beside her and made herself comfortable again in the bed. Two fat pillows cushioned her back, and her thick comforter was tucked snugly around her legs. Ada smiled the instant he said her name. She heard the smile in his voice, as well.

"Hey, beautiful, what are you up to?" he asked.

"I'm trying to write," she told him. "But I'm not having much success."

"Maybe you need some down time. I could come over and massage your back. That might help." It was just an excuse, she knew, so he could come see her. Ada never took him up on it, and it became a running gag between them. "No thanks," she said. "I'll muddle through."

"Well, I really just wanted to hear your voice," he admitted, and she believed him. "I miss you," he said.

"You know where I'll be tonight," she reminded him. She was glad she was performing that evening, and she knew he'd show up. She'd canvass the room and see him, and her face would erupt in a smile. His would, too. Ada opened the small laptop again. It jarred her, this new feeling that washed over her. She had to laugh out loud as her fingers danced around the keyboard, and she watched herself type:

Chapter 31

Happy

Culturatti Ink and Barbara Randall are pleased to donate the proceeds from this novel to Culturatti Kids.

Culturatti Kids is a national non-profit organization that works to inspire young writers and advance literary arts education. For more information, visit www.CulturattiKids.net.